Relief floo____ ____ough me and I staggered back a few steps, bumping into the open door. I took another breath through my mouth, stepped forward again and carefully went through the victim's pockets. But he was clean—no identification. A message—that's what he was.

I thought back to the two wineglasses. If Ma had been here, she would have started cleaning the apartment and gotten rid of the evidence. I was tempted to, but something held me back—I was pretty sure Albert hadn't killed this man, and it was becoming clear to me that Albert had been set up for something. I didn't know for what, but I did know something was going on.

─────────── ★ ───────────

Previously published Worldwide Mystery titles by
WENDI LEE

MISSING EDEN
DEADBEAT

He Who Dies

WENDI LEE

WORLDWIDE.

TORONTO • NEW YORK • LONDON
AMSTERDAM • PARIS • SYDNEY • HAMBURG
STOCKHOLM • ATHENS • TOKYO • MILAN
MADRID • WARSAW • BUDAPEST • AUCKLAND

For Terry,
who keeps me sane
with love

HE WHO DIES

A Worldwide Mystery/June 2001

First published by St. Martin's Press, Incorporated.

ISBN 0-373-26386-4

Printed in U.S.A.

"He who dies
with the most toys wins."
—*Anonymous, 1980s*

ONE

IT HAD BEEN A QUIET DAY at the office but then, it was a Monday. I'd just faxed some paperwork over to Bob Leone's insurance agency, and filed two paid invoices from Repos R Us for a couple of cars I'd helped repossess a week ago. The clock on my desk read 3:29. I was contemplating closing early when the door flew open and Ma stepped in. For a stranger who was getting his first glimpse of Ma, she was quite a sight. She stood less that five feet tall and had a helmet of Loving Care raven black hair that perched on top of her skull. Although she had washed away the gray, her face was still a careworn map that told the story of a woman whose son-of-a-bitch husband left her to raise six children alone.

A large black patent leather purse, a remnant of the sixties, hung on her frail-looking arm. I fondly called her purse the "Black Hole" because it held everything anyone could possibly need. There had been times she pulled things out of that purse that I'd had no idea I would need. For instance, when we went to Easter service last year, she pulled a Beanie Baby out of the "Black Hole" when one of her grandchildren got fidgety. After service, the plastic frames of Carla's glasses broke and Ma pulled superglue out of her Black Hole to mend them. When someone sneezed and blamed it on allergies, she groped around and brought out some allergy medication.

I am often told I look like Ma, but I'm taller and my shoulder-length hair is a natural golden brown. Okay, the golden highlights are from a bottle, but it looks more nat-

ural than Ma's Grecian Formula hair. Did I mention how
fond I am of Ma? Even in the face of her bitter disappointment that I hadn't yet married and had children—a fact of
which she reminds me at least once a day—she still loved
me.

It occurred to me that she hadn't called me today—usually, we talk on the phone about once or twice a day. So
it was a surprise that she had come to my office. In fact, it
was surprising that she'd actually gotten out of Malden. Ma
didn't drive, hadn't driven for over twenty years. Malden's
transportation system was difficult to understand, at best. If
Ma wanted to go someplace, she either caught a ride from
a neighbor, or browbeat one of her children into picking
her up.

"Hi, Ma," I said with a big grin. "This is a surprise.
You must have gotten a ride with a neighbor. Want to grab
an early dinner or something? I can drive you home after-
ward." The prospect of taking Ma out to eat began to take
on a golden glow—there were so many good restaurants, I
would have a hard time choosing where to take Ma to eat.

Ma shook her head distractedly. It was then that I first
noticed Ma was almost in tears. She hadn't looked this
upset since her sixty-year-old brother Sonny married a
twenty-seven-year-old Nordic Lutheran girl from the Mid-
west by the name of Tricia Tronsgaard, who was an obvi-
ous golddigger. The fact that Sonny didn't have two nickels
to rub together until the third of every month when his
pension check came in seemed to sail past Ma and the rest
of the relatives.

I steered Ma to my pink and green sofa, a partial pay-
ment from a former client. "Ma, you okay? You weren't
mugged or anything, were you? You feeling all right?" She
couldn't be feeling all right, because she hadn't commented
on how the violent lilac walls clashed with the green and

pink sofa. Until a few months ago, my office had been a soothing shade of dull beige. But in a fit of domesticity, my sister Sophia had painted the new apartment she and David shared with her two children, Stephanie and Michael. Stephanie had her bedroom painted lavender and there was enough left over to paint a sixteen-by-sixteen room. I nixed the idea of painting anything in my apartment lavender, and Sophia, with my sister Rosa in tow, had turned to my office to use up the paint. I often felt as if I was entering a Barbie-doll office and I keep looking for the Mattel stamp on my desk or my phone.

Ma hadn't seen it until now, and she wasn't commenting. So she must be feeling pretty bad.

Ma took a hankie out of the Black Hole, which now perched on her lap like a vulture. "I'm all right, Angela. Just upset, worried." She dabbed at her eyes.

"Okay, Ma. What's the problem?"

"Angela, have you heard from your brother?"

I had three brothers. She expected me to know which one she was referring to? "Uh, I heard from Carla this morning. Vinnie's fine, according to her." Carla was Vinnie's second wife. She'd called to ask what she thought she should bring to Ma's seventieth birthday party. We were having a big blow-out party for Ma, inviting all the relatives, renting a church hall, and everyone was bringing pot-luck. I was in charge of videotaping the event—I'd recently purchased a new camcorder, courtesy of my uncle Sol, who worked at a discount electronic store in Boston proper.

Ma waved a hand dismissively. "No, no, not Vinnie."

I searched my memory. "Ray was at dinner last night," I ventured.

She looked at me as if I was her idiot child. "Of course Ray was there. I saw him, too. You two were whispering in my den about that surprise party you're throwing me."

Ma wasn't supposed to know about the party, but she was one of those people you couldn't keep a secret from.

Still, I tried. "What party?" I asked as innocently as possible.

She tilted her chin down and looked fiercely up at me from under her black (dyed) eyebrows. If she hadn't been my mother, I would have said that she looked a little like Groucho Marx at that moment.

That left Albert. He hadn't been at dinner last night. I sighed. "No, I haven't heard from Albert lately. But you know that's not so unusual."

Ma blinked fast, her expression returning to the softer, more vulnerable look she had originally when she came into my office. I thought she was going to cry right then and there. I reached for the tissue box. Ma shook her head and I took my hand away as fast as I'd reached for it.

"Ma, tell me. What's going on?" It wasn't uncommon for me to go without hearing from Albert for weeks at a time. It wasn't the first time he hadn't made it to the Sunday dinner. He knew about Ma's party, and he was good about showing up to important events, although he'd been known to make a late entrance.

Ma looked down, hesitant all of a sudden. I waited patiently. No use trying to rush Ma when she didn't want to be rushed—which was most of the time. "He didn't call me like he always does on Friday night," she said.

I blinked. This was news to me: I had always assumed that Albert didn't keep in touch with anyone in the family on a regular basis—including Ma. Ma had never mentioned it to me. Albert had always been in and out of our lives at his own leisure, and I had assumed that it wasn't any different with Ma. How I could have assumed that, I don't know. Now I was at a loss for words. But that didn't stop me. I didn't want Ma to know what I had taken for granted. "Okay, so he didn't call, Ma. That's not a crime."

Ma winced at my words, and inwardly, so did I.

The Matelli clan had always believed, in a collectively unspoken manner, that Albert was involved with something illegal, something we didn't want to know about.

"He always calls me on Friday night, just to touch base. And if he wasn't coming to Sunday dinner, he definitely would have called to let me know."

When I couldn't make Sunday dinner, which was rare, I always called. All of us children had been brought up to show respect for our elders, and to always RSVP, even if it was a standing invitation. Albert would have called unless he couldn't.

"Angela, I want to hire you to find out where he is. Make sure he's all right." She opened the Black Hole and took out her checkbook.

"No, Ma," I said, meaning for her to put away her money.

She fixed her dark brown eyes on me. Her stare could have cut me in half if it was a razor. "No? Are you saying no to me, Angela Agnes? You won't put my worry to rest by taking this case?"

I smiled, despite the fact that she used my hated middle name. "I mean, no, Ma, you don't have to hire me. You're family. Albert's family. I'll look for him for free."

I figured this was a piece of cake. My little brother was probably on a business trip or on a long weekend with a new love or doing something I didn't even want to think about. Albert is Ma's youngest son and she worries about him more than she does the rest of us. He had pneumonia when he was four and almost died, and since then, she's been under the impression that Albert is delicate. I happen to know that Albert works out every day, either running

five miles or spending an hour at his local gym, sparring
with a punching bag.

We don't talk about it much, but Albert works for the
Mob in Rhode Island. Yeah, it's kind of hard to believe
that I could be working for one side and Albert has been
working for the other side. But as far as anyone knew,
Albert was no soldier or enforcer. I cornered Uncle Iggy
once at a family get-together—actually, it was Aunt Rose's
funeral. Uncle Iggy is about the most "connected" Matelli
we have in our family and he assured me that Albert's
hands were still fairly clean—no blood on them, anyway.
He'd started as a bagman, then ran numbers, delivered
packages, and now he ran front operations for the Mob.

In other words, if he were ever arrested in any of those
situations, he would probably be set free for lack of evidence. "I was holding it for a friend" or "I thought I was
running a take-out chicken place, I didn't know I was fronting for the Mob," would get Albert out on bail, maybe get
him a finger-shaking from some judge if it ever went to
court. But so far, Albert hadn't been arrested or caught in
a raid. He led a charmed life. Maybe that was why the Mob
kept him around.

"Look, let me take you out to dinner, and we can talk
about this, okay?" I slipped my arm around her.

She patted my hand and nodded. "You're a good girl,
Angela."

I took Ma to an early dinner at an Italian deli down the
street and, while we were waiting for our orders, she told
me all the latest dope on the family.

"Aunt Sarah just had hip replacement surgery. She's going through physical therapy and Uncle Martin tells me that
every time she takes a step, he can hear the squeak," Ma
said after swallowing a mouthful of chicken salad. She was
using her fork like a maestro uses his baton to direct an

orchestra. "He asked the therapist about it and she told him the squeak would go away in time."

"If it doesn't go away, maybe they could go in and oil it every once in a while," I replied. I was being facetious. I had skipped lunch to get all my paperwork done today, so I ate heartily.

Ma nodded solemnly. "I'll ask if that can be done."

I started to tell her I was kidding, but thought better of it. That would lead to a lecture on how important family was and how I shouldn't make fun of old people and their hip replacements because "someday, mark my words, you will be under the knife and you'll be praying to God that everything goes smoothly." So I just smiled and chewed another mouthful of pastrami, sautéed onions, and provolone on rye.

"Speaking of Sarah and Martin, you know his sister, Beatrice?" I didn't even have time to nod before Ma continued. Beyond my sisters and brothers and their immediate families, family relationships turn a little muddy for me and I find it easier to just feign knowledge where there was none. "Well, she wrote a letter to her son, John, telling him that she was divorcing him."

I frowned. "Beatrice was married to Sarah and Martin's son?"

Ma snorted impatiently. "Beatrice is divorcing John, her son."

"Beatrice was married to her own son? Isn't that illegal?" I was beginning to take a trip to fuzzy-town with all the soap opera goings-on.

Ma rolled her eyes. "She's not divorcing him in the conjugal sense, Angela. It's a symbolic divorce. Sarah confided in me that there's been a lot of abuse between the two of them."

"Sarah and John or Sarah and Beatrice?" I couldn't believe I'd allowed Ma to pull me into her gossip mill. I barely knew these people. I'd probably seen John and Beatrice a total of three times in my whole life. Why should I care? But now, I wanted to straighten this whole thing out for my sanity, then instruct Ma to never mention these people again.

"For heaven's sake, Angela, if you opened your ears, you might learn something. I was talking about Beatrice," Ma said through clenched teeth. I could see she was beginning to regret having brought up this subject. "There has been abuse between John and Beatrice."

"John's been hitting his mom?" I asked. I didn't know Cousin John very well, but I had just seen him that third time in my life, just last Christmas, and he'd struck me as a fairly mellow guy for a stockbroker.

Ma shook her head, her gold earrings dangling from beneath her short black hair sprayed into the likeness of a motorcycle helmet. "No, Sarah told me that Beatrice feels that John doesn't pay enough attention to her."

I recalled that John had taken his mom on an all-expenses paid three-week European holiday last year, just because he loved her. For Christmas, we had all been witness to the recliner and big screen TV that he'd given her. I remembered that Ma had mentioned in a big fat hint to all of us that John had taken his mother to New York City for a four-day weekend and wined and dined her on her birthday. I reminded Ma, and felt proud of myself for being able to dredge all this up in an instant.

She dismissed all my handiwork with a wave of her hand. "That's just things," Ma said loftily. "He doesn't talk to her. When he calls her on the phone, he listens to what she has to say, then says, 'Uh-huh. That's nice, Ma. Well, I've got to turn in early tonight. Big meeting in the morning. Love you. Bye.'"

"So you're saying he doesn't talk to her. And that's abuse?" I was getting a headache from trying to figure out what Aunt Beatrice was so upset about. I was of John's generation, so I guess I wasn't able to see what was the big deal. As a child, teenager, and adult, John had never struck me, in the few times I'd seen him, as much of a talker. It seemed to me that if Aunt Beatrice wanted someone to gossip with, she should have had a daughter. Besides, once you did get John talking, as I had finally done at the holidays after a few mugs of Tom and Jerry, he could be downright dull when he started in about stocks and his toy train hobby. But I refrained from saying anything to Ma. I was no perfect daughter and I was afraid she might start in on my less-than-wonderful qualities.

It was time to change the subject. "So Ma, what do you know about Albert's plans for this week?" I hadn't wanted to take this job too seriously at first, but now I was beginning to think about it—Albert was a good son. He called Ma every week, talked to her, unlike Cousin John. Maybe there was something to Ma's worry. Of course, this was coming from someone who got a call from Ma every time I got the sniffles: "This is the third time I've called, Angela, and I'm worried you're not answering the phone. You could be lying there, sick as a dog, feverish, dead for all I know. Please call me when you get this message."

She shrugged and looked down at the remnants of her chicken salad. "Aah. I don't know. Albert's good at talking to me every Friday, but he never really says anything."

I leaned toward her. "Ma, as an investigator to her client, I have to tell you, holding out on the investigator is going to make her job much more difficult."

She closed her eyes. "But, Angela, you're my daughter. There are some things a mother must keep from her children."

I leaned back in my chair. "Ma, whatever you're holding back from me won't shock me. Remember, I spent eight years in the marines."

She looked up and gave me a half smile. "Yeah, you don't have to remind me, Angela." Her voice took on a wistful tone. "Sometimes I wish you weren't so self-sufficient, that you relied on me more."

I suppressed a smile. "You mean, you want me to be a kid again."

Ma rolled her eyes and shook her head. "No, but your independence scares me."

That's why you rely on me so much, I thought. I'd always been the dependable one, the one Ma called when something was wrong with another member of the Matelli clan. I was the fixer, just like now.

Her shoulders squared and she said, "Albert works for the Mob."

I suppressed the urge to say, "And—?" Instead, I raised my eyebrows in mild surprise. But I could never fool Ma. She waved her hand dismissively. "Of course, you knew that. But Albert told me he was thinking about leaving the Family. Now he doesn't call me and I can't reach him."

"Oh," I replied into the heavy silence that followed. "That could be a problem."

I often found it difficult to believe that he was working for the Mob in the first place. He had earned a degree in business and was putting it to use for a crime organization. Of course, the Mafia had paid for his college education, so that probably explained why he'd gone to work for them after he'd graduated.

She gave me a sharp look, but didn't say anything.

I asked her the questions I would normally ask a client. "When did you last talk to Albert? What did he say to you? Can you remember anything that maybe didn't seem important at the time, something he might have said that seemed unusual? Was there anyone who wanted to do him harm? Where was the last place he was seen by anyone? Who did he hang around with?''

Ma seemed overwhelmed. I was thinking that she didn't realize exactly what I did for a living, and it kind of impressed her. She was silent after answering my last question.

"Are you okay?" I asked as I wrote the last name of Albert's school chum in my notebook.

"Yeah, but I was thinking—"

I sat up a little straighter and prepared to be showered with praise.

"—maybe I'd better come with you. I'm not sure you're gonna be able to investigate this case on your own."

"Ma—," I started to say something, then broke off. I could hear the air deflating from my grandiose idea that Ma might be impressed with my work. "—I don't think that'd be such a good idea."

"Why not? I know Albert better than you do. Besides—" she dug around in her purse and produced a key "—I have a key to Albert's apartment." She waved it like a carrot in front of my nose before dropping it back into her purse. It would be a good place to start.

I sighed, knowing I'd been bested. "Okay, Ma, you can come along on the apartment search, but that's where it ends."

Ma smiled for the first time since she'd come into my office, but I didn't like her smile much. It was too smug.

TWO

SINCE MA DIDN'T DRIVE, we took my three-year-old Bronco for the hour-long trip to Albert's neighborhood in Providence, Rhode Island. It took us longer than usual because the roads were clogged during rush hour. Ma spent most of the time catching up on more family news. It seemed to be a never-ending list of maladies, surgeries that went wrong, and grudges against other family members. I was beginning to think Ma could sell the Matelli family story to some network as a soap opera.

I was also getting the impression that Ma looked on this time with me as a treat instead of business, and I had to admit that this was how I was treating Albert's "disappearance" as well. Even with the information that the Mob might be involved, I found it hard to take my missing brother seriously.

Although most of the Italian faction of modern-day East Boston had some Mob connections buried in the family, we tried not to think about it too much—until and unless it was needed. I guess a lot of Italian-Americans who lived decent, law-abiding lives liked to think of the Mob as something from the past. We knew it still existed, but as long as it didn't touch our lives, we pretended it didn't. Maybe that was why Ma and I spent most of our drive to Rhode Island acting as if we were spending a day down there on a holiday.

I hadn't been to visit Albert since he'd moved in several weeks earlier, right after the divorce and the sale of his and Sylvia's house. My brother now lived in a nice condo complex that overlooked the ocean and was called, appropriately enough, "Oceanview."

The sun had set by the time we pulled up and parked in front of the building. Despite the darkness, I could see enough of the condo to note the minimalist look. It was basically a cube with windows, much like a hotel. Upon entering the lobby, I noticed that the tang of salt air permeated the inside of the building. I wondered how much of the rent money had gone to the upkeep of the inside of the building. It was warm in the lobby and the security guard on duty was dressed for the Caribbean, wearing a tropical shirt, khaki shorts, and shades. His physique was overly muscular for a guy who sat in a lobby all day, playing a glorified doorman. I mean, how much work was it to sign in service people, answer phones, and open doors for the residents of this high-class condominium?

"Can I help you ladies?" he asked, taking off his shades to give us a gander at his baby blues. He flashed a smile. I got the feeling that he flashed the same smile at everyone. His nametag said Biff.

Ma took over. She'd been to Albert's new place once before. "We're here to see Albert Matelli. He should be expecting me."

Biff consulted a computer behind his desk, picked up his phone and punched in a number. After a minute had gone by and no answer, he frowned and hung up. "I'm afraid he's not in right now."

"That's okay, we can wait in his apartment. I have a key." Ma started to rummage around in her purse.

Biff's smile stayed in place. "I'm afraid I can't allow that." He glanced at the computer monitor again. "You aren't authorized to have a key."

"What is this," I asked, "some kind of Gestapo condo?"

He favored me with a superior smile, the kind that makes me want to smash a cream pie in his face. "This is a high-security condominium. The residents don't want strangers wandering around the halls of this building unescorted." He said the word *strangers* as if he really wanted to call us *riff-raff.* Funny, coming from a guy built like a muscle-worshiper. He ought to be out on Venice Boulevard, pumping iron on Muscle Beach with other steroid-bound freaks while thong-clad girls roller-skated by. I noted that his hair was thinning on top—probably due to steroid use—and he combed it back with plenty of gel to separate each stand, hoping to cover as much area as possible with what little he had left.

"But I'm his mother!" Ma said. "I should be on his list."

"What's your name again?" he asked. She told him. Biff looked at the screen again, then shook his head. "I'm sorry, but Mr. Matelli just moved in a few weeks ago, and it's possible he hasn't had time to put you on the list."

"I have ID to prove who I am." She took out her wallet and showed him, but Biff remained unmoved.

He barely glanced at her ID before stepping around the desk and sticking his hand out. "I'm sorry, ma'am. It's against the association's rules for anyone who isn't on the authorized list to have a key to a resident's unit. Please turn the key over to me, ma'am."

Ma surprised me by setting her lips in a thin line, lightly rummaging around, and then looking up defiantly at Biff. "Oh, dear, I'm afraid I left my key at home in Malden. That's in Massachusetts." She smiled sweetly at him before turning to me, a helpless look in her eye, and shrugged. "Maybe we can go shopping and have some coffee while we wait for him."

This wasn't the Ma I knew. She was usually accommodating to people in positions of authority. Even officious muscle-bound jerks like Biff, who did not look a bit convinced by Ma's forgetful little old lady routine. Ma has a mind as sharp as a stiletto and just by looking at her, it showed. At least, I'd always thought so. But I stayed in character, the good and patient daughter waiting on her dotty mother. "Whatever you say, Ma." I turned to Biff. "Do your residents always check in with you?"

"Yeah, ninety-nine percent of the time. It's easier for them when they're expecting service people and guests."

"Can you tell me when my brother checked in with you last?" Biff was caught off guard and nodded. He tapped a few keys and frowned. "Says here that he hasn't checked in for three days."

I glanced around, noting the security monitors behind Biff. One camera was focused on what looked like a side door.

I thanked him and we left.

"What was Albert thinking, not putting me on the list to have a key to his apartment?" Ma grumbled when we were outside.

I had an idea, but I had to wonder how Ma had acquired the key in the first place. So I asked the million-dollar question. "Does Albert know you have a key?"

She shrugged. "He forgot his spare set of keys at my place a few Sundays ago, and picked them up a week later. I thought it would be prudent to have a spare key made in case he forgot *his* spare set, and lost his originals."

Spoken like a true mother. Always looking out for us, even when we were in our twenties and thirties.

"Well, that makes sense," I said, trying to remember if I'd ever left my keys with Ma at any point in the last few years.

"What's next?" she asked.

"I thought we'd go out for coffee. That's what you told Biff in there."

Ma shot me a narrow look.

"We have to make this look like we're really going to go to coffee." Besides, it was almost seven o'clock and I was hungry again. That sandwich I had two hours ago might as well have been Chinese food.

We found a Starbuck's about a mile down from where Albert lived. While Ma ignored her Earl Grey, I enjoyed my hazelnut latte and almond biscotti.

"Your tea isn't good?"

She looked up at me, her face ashen and drawn. "It's good," she replied with a shrug. "I'm just not thirsty." Ma was worried.

"Ma, it's only been a few days. Albert probably met some girl, fell in love, and he's with her now." I felt self-conscious saying it to my own mother, but I had to make her feel better. I pushed away my clean plate and sipped my latte. I had to distract her in some way, and I thought I knew how. If the Mob was involved and there was foul play, I didn't want her along while I was breaking and entering. On the other hand, I had agreed to take her with me. I had a set of walkie-talkies that I'd recently used in a job I did with Chuck Eddy, a private eye I teamed up with on occasion. Fortunately, I hadn't had the occasion to return them to Eddy yet.

Ma could stay by the car and act as lookout. We went back to the Bronco. There was a chill in the air as I drove back to Albert's condo.

"He could be lying in his condo, unable to get to the phone to let anyone know that he's hurt," Ma was saying. She'd already come up with a dozen of scenarios about what could have happened to Albert. Every once in a while,

I managed to interject a "hmm" or some other nonspecific sound to let Ma know I was listening.

We parked on a side street near the condo. I spotted the door I was searching for on the side of the building. I got out of the car and walked up to inspect it. A safety bar kept unauthorized people from wandering in from the outside and a card slot was installed for residents who wanted to enter. A Dumpster sat to one side of the door. Residents could walk out the door, throw their trash in the Dumpster, and then use their card to get back in. As if on cue, a tall, slender, blond-bearded man came out of the side door, carrying a trash bag. Fortunately, I was on the other side of the Dumpster when he tossed his burden into it with a basketball-like dunk.

Not wanting to waste my chance, I pulled out my wallet and took a credit card out. As soon as he had opened the door again and walked inside, I hurried up and slipped the credit card across the lock while the door slowly closed. It held. I waited a minute before peering inside to make sure no one was coming out, and found the hallway empty.

"What's going on?" Ma's voice came from behind my right shoulder and made me jump. Fortunately, I wasn't still holding on to the credit card, or we might have had to wait for someone else to take out the trash.

"Ma, don't do that to me." I turned to look at her.

She looked genuinely perplexed. "Do what?"

"Sneak up on me like that."

She shrugged. "I thought you investigators had some sort of super-sense or something. I thought you would have heard me coming."

"I'm not a superhero, Ma," I replied, hoping she couldn't see me blushing furiously in the dark. Despite my explanation, I was a little embarrassed that I hadn't heard her come up behind me.

"What's next? What'd you do to the door?" She started
to reach for it. I stopped her as gently as I could.

"I've made it possible to get inside. But for now, I need
you to do me a favor."

"What?"

"I need a lookout."

Ma looked disappointed. "You want me to stay outside,
not go with you where the action is?"

"Ma, someone needs to distract that security guard from
the monitors while I go up to Albert's apartment. You have
to keep him occupied."

"How can I do that?"

"Ma, you're good at that. Ask lots of questions. Get him
talking about himself. Just make sure he doesn't look at
those monitors for at least two minutes." I would be cutting
it close, but I could sprint for the stairs if the elevator
wasn't quick enough. I stuck my hand out. "I need the
key."

She sighed. "Okay. But I have to tell you that I'm not
happy about being left behind." She got the key out of her
pants pocket and handed it to me. Apparently all that
searching in the Black Hole had been an act for Biff's sake.

"Now I have to teach you how to use a walkie-talkie."

She brightened up at the thought of walkie-talkies. I took
them out of the Bronco's glove compartment, gave her one,
then we tested them. They seemed to be working, but it
took me a few minutes to show Ma which button was the
"on" button. She kept hitting the "off" button.

"Now go do your part to let me in," I instructed Ma.
"After a few minutes, leave the lobby and watch the building from across the street." I pointed to an empty bus
bench. "If anything funny seems to be happening—cop
cars or an ambulance or men in black—let me know."

She grabbed my arm before I turned to go. "Be careful,

Angie. I got a bad feeling something has happened to Albert and I'd never forgive myself if anything happened to you, too.'' She gave me a peck on a cheek and it felt as if I'd just donned armor. I don't know how mothers do that, but there's something about the way a mother worries about you and kisses you.

A few moments later, as I was crossing the street, my walkie-talkie squawked to life and I jumped. An older couple, out for a stroll, were passing by and they gave me a strange look. I turned away from them, took out the infernal device and turned down the volume. "What's up, Ma?"

"I'm about to enter the lobby," she whispered into her end of it.

"Okay. I hope he can't see you talking into that thing."

"You must think your mother is an idiot."

"No, Ma, but—"

Before I could explain myself, she butted in with, "Roger and out."

Ma must have thought we were *Adam-12* or something, using TV cop show phrases like "Roger and out." I shrugged, trotted up to the side door and pulled it open.

I felt as if I was breaking into Fort Knox, but it was only a condominium, a place I should have been able to get into in the first place. Why should I feel guilty about breaking into my own brother's home?

As I waited for the elevator to open, I studied the layout—wide halls, deep blue carpeting, pale sand-colored walls, and seashell-shaped, deco-inspired wall lighting sconces. Each unit had a door that was recessed, giving each resident a private little alcove. I looked for the security camera but as I expected, I didn't see it—probably fiber optics. Ma had kept the channel open so I could monitor her conversation with Biff. I kept the volume low.

The elevator doors finally opened and I was transported

to the third floor, which was much the same as the first
floor. Albert's unit, 311, faced the ocean and was near the
end of the hall. I knocked on the door, not expecting an
answer, and after half a minute, I used Ma's key. It stuck
a little, but I jiggled it and was able to gain entry before
anyone entered the hallway.

Albert's place was dark, and it smelled stuffy and sour,
like old garbage that hadn't been taken out. There wasn't
any reason I shouldn't turn on lights, so I felt around the
wall until I found a light switch. I'd never been in his new
condo, but from having visited Albert in his other surroundings, I was pleasantly surprised at the additions to his living
room.

Right after his divorce from Sylvia, his living area had
consisted of old kitchen chairs, a black and white TV, and
his old stereo from high school. He had a sofa now, along
with a matching easy chair and recliner, a state-of-the-art
entertainment center that included a CD player, a laser disc
player, VCR, and a tall CD rack of jazz, blues, old rock,
Motown, and alternative music. He even had one of those
flat TVs that hang on the wall. I added up the cost of all
the furniture and electronic equipment, and it came to
thousands of dollars. I figured at least in the middle five
figures.

Albert had been divorced for a few months, and his ex-
wife, Sylvia, maintained an amicable relationship with him
while managing to squeeze alimony out of him as she went
back to school to get a degree in business. Our family had
never really had a chance to like Sylvia. She was always a
little snide, always seemed to be looking down her nose at
us. And perhaps she was—her family came from Rhode
Island "old money." So I thought it was more than mag-
nanimous of Albert to support her even though the monthly

stipend from her trust fund was more than a modest lawyer made in a month.

I knew he had given her practically everything they had accumulated together—hence, kitchen table chairs and old stereo system in the living room, I recognized as stuff that had once been stored at Ma's house. I looked around, taking in the sleek, contemporary coffee table, the entertainment center, and the bookcases in an obviously expensive apartment.

"Albert," I muttered to myself, "how did you come into all of this?"

I wandered into the kitchen and found state-of-the-art kitchen appliances, a fabulous chrome Wolf gas range and grill, oven, and refrigerator, and a top of the line microwave. Albert liked to cook, and I wasn't surprised that his kitchen cabinets were well stocked with all sorts of gourmet spices and sauces, pastas and grains.

On the Wolf range was a skillet with something in it. I leaned over it and turned on the overhead light to get a better look at it. He'd been in the middle of cooking minced garlic before he disappeared. A large hunk of Parmesan cheese sat out, a hand grater next to it.

I moved over to the butcher-block island. A bowl of raw eggs sat out, along with a hunk of dried out prosciutto. The eggs were probably what stank. Albert had been making a carbonara. I'd make a great meal detective—just call Angela Matelli and she'll tell you what they were planning to make for dinner before disappearing.

A small alcove off the kitchen held an elegant dining room table and chairs. It was set for two people, but there were three wine glasses. Two of the glasses had the remains of a red Napa Valley cabernet in them. I didn't have to make any great deductions about the wine—the open bottle was sitting there, still half-full. On a whim, I moved over

to the refrigerator and opened the door, half-expecting to
see a body crammed into the space. Of course, it was just
a refrigerator with a couple of veal steaks sitting there.
They were off-color, indicating that they'd been in the refrigerator a day or two too long. In the door of the cooler,
along with the heavy cream that went into the pasta dish,
sat an unopened bottle of Gamay Beaujolais, a '96 vintage,
very nice, much lighter red than the cabernet—a better
choice as a companion to the pasta carbonara. Of course,
Gamay should only be in the refrigerator for an hour or
two before being served. Albert knew that—he was an even
bigger wine snob than I was. It was beginning to look as
if Albert was called away unexpectedly, or was forced to
leave.

I went back to the dining table and, with the aid of a
nearby napkin, picked up the glasses to inspect them. There
was no trace of lipstick on either. The third glass and the
open wine bottle told me that someone had shown up unexpectedly. I concluded that the mysterious third party had
been a man or a woman who didn't wear lipstick. I wondered who Albert's date was and if she'd seen Albert that
night. If she had, she hadn't stayed long enough to have
even a glass of wine.

I moved into one of the bedrooms. Despite the fact that
the smell seemed to follow me here, the room was neatly
put together with a nice black lacquer ensemble, and many
of Albert's trophies from high school were there. He'd been
on the swim team and the school had won a lot of meets
then. Albert had been one of the stars.

The bed was one of those waterbeds filled with gelatin.
Ick. I tried it, bouncing on it for a minute, and it seemed
comfortable enough. I stretched out on it and lay there,
staring up at the ceiling, thinking about Albert and where
he could be and why he'd left without a word. The walkie-

talkie squawked to life. I leaped from the bed like a cartoon character and fingered the volume.

"Angie! Angie? Are you there? Ten-four."

I tuned in. "It's 'over,' Ma."

"What's over?" I could hear the sounds of cars passing in the background. She was probably in or near my car.

"You don't say 'ten-four.' You say 'over' when you're finished saying something and want a response."

"Oh." There was a pause, then, "Over."

I sighed and pressed the button to talk. "Was there something you wanted, Ma?"

"No, just wondering what's going on up there. You're taking a long time." Pause. "Over."

"Sorry. I don't really have any timeframe, and I'm giving his place a thorough going-over. I'm sorry you can't join me. Over." I hoped she couldn't detect the insincerity in my voice.

"Okay. I'll just sit here. I brought along some knitting. Over."

"Ten-four," I replied. "I'll finish up here in about ten or fifteen minutes, then I'll lock up. Over and out."

I opened the drawer to his nightstand and found a package of condoms, some of the packaging empty, and a Lawrence Block Scudder novel that he'd read halfway through.

I moved over to the closet space. His clothes—Calvin Klein suits and matching shirts, silk haute couture ties, Hilfiger warm-ups and sports stuff, Gucci dress shoes, and Adidas running shoes—were organized in a wall-size closet. Albert had always been something of a neat freak. I was a little creeped out going through my brother's dresser drawers and highboy, but something might be hidden among his socks, cotton jockstraps, silk boxers, and linen handkerchiefs.

On top of his dresser was a mahogany box for his jewelry, which consisted of a Movado watch, a gold ring with a diamond chip in it, and an 18-carat gold-link ID bracelet that was inscribed "Always and forever, Sylvia." I thought how ironic it was that the memento he'd kept from his ex-wife was engraved with such a large promise, all of it unfulfilled.

The bathroom, which was off the master bedroom, was as neat as a pin with the exception of a bath towel that had been used and a few cotton balls and tissues in the wastebasket. His medicine cabinet consisted of over-the-counter painkillers like ibuprofen and acetaminophen, some mentholated cream for aching joints and shaving paraphernalia.

I moved back into the hallway, walking toward the other bedroom. I had been idly thinking about Albert and how little I knew of his life. He was my favorite brother, something I would never admit to the other members of the Matelli clan, but despite the fact that we all knew he worked for the Mafia, we didn't know much else about him. He maintained an enigmatic status.

The other bedroom was an office. The door was closed and when I opened it, the first thing I noticed about it was the corpse.

I'd thought it was rotten eggs that smelled, and all the time I'd been in this apartment, this corpse had been laying here on the floor of Albert's office. I gagged at the stench, then remembered there was a jar of Vicks VapoRub in Albert's bathroom. Stumbling down the hall, I tried to figure out what I was going to do. Should I call the cops? Yes, of course. But who was this guy in Albert's office? Had Albert killed him? Could I turn in my own brother?

I entered the bathroom just as my stomach did a somersault and I fell to my knees, now fully understanding the term "praying to the porcelain god." When I had nothing left to give, I flushed the toilet, then remembered to wipe down the toilet handle for fingerprints with a handkerchief I kept handy in my purse.

I tried to recall the face of the victim as I reached for the Vicks. My strongest reaction was that I didn't want to think about it at all, but here is where my military training, being a marine, comes in handy—I went on automatic pilot. I'd seen a few dead bodies in the service and in my current line of work but until now, I had had the good fortune to avoid discovering a ripe body before. I took a few deep breaths, then gagged again, ending in an unpleasant cough. Yuck. Three-day-old corpses smelled bad, and remembering that didn't even begin to cover how bad it was to look at them.

But I had to steel myself to look at the dead man again—I couldn't be certain but from my quick look at it, he wasn't Albert. Everything in my being said it wasn't him. I only hoped my instincts were right this time.

After fortifying myself with more Vicks on cottonballs stuffed in my nose, I went back into the office. I made sure all the lights were turned on, then leaned over the dead guy to get a better look. He was crumpled up like a human accordion, clearly shot from behind. His face was toward the office door, and he already had started rotting. The large bluish "bruises" were actually where the blood had started pooling under the skin. I concentrated on the swollen features, trying to determine if this was my brother or not. A few moments of indecision for me, then I noticed a small mole to the left side of his nose. Yes, he resembled Albert, but Albert didn't have a mole on his handsome face. He also didn't have the small hole behind the left ear where the bullet had entered.

Relief flooded through me and I staggered back a few steps, bumping into the open door. I took another breath through my mouth, stepped forward again, and carefully went through the victim's pockets. But he was clean—no identification. A message—that's what he was.

I thought back to the two wine glasses. If Ma had been here, she would have started cleaning the apartment and gotten rid of the evidence. I was tempted to, but something held me back—I was pretty sure Albert hadn't killed this man, and it was becoming clear to me that Albert had been set up for something. I didn't know for what, but I did know something was going on.

I decided to call the police after I'd been through the apartment—maybe somewhere safe like back in Massachusetts at some pay phone at a rest area along the way. I had to get Ma out of here—she shouldn't have to be involved. If I stayed and called the police, I'd have to explain why I was in my brother's apartment without his permission—Biff would make the police throw the book at me, that much was clear. I wouldn't be able to investigate from a jail cell.

I got on the walkie-talkie. "Ma."

"Roger, Angela, what's up? Are you leaving?"

"I just found, um, something, and I'm gonna have to check into it a little more." I couldn't tell her. Not yet. Maybe not ever, if there was a way to do it. Even as I thought it, I knew there was no way to keep this news from her. But maybe for just a little while—maybe just until we were back in Massachusetts, and I had cleared this mess up, and maybe when I was married and had given her the grandchildren she'd always wanted from me. Then I would tell her. But I knew that was unrealistic as hell. I could at least wait until I absolutely had to tell her.

There was silence on the other end. I wondered what she was thinking. She finally told me. "I'm comin' up there to help. You need some help."

"No, Ma," I spoke frantically into the walkie-talkie.

"Angela, don't tell me what to do."

"Ma, I'm not staying here. I'm leaving in a few minutes. Please do as I say." I told her to take the car and drive a block away. I would meet her. I prayed she'd kept up her driver's license without owning a car—and that her driving wouldn't draw unneeded attention.

"All right," I heard her say reluctantly. "But Angela, Albert's not there?"

"No, Ma, he's not here." What the hell was she thinking right now—Albert was hiding in his own condo, impersonating a floor lamp? The guy in his office was doing a damn awful job of impersonating a throw rug.

More silence, then, "All right, we'll do it your way. But I don't like it."

"Neither do I, Ma."

Before I left, I had to go through Albert's office. I knew I wouldn't get another chance. I also had to do it fast for two reasons: Ma wanted to come up to help, and the less time I stayed with the corpse in the room, the better off I'd be.

I looked around. There was a desk with a printer on a new computer desk, but no computer. It was probably a notebook computer and either the person who killed this guy had taken it, or Albert had grabbed it before fleeing the scene of the crime. Boxes were stacked against the far wall. A cell phone rested on the desk, and I thought that was odd, considering that Albert almost never went anywhere without his cell phone. Even when he was going through the divorce, Albert kept the cell phone. I noted that his briefcase was gone. He carried it to Boston whenever he came to visit. Sometimes he had it when he came to Sunday dinner at Ma's. I was just starting to go through his desk when my walkie-talkie squawked to life again.

"Angela! Angela? Are you there, Angela?"

I spoke into my end. "Yeah, I'm here, Ma. Jeez, you scared the crap out of me. It's so quiet here. Where are you?" I was avoiding looking at the corpse, but it was hard to get past the vision of what I first saw when I opened the door to Albert's home office.

"I'm in the car. Did you find anything?"

"It looks like he left in a hurry, wherever he was going. And it looks like he had company. There's no sign of a struggle, so he went willingly, or at the end of a gun—" I forgot who I was talking to for a moment, and I heard an audible gasp. I decided it wasn't the time to apologize. "It also looks like he was planning some romantic dinner and his plans were interrupted. I just have to figure out who he was having over for dinner—"

"Albert was seeing someone, I think her name was Karen. What was he going to make for dinner?"

Before I thought about the idiocy of the question, I answered, "Looks like a carbonara."

"Did he use prosciutto or pancetta? A lot of my friends swear by pancetta, saying that it doesn't overpower the flavor of the carbonara—"

"Ma—"

"—but I like prosciutto—"

"Ma!"

There was silence for a moment followed by, "What?"

"Enough about the prosciutto. Albert's missing and I have to finish up here so we can call the police."

THREE

I FIGURED THAT if anything would give me a hint of what he had gotten himself into, it would be in Albert's office. The dead body was about the biggest hint I'd ever seen. It was difficult to ignore, but I did my best as I looked through the desk drawers. I found nothing, no taped envelopes stuck under the drawers, no cryptic messages.

There was a box of diskettes, some labeled and some not. I know I don't always label diskettes that I use, so I dumped all of them in my purse.

As I reached for the phone, I noticed that the answering machine was blinking. I played the tape back. There were seven messages.

The first message was from someone who didn't identify himself. The content made my blood run cold. The voice itself made me think of a bulldog. "Al, you there? I see your car is here. Me Nick and Eddie will be paying you a little visit in the next hour if you don't—"

Albert picked up. "Yeah, I'm here, Johnny. Look, I'm expecting a young lady. Can't this wait?"

"No. No, it can't wait. You haven't given Sal an answer, Al. He needs an answer right now."

There was an audible sigh from my brother. "Come up for a minute. Alone. Leave Eddie out of this. We'll talk." Click. That was the end of it. Now I had a few names: Eddie, Nick, Johnny, and Sal. Was Eddie the guy on Albert's office floor or was it Johnny? Maybe it was Nick or Sal. Maybe it was someone else who wasn't mentioned on the tape. I continued to listen to the messages.

Beep. "Albert? Karen. What happened to you Friday night? I came to your apartment, but the security guard said you'd gone out. I hope you have a good excuse." She didn't sound happy, but she didn't sound angry either—more curious and worried than anything else.

Beep. "Hey, Rick here. You didn't pick up our clients at the airport. I'm taking them to lunch. I hope you're here for the two o'clock meeting today. This could be very important to the future of our business. Hope you pay me back for the taxi."

Beep. "Albert? This is your mother. I haven't heard from you. Call me. Soon."

Beep. "Albert. Rick again. It's three o'clock, man, and you didn't show up for the meeting. By the way, I took our clients to an expensive lunch, on you. You get cold feet or something? Never thought I'd see the day you were intimidated by big money. But guess what? They're still eager to buy. We can't make a move without you, though. You know that. What's going on? Call me." Hmm, curiouser and curiouser.

Beep. "Albert? Karen. I'm worried. You haven't called. Unless aliens abducted you, call me."

Beep. "Al? Sylvia. I wanted to know if you're free on Wednesday night for dinner. Give me a call and we'll get together."

I didn't know who Rick was or why Albert had a meeting with him, or why he was even chauffeuring clients of some sort. Karen was clearly the guest on Friday night. Sylvia, the ex-wife, was obviously still on good terms with my brother. I put the tape in my purse along with the diskettes.

Damn, Albert couldn't be an open book. He had to be an enigma. If he threw a party and invited everyone he knew, I'd bet that they would all meet each other for the first time. He wasn't much for crowds, the exception being family.

I gazed at the desktop and realized that there was a small rectangular place where a notebook computer had once sat. Someone had either taken the computer, or my brother had grabbed it before he disappeared. My eye caught sight of a white envelope in the wastepaper basket. I picked it out and smoothed it on the desktop. The return address was ToyCo, a major toy company. I dug around in the trash, past the apple cores, banana peels, and junk mail to the bottom of the basket, but didn't find anything else.

The file cabinet was a two-drawer affair set to one side of the desk. I looked up the T's in the bottom drawer, and found a ToyCo file. But it was empty. With an empty envelope and a file with the ToyCo name on it, I reasoned that someone—Albert—had taken the letter. The killer? One and the same? I didn't even want to think about it. I just wanted to get out of the office with the rotting body in it.

But someone had taken the letter that had been inside the envelope. I stuck the envelope into my purse and sat back in the comfortable office chair. Spinning around in the chair while I mulled over what I had found, I caught sight of the slightly open closet door and the stack of boxes just inside.

I reluctantly left the chair, stepped around the corpse, and opened the closet door. Hauling one of the boxes out, I took out my handy folding knife from my purse and slit open the tape that held it closed. It was filled to the brim with Itty Bitty Kittys. I recognized the cat-faced doll with three changes of clothes that Albert had given our niece, Stephanie, for her tenth birthday last year. In fact, she had received one before Itty Bitty Kittys hit the open market a few months later. The doll became an instant hit at Christmas, selling over a million of the suckers to little girls throughout the United States. It had been this year's Furby or Cabbage Patch Doll.

I opened another box and it was filled with the same thing. Not all of the boxes were the same size, so I opened one of the smaller boxes. It was filled with Itty Bitty Kitty clothes. The sickening pink and purple and green colors swirled together made me grimace. Why were all girls' toys the same icky colors? Why did girls fall for that stuff? I'd never understood it, even when I was a little girl. I was always more attracted to Lionel trains and chemistry sets, but my relatives and their friends and I ended up with Barbie dolls and baby dolls and makeup and nail polish.

I fingered a couple of the outfits. They were kind of cute. I looked over at one of the Itty Bitty Kitty boxes. The doll *was* kind of appealing, in an ooky way. I picked it up and selected some of the clothes, telling myself that it was odd that my brother had so much of this stuff. It must mean something. I should take one of everything back to Boston and study it. And if I got bored looking at Itty Bitty Kitty in her pink-and-purple polka-dotted playsuit, I could always change her clothes.

Ma spoke to me again from the walkie-talkie. "Angela, I can hear sirens in the background. I don't know if it has anything to do with Albert's condo, but you should get outta there. Over."

"Okay, Ma. I'll be coming out the side door. Over." I had to get out of there. Chances were that the sirens were for someplace else, someplace near here, but I didn't want to take any more chances. I'd just about finished my search anyway.

I deliberated for a moment—should I wipe down my fingerprints? I was his sister, and why shouldn't my fingerprints be here? I quickly wiped down the closet door and the light switch. There was no time to do anything else.

As I left the office, I grabbed one of the boxes of dolls and another box of outfits. I took the elevator to the ground floor, praying that I wouldn't run into the cops. The coast was clear—I'd always wanted to say that—and I was about to slip through the side door when I thought about access to the garage. I moved down the hallway toward the front, remembering that the garage was on the left side of the building and unmindful of security cameras at this point. I turned right and saw the door to the garage ahead, clearly marked.

The garage was filled with cars, as was expected, and there were dim lights in every concrete post so the residents could find their cars and unlock them. Albert had a vintage black Trans Am, and I looked for it. The spaces, fortunately, were clearly marked for the residents and I easily found Albert's space—empty.

Although I didn't meet anyone on my way out of the garage, I swear I could feel eyes on me as I walked around the corner to where Ma had been ordered to park. Ma had her eyes closed while seated in the passenger seat. When I slammed the door shut, she bolted upright, opening her eyes.

"I thought I'd have to bail you out of jail," she said. "Did you find anything besides rotten eggs and prosciutto?"

Again, I debated on whether to tell her, then decided against it. She didn't need to worry about it.

"Someone was definitely in there," I said. "Someone besides Albert. It's difficult to tell, but if he was taken against his will, the other guy had a gun. There wasn't any sign of a struggle." It was wonderful the way the words flowed from my lips—not lying, exactly, but not telling the whole truth.

I started the car, itchy to get out of Providence and out of Rhode Island. I would imagine the police were on my tail all the way to the border of Massachusetts. But what scared me the most was the fact that Ma had been right— something was definitely wrong with Albert's disappearance.

The lookalike corpse was the clincher. It was as if someone had wanted to deliver a message to Albert. I wondered if Nick, Johnny, Eddie, or Sal had anything to do with the dead man, or if this had happened later, the next day. Albert might have disappeared of his own free will once he discovered the corpse.

My next questions had to do with my own involvement: Would I be able to find an ex-Mafioso, and if so, did I want to? If I did, I would definitely place my family and myself in danger, and quite possibly, if Albert had been able to go deep enough underground, my meddling would compromise his safety. On the other hand, Ma probably couldn't live without seeing or talking to one of her children. It was going to be hard next Sunday if he didn't show up to dinner.

Before we left, I swung around the block, slowing down when I came to the street the condo was on. Yes, there were several police cars parked there, red lights blinking merrily away. What I couldn't understand was how the police had found out. No doubt it was an anonymous phone call. But who had known? Ma, and the security guard— Biff? Was he worth talking to? And what would he know? Did he call the police because he suspected I'd gotten up to Albert's condo after all, or did he know about the corpse? Questions, questions. And no answers.

Ma had fallen silent, unusual for the old gal. I wondered

if she knew I was deep in thought, or if she was deep in thought as well. We didn't say much on the drive back, except when she said I was driving too erratically, which seemed to be every time she thought I was cutting off a truck or drifting toward the shoulder of the interstate.

Surprisingly, I didn't drop her off at a rest area. I actually drove her all the way back home to Malden.

"You want to come in for some late dinner, Angela? Nothing fancy, just leftovers."

Now I was never known, in my entire life, to turn down a meal at Ma's, even leftovers.

I followed her inside and she heated up my favorite, stuffed artichokes and large wedges of northern-style lasagna, in her new microwave oven, the one Albert had given her for Christmas. I set the table in the kitchen. She sat down with a couple of glasses of cold red table wine and pushed one toward me. Most Italians seem to keep the red table wine cold. Go figure. I finished up the silverware and slowly sat down, then took a sip of the wine. It was comfortable, sort of like the stuffed artichokes and Ma's lasagna.

"So, tell me in more detail—what did Albert's place look like? Were there any clues? Anything you could look into? Did you find an address book?"

Maybe she knew. Ma had a sixth sense when her children weren't telling her the whole truth. I still couldn't tell her. But I did launch into theories and described the condo in detail.

Ma stayed silent, a feat that was probably difficult for her. She didn't yell at me like I thought she would. She just nodded. "It's time to see Don Testa."

The microwave took that moment to beep. I thought I hadn't heard her. "What did you say?"

"I said," Ma said as she got up and calmly walked over

to the microwave to take out our food, "it's time for me
to go see Don Testa."

I got up and helped her dole out the lasagna, making
sure I gave myself an extra portion. She put the artichokes
on our plates, making sure I got the bigger one. It's a wonder I wasn't three hundred pounds by now, but I attributed
that to the fact that I had a high metabolism. And the two
hours of Aikido and kickboxing aerobics that I did five days
or more a week.

The garlic, lemon and nutmeg aromas mingled and I in-
haled the fragrance, but suddenly, I wasn't hungry. A first
for me. "Wait a minute, are you talking about a guy named
Don, or the Don?" The Don, Don Testa, was the boss of
the Rhode Island Mafia family. Albert worked for him.

"The Don, We went to school together." Ma had been
a pistol in her time, from what I've heard from Uncle "No-
Legs" Charlie.

I sat down in my chair a little harder than I wanted to.
She looked at me. "You don't look well, Angela. Maybe
you should stay here tonight."

"No, it's just that, well, I guess I never thought much
about the Mafia. I always knew it was a part of our history,
and I knew Albert was involved in a peripheral way. I guess
I just never thought of the guys at the top as having gone
to school with my mother."

"He used to carry my books to school," Ma continued.
"He took me to the homecoming dance, too."

"Uh, that's great, Ma, but I don't think carrying your
books to school is going to bring up so many sentimental
memories that he's going to forgive Albert whatever he's
gotten himself into."

Ma didn't answer. She just started to eat. Despite my
earlier lack of appetite, I'd regained it and attacked my
artichoke with gusto. When I was down to the heart, Ma

brought up the subject again. "Of course, you would go with me, Angela. I couldn't go alone. But I'll have to talk to him." Right. She said this as if I was a tag-along kid who was privileged to go with her. I choked on a bite of lasagna.

"Look, Ma, that's a good idea. But let me try a few other things first. Okay?"

Ma blinked back a few tears. "He's such a good boy, is Albert. I hope he's all right. I think I'm supposed to feel it if something's, you know, wrong with him."

I knew what she meant—she just couldn't bring herself to say the word *dead*.

I hoped he was okay, too.

FOUR

IT WAS VERY LATE when I left Ma's house and drove home. I took Albert's boxes to my house because it was closer than my office. I lugged the boxes up three flights to my apartment.

Very early the next morning, I dug the diskettes and cassette out of my purse, stuffed them in a large bag, and took the blue line T to my office building. Now that I had essentially broken into my brother's apartment, I wasn't sure how to proceed. I knew I would probably have to call family members and ask if they'd heard from him. I was hoping one of the diskettes would contain an address and phone number file of Albert's business contacts.

I took the elevator to my floor. Every time I entered my office these days, it was hard to believe this was the same place I had moved into a few years ago. I sat down on the green and pink sofabed, which was pretty comfortable.

I glanced at the answering machine, but it was still quite early, so not even Ma had called me yet.

I started making a list of names, trying to match addresses to them. There was Rick, Eddie, Nick, Johnny, Karen, Sylvia, all my brothers and sisters, Ma, me. And Testa. As an afterthought, I added Biff's name. Why I added the security guard at Albert's building, I didn't know. I didn't like him, for one thing.

I had no last names for the first four on my list, although I was sure I could get Karen's last name from Ma. Biff didn't need a last name. I knew where I could find him.

I'd just turned my attention to Albert's diskettes when

the phone rang. I looked at the box of stuff and thought about my brother. I sighed. The phone rang again. I picked it up.

"Hello?"

Breathing. I hated obscene phone callers.

"Listen, buddy, I got more important things to do than—"

I almost missed it. "Angie?" The voice was breathy. I couldn't tell if it was a man or a woman with a low voice. There were car noises in the background.

"Albert?" I asked, sitting straight up. "Where are you?"

Click. The phone went dead. What the hell was that all about? I dialed star 69 to get the number of the person who'd just called. I wrote it down and called it back. It rang and rang and rang. I put my feet up on my desk, being very careful not to tip over in my temperamental chair. Finally, someone picked up. I could hear street noises in the background.

"Whatta you want? This is a public phone." It was a growl, the voice of some passerby who wanted to use the phone but found himself stuck answering some random call.

"Don't hang up," I said hastily. "I need to know something—what street is this phone on?"

"Copley Square," the voice said. "Outside Bixby's Bagels."

"Thanks."

"Don't mention it," he growled. Then the line went dead.

I sat back and tapped my fingers on my desk, an annoying habit that I only did in a room by myself. There was no point in following up on that call. If it had been Albert, he'd be long gone by the time I took the T there.

I took my list of everyone that knew Albert and started

eliminating those who probably weren't harboring him. I started with my brothers and sisters. Rosa was away in Italy for two weeks with her art history class. I'd personally put her on a plane a few days ago and I knew Albert wasn't hiding out in her apartment. Since I picked up all her mail and went into her apartment on a regular basis to feed her goldfish and water her plants, I think I would notice if one of my brothers were hanging around.

I called Sophia. I knew her school schedule, and today was one of her days at home.

"So has Albert turned up yet?" she asked.

"Ma told you, huh?"

I could almost hear her shrug over the phone. "She got to thinking about it and decided to tell all of us in case the Mob was after him."

So much for the "ignorance is bliss" part of my conversation with Ma. But she was right in telling Sophia.

"I already told Ma everything I know, which is nothing."

Great. Ma was doing my work for me. I just hoped she'd leave off her investigation with the family. I didn't need her digging into my case files and going out asking all sorts of impertinent questions—that was my job.

"So tell me what you told her," I replied.

"Angie, I just told you. I don't know anything helpful. He hasn't called here, and you know Albert and I weren't that close."

I stopped myself from saying anything to her about the past tense she used—I wanted to convince myself that Albert was still alive. I had to believe it. The dead body in his condo building was just a coincidence—wasn't it?

"Look," I said in a rational tone, "you may not be close to Albert, but that would be a reason why he would contact you. The Mob knows who he's close to, and he wouldn't put their lives in danger. But you—''

"Oh, so he'd put my life in danger, but not yours or Vinnie's?'' Sophia asked in a dry tone.

"That's not what I was saying.''

"Yeah, good old expendable Sophia. She'll help me,'' Sophia mimicked in a very poor imitation of Albert.

I chose to ignore Sophia's attempt at a pity party. "So he hasn't called or dropped a postcard in the mail?''

"Nope. But while you're at it, why not try Dad? Maybe Albert went to him.''

She had mentioned Dad to annoy me, but as ideas went, it didn't sound half bad. I wondered if Albert had gone to our dad to hide him out. My father had a phone, but when he was in, it was busy, and when no one answered, he was down at the racetrack. Uncle "No-Legs'' Charlie lived in the same apartment building, and I began to wonder if a trip down there would be worth my while.

Seeing my father wasn't something I looked forward to. On the other hand, I didn't dread it. I had come to terms with the fact that I hadn't had a strong father figure growing up. He was just one of those sad characters who lived on the periphery of my life, circling my existence like *Sputnik*.

After saying goodbye to Sophia, I called Ray, another long shot who could turn out promising—he lived in a small town on the Massachusetts–New Hampshire border, and worked out of Nashua, New Hampshire, where he owned a small electronics company, a computer chip manufacturer. What better place for Albert to hide out than in a small border town?

Helene answered. She was a lawyer who had taken time off to be a homemaker until their boys were more independent. She always talked about going back to work—it was clear to me that this was a sacrifice for her, but with a husband who was as successful as Ray, she became the homemaker by default.

"Hi, Angie, what's going on?" The cautious tone in her voice told me that Ma had talked to her already, or maybe Albert was up there with them.

"Ma's gotten to you already, right?"

"About what?"

"Albert."

"Yes, she called earlier," Helene said. "Ray came home for lunch and took the call. He told me everything."

"Everything?" I asked.

There was a pause before Helene said, "Well, let's put it this way: if we do find Albert, he'd gonna need a really good lawyer. I'm not sure how much we want the kids to know. I don't want them thinking Albert is some bigger-than-life character." Did I mention that Ray and Helene were a bit overprotective?

I groaned. "Helene, they don't need to know. You know that."

"Angie, what can I do? I love Albert, he's very charming and great with the kids, but I don't like what he does for a living. I told Ray I don't like Albert's influence on the kids. And even if we don't say anything, they'll find out eventually. The way your mother is going about it, she's going to ask every single soul in this family, including Carla and Vinnie's nine-month-old baby, if they've seen Albert."

I pinched the bridge of my nose, hoping that a headache wasn't forming right now. "Look, Helene, I understand your concern, but you gotta understand Ma's concern for Albert. He's the baby."

Helene snorted. "Some baby—hooked up with the Mob, fronting for them, and now, who knows? For all I know, he's killed people."

"Stop it," I said sharply. I immediately regretted my tone. Helene didn't deserve it. She was just trying to protect her boys. "Sorry. I didn't mean for it to come out that way."

"Angie, I'm sorry, too. I like Albert. I really do. He's a good guy. But he's made some bad choices and I'm not sure we can support him right now. Our boys are so impressionable these days with the things they see on television—all the gang violence. If they knew what Albert did for a living, they'd probably want to know how much he cleared a year as a Mob guy."

I refrained from pointing out that my nephews probably already knew what Albert did for a living.

"Ain't that the truth," I sympathized. "Look, if you hear from him, let me know immediately."

"And if he shows up, you let me know," she replied. "Ray is worried. And despite what I just said to you, so am I."

I thanked her and hung up.

Both Carla and Vinnie worked, so I wasn't about to call them until this evening from my home. Rosa was out of the country for another week and a half and I doubted that Albert even remembered that she was gone or where she was. Besides, if Albert were running from the Mob, why would he run to Italy or anywhere near it? I took the T back to East Boston.

Okay, I didn't like to do it, but I'd have to go see my dad—and "No-Legs" Charlie, my uncle. Fortunately, I could wash the taste of seeing my father out of my mind by visiting Charlie. It was a short distance from my apartment to the waterfront apartments on Gold Star Street near the Orient Heights Beach area.

I took my Bronco in case I wanted to make a fast getaway. When I pulled away from my parking space on Mar-

ginal, a black LeSabre pulled away as well. It may have
been coincidence, but I had a bad feeling about it. I made
an unexpected turn right, and the car made the same turn.
Whoever was in the LeSabre wasn't doing a very good job
of tailing me. I'd already made them. I didn't want to lead
them directly to my uncle, so I made the decision to lose
my tail. As far as my dad was concerned, I didn't give a
damn. He left us years ago, lived nearby, but we hardly
ever saw him.

The strong male figures in my life did not include Vincente Matelli. "No-Legs" Charlie had been there for me,
as had Ray and to a certain extent, Vinnie. Ma's priest,
Father Tim, had always had time for me and my siblings
after Dad left, and had even tried to enroll me in a Catholic
school, telling Ma that I'd make a great nun, if I decided
to take it up as a vocation. Boy, did he have me pegged
wrong. But he was a nice man and I always remembered
his small kindnesses, like he'd always have a pocketful of
candy for us after mass.

Vincente Matelli was devout in another way—he reli-
giously attended Suffolk Downs, our local racetrack. After
many years of watching the money our father made being
lost at the tracks, Ma finally kicked him out. It didn't cure
him—in fact, it made him a deadbeat dad. He just felt he
had more money to spend there. And when he did have
some winnings, he would spend it on himself. He just kind
of forgot he had a family.

We didn't miss him much when he was ousted from our
home. Ma went on as usual. I think she was secretly relieved that she didn't have to pretend anymore that they
had a great marriage.

I glanced in my rearview mirror again and turned up a
tiny street that would lead the black Buick on a merry
chase. The streets up in this particular part of East Boston

rivaled San Francisco in their twists and turns. After a few right turns and one left, I'd lost the tail and doubled back to Saratoga Street, where I turned right on St. Edward, then took a left on Gold Star.

My adrenaline was pumping from the chase, and I got out of the car to breathe in some of the salty air. This would be a great place to build nice condos, if it weren't for the airport directly across the water. I knew that the only reason my dad lived there was because it was close to Suffolk Downs. In fact, if there had only been a shack near Suffolk Downs, Vincente would have gladly lived there.

Uncle Charlie lived there because the condos had handicapped apartments, and he got a great deal. Besides, he didn't mind the noise from the airplanes taking off. He just turned off his hearing aid and went to sleep.

Unlike Albert's condo building, Dad's place was a walk-in. I knocked on the apartment door. My dad was home. When he opened the door and saw me standing there, he nodded briefly, turned around and went back to what he was doing in his apartment, leaving the door open for me to follow him. What a gracious host, I thought. The apartment was tiny, smoky, and noisy. Vincente had the TV on—it was blaring some soap opera—while he sat in a smelly lounge chair and circled the bets he would place when he went to the track later in the day.

"So, what brings you here?" he asked, not in a pleasant or unpleasant manner. He was neutral now, just like he was in my life. A neutral presence.

I got right to the point. There was no beating around the bush with him—he wasn't that sort of guy. Don't try any histrionics with him, either. He didn't have time for it. When it was time to go to Suffolk Downs, he'd just pick up and leave, even if you were in the middle of something.

"Albert's disappeared. Ma and I went to his condo in

Providence and it looked as if he'd left in a hurry. We think he might try to contact some family member.''

Vincente looked up. "Why would he come here?'' I'd gotten his attention.

I shrugged. "I don't know. I'm talking to everyone he knows or who might have seen or heard from him over the last few days."

He studied me briefly as if he were trying to figure out my odds and how good they were. I got the impression that he had something to say, but instead, he went back to his racing form.

"You some kind of private eye or something?" I noticed he hadn't used my name at all, which probably meant that he couldn't remember it. It didn't make me angry, just kind of sad for him.

"Yeah, Vincente, I am," I replied in a neutral tone, the kind I once used when I was in the marines in the Investigations Division. "I'm your middle daughter, Angela. I was in the marines for eight years. Got out a few years back and started up my own business." Okay, so maybe I didn't sound so neutral toward the end there.

He looked up at me. "I know who you are, Angela," he replied, frowning a little. "I know about what you been doing."

I backed down. Okay, so maybe I wasn't totally okay with the way my father turned out. Maybe I did want him to acknowledge me and my brothers and sisters. But I'd never let him know that.

I nodded, keeping my face as impassive as possible. "Then we understand each other." I took out a business card and left it on the cardboard box that served as an end table to the lounge chair.

"Call me if he gets in contact," I said. I caught his eye.

There didn't seem to be anything behind his blank expression but desperation. "Tell Albert I can help him."

My dad mumbled something about getting in touch with me if my brother contacted him, then he went back to his form while I let myself out. I leaned against the wall outside his apartment and took a few moments to collect myself.

My next stop was a few apartments down. "No-Legs" was in, eating a bowl of soup for lunch.

"Hey, Angie, how ya doing?" He backed up his wheelchair to let me in. "So, you here for a visit or is this business?" Uncle Charlie had been a huge help on my first case, and I had always been fond of him. He was an ex-cop who cared deeply for our family, unlike my father. In some ways, he was probably trying to make up for Vincente's deficiencies. He'd never married, so he had a ready-made family to watch grow up and to influence. And Charlie was a great influence. He was one of the true good guys.

I sat down with Charlie and asked about Albert. Ma had called Charlie already. I was beginning to wonder why Ma had bothered to hire me in the first place—she seemed to be doing fine on her own.

But Charlie was happy to talk about my brother anyway. He was the only person I felt comfortable telling about the dead guy in Albert's apartment. Being an ex-cop, he didn't feel obligated to report it, and he trusted my instincts. I described my visit to Albert's condo, my search of his premises, the dead body in the office.

"You thought it was Albert?"

"At first. But the security guard had mentioned that Albert hadn't been around since Friday."

"It wasn't Albert," Charlie stated. It was good to talk to someone who had had investigative experience. He understood me.

Still, I shook my head. He looked relieved.

"No, but the victim looked like Albert," I replied. "Same height, weight, hair color, et cetera."

Uncle Charlie was silent, absorbing what I had just said. "So this vic might have been killed by mistake."

"He was killed execution-style."

Charlie took a deep breath and let it out slowly. "Ange, I know your brother has been working for the Mob, but he wasn't at a high enough level to be killed that way. Not unless he'd decided to turn state's evidence, and he never expressed that desire to me. You know we talked on a regular basis."

"Everyone seems to have talked to Albert on a regular basis except me," I grumbled. "I've always considered us fairly close, but now—"

Charlie held up a hand. "Angie, to be honest, Albert didn't come around all that regular back when I was in the precinct. It was only these last few years, since I've been away from the blue brotherhood, since most of my contacts have died natural or unnatural deaths, that Albert and I have found some common ground."

I shrugged. "Yeah okay, Uncle Charlie."

Charlie reached over and squeezed my hand. "Ya know, Angie, I think Albert is a little awed by what you do, maybe he's not sure what you want when you talk to him about his business."

I nodded, head and eyes down for a moment. "I get what you're saying. In the meantime, let's brainstorm."

Charlie sat back and crossed his arms. "You say the body was left in his apartment. There are several ways to go with that. He could've killed the guy and took off, someone else was there and killed the guy, then made Albert go with him, or while the guy was being killed, Albert made his escape." Charlie paused, then added, "The other possibility is that the guy was killed in his apartment while he was away, and Albert found him when he came back, then took off.''

"Okay.'' I ticked points on one hand as I talked. "Why would Albert kill a guy in his place, then run away? There didn't appear to be a struggle. If Albert had the gun, why wouldn't he take the victim away from his place? And if he did kill the guy there, it would be easy enough for him to move the body. He worked for Testa. He could have figured something out. As for the third theory, Albert would have had to make a very quick escape, and it appears that several things are missing from his files, which means that the second theory is the more probable. Your last theory, again, has some holes. There's security guards and cameras set up in the building, so it would be virtually impossible for anyone to get into Albert's apartment without being seen.'' I didn't mention my own break-in, because it would be caught on tape if anyone went to the trouble of looking for it.

Charlie was frowning. "That all sounds good, but why would the shooter leave Albert alive?''

"Why kill someone else in Albert's condo in the first place?'' I looked up at Uncle Charlie. "Is there some Mob war in Providence that we're not aware of? Albert's look-alike might have been killed as a warning or as retaliation for some other low-level killing. Do they do that sort of thing?''

"Sure they do,'' he replied. "How much do you know about your brother's business?''

"Not much,'' I admitted. "And I wanted to keep it that way, but Albert's disappearance seems to have left me no choice.''

My uncle and I weren't much for displays of affection. He was more of a physical guy—punching my shoulder lightly or maybe putting an arm around the back of my chair. Which was okay with me. I'd never been much for displays of affection either, which is weird when I consider my Italian background. I suppose the marines drummed it out of me. But for the second time this afternoon, Charlie reached out and touched me, patting my cheek. "Ange, I don't know if this is such a good idea. I don't like the idea of you out there asking questions about the Mafia in Rhode Island. It could get you killed."

I reached out and squeezed his hand. "I'll try to be discreet." Although how discreet could I be when asking questions about the Mafia was all in how you looked at it. I decided not to look at it at all.

"You know I'll do what I can from my angle," he offered. "I know a couple of guys in the PPD. You want I should talk to them about this stiff?"

I nodded. "That'd be great, Uncle Charlie."

He shook his head. "Six of you growing up without Vincente there. I did my best. You all turned out okay, except Albert."

I felt I had to defend Albert, even though I knew what Uncle Charlie was getting at. "Look, Uncle, you know Albert's all right."

He heaved a sigh. "Yeah, I know. But he always liked to watch them *Godfather* movies, always wanted to be the bad guy when you were playing cops and robbers. And he's a nice kid. Always has been. Doesn't have the stomach for killing. But he's living out his dreams now, and it may have gotten him in deeper than he thought was possible."

"Yeah, I guess so," I replied in a reluctant tone. "Well, I gotta go, Uncle. You take care. I'll be in touch."

As I got to the door, he called out, "Angie?"

"Yeah?" I turned and caught my uncle with a serious expression. He was seated in his wheelchair, a shaft of sunlight slanted across him.

"You saw your dad, right?"

I managed to smile, shrug, and nod at the same time. "I had to. Albert might have gone there to hide out."

"Don't blame him for the way he is, kid. There isn't much there anymore."

I stopped. "Charlie? Is everything all right with my dad? He seemed a little...different. You know?"

"Yeah, I know. He seems a little more preoccupied lately. I'll keep an eye on him."

"Yeah, well, I know, Charlie. I don't expect much from him." I said goodbye again and left.

I DON'T KNOW WHY, but my heart was a little heavier when I got home. I was about ready to make something to eat when the phone rang.

I picked it up. "Yeah?"

"It's all set up." Ma did this to me. One moment I'm well grounded in reality, the next moment, she's talking about something in vague terms and expecting me to get it.

"What's all set, Ma?"

"Our meeting with Giovanni Testa. If we leave now, we'll be there by noon. He's invited us for brunch. Isn't that nice?"

"Oh, goody," was all I could manage before telling her I'd pick her up as soon as I got my car. Ma was behaving as if this was something she did all the time, having breakfast with the head of the Providence Mafia. She even sounded a little excited. I refrained from reminding her that her youngest son, Albert, was missing. There would be time enough to point that out on the way to Rhode Island.

"Say, Ma, do you happen to know the last name of the girl Albert was dating? You said her first name was Karen."

"Hirsch. Her name is Karen Hirsch. She lives in New-port." Albert's ex, Sylvia, lived in Newport also. Thinking of Sylvia made me almost look forward to meeting Karen Hirsch. I was not in a hurry to talk to either woman—Karen clearly had not been there when the victim was killed or when Albert was abducted or escaped from the killers or, although it was hard to think in these terms for me, when Albert had killed the victim.

"Thanks, Ma. Be there soon." I hung up.

Fredd, my pet iguana, was looking at me like, "What did she want?"

I went to the kitchen and poured myself a glass of cold red wine. I thought of draining it, then realized I'd be driving. And, it was still morning. Fredd was giving me a strange look. "I decided I'm not thirsty," I explained, shrugging off the fact that I was reduced to talking to an iguana now that Rosa was gone for a few weeks.

As if on cue, the phone rang again. It was Rosa, calling from Rome.

After the "I miss you's" and telling her how her apart-ment was doing, I told her briefly about Albert. She was about the only person Ma hadn't gotten around to telling.

"Jeez, Angie, do you think I should catch a flight back home?"

"No, I don't think that's necessary at this point. How about you just have a great time, and let me do the wor-rying?"

There was a small silence on her end. "Look, just don't let me languish here in Rome if something important hap-pens, okay? Truth is, as much as I love it here, I miss Eastie, and U-Mass, and even Fredd."

We laughed at that.

"So what's Ma up to these days, besides helping you

break into Albert's place?'' Her tone was light and I matched it with a light tone of my own.

''Uh, I gotta pick Ma up for lunch.'' I thought it was pretty clever of me to leave out the part about the Don joining us. Telling her didn't seem like a very discreet thing to do.

FIVE

I WAS TEMPTED TO CALL Ma back and tell her I didn't think it would be a good idea for us to go down there, but it was an even worse idea to decline the invitation. I drove up to Malden to pick up Ma. She was more than ready, she looked nervous, asking how her hair looked, did the dress make her look fat, et cetera.

"Ma, calm down," I finally said. "This isn't a high school prom, and Don Testa isn't your date." Ma got awfully quiet about then.

Traffic was fairly light—commuters tended to go from Rhode Island into Boston, and we were going the opposite way. We passed lines of cars idling on the freeway, all headed north. Some commuters were reading books, talking on their cell phones, or applying makeup. I even saw one commuter doing a Mr. Bean trick—putting his socks on while waiting for the traffic to start moving again.

As we got nearer to Providence, Ma became talkative. But the way she talked to me took me back to when I was nine years old and Sophia's namesake, Aunt Sofia, came to visit from the Old Country.

"Don't get too familiar with Giovanni," she instructed. I couldn't help but notice that she was addressing him in familiar terms, and I wondered if she would be taking her own advice, or would slip up. Or would it even be a slip? I tried to picture Ma conversing in the style I had always stereotyped as Mafia language, with the "dese" and "dose" and the "rub him outs," but I couldn't see it.

"Remember your manners," was another gem Ma prodded me with. Like I was gonna say, "Pardon me, Don Testa, but I must reach across the table to grab your collar and shake an answer out of you," or something like that. I assumed she meant that I should use my napkin to dab my lips after partaking of eggs and bacon or ham and cheese or whatever. I just nodded.

"And don't ask any rude questions."

I turned to stare at her. Her eyes were on the road ahead of us and there were two red spots on her cheeks. "Ma! How am I supposed to get anywhere with his guy when I can't ask any rude questions? As it is, I was reluctant to have you come with me and the only thing that keeps you in this car—"

"Watch out, Angela Agnes, our exit is coming up in a mile," Ma interrupted as if she hadn't heard me.

But I wasn't finished: "—is the fact that you were the one who set up this appointment and it sounds as if Don Testa knows you well enough and is looking forward to seeing you. I'm not crazy about involving you in Albert's disappearance."

Ma crossed her arms and her face became expressionless. Not a good sign. "Angela Agnes Matelli, you should know better than to talk to your mother that way."

I almost missed the exit. Here we were on the interstate, having an argument. Ma had dug in her heels and I was fast getting ready to drop her off at a mall and pick her up after the meeting. Once we were down to thirty-five miles an hour, I took the opportunity to pull over to a gas station and let the car idle.

"What are you doing?" Ma's voice had gotten high and angry. I was definitely treading the shark-infested waters.

I kept my voice soft. "Ma, I know you care about what other people think about your family, but this isn't the time to keep up appearances. If Don Testa doesn't give me the

answers I'm looking for, I may have to get tough." But
how tough I got depended on how many bodyguards surrounded him.

"I just don't want another child disappearing on me." I
could hear the quiver in her voice and I realized that Ma
was scared, probably more than I was. She wasn't afraid
of appearances, she was afraid of disappearances.

I looked at the time. We were way ahead of schedule. I
took a few moments to reassure Ma. "Okay, Ma, tell me
what you know about Testa."

She had gone to high school with him. He was smart,
much smarter than his father, who had been a businessman,
at least according to her. Being a businessman could mean
anything from, well, being a businessman, to being the don
of a highly organized Mafia structure. It wasn't much to go
on. Oh yes, and Don Testa had taken Ma to the homecoming, or whatever they called the dances in those days.

"Giovanni was editor of the yearbook, and got A's and
B's in school. He played football and was a quarterback,"
Ma prattled on. "He took me to the prom, too, and gave
me a corsage of white orchids that his father had grown in
a hothouse in back of his mansion." Shades of Don Cor-
leone. "He was very polite and played the gentleman at
the prom. He was a good dancer, probably had lessons. And
he had his own car. And there were bodyguards that came
with us to the prom and the homecoming. I remember that.
Everyone thought we would get married. After graduation,
he went into the service, I think he was an officer in the
navy, and he was released from service early because his
father had a heart attack and he had to come home to take
over the family business. By then, I had married your father, and Giovanni had found Francesca."

"They allowed him to do that? I mean, the Mafia business?'' I was confused. The United States Armed Services wouldn't allow a soldier to go home to run the Mafia.

Ma looked at me as if I was out of my mind. ''You think that's what he told them? Of course not. His father ran a legitimate business, a butcher shop.''

*Ooo*kay, I got the picture. Businessman, nothing. Once Ma got going, the memories fairly spilled out of her. Now I knew a lot of useless information about the Don—it sounded as if he had wanted for nothing while growing up, he was a gentleman, and he was head of the Mafia in Providence before he turned thirty. Straight out of *The Godfather*.

I got back on the road and headed toward the swanky area of Providence, near the ocean. Testa lived in a gated community with a security guard who stopped everyone who entered and made sure they belonged. The only old cars parked in this community were either antiques or belonged to the hired help.

The house was a testament to excess. Pure white with a uniformly green, one-inch lawn and shrubbery along the windows that were decorated, by the way, with white-painted cast-iron bars. The Mediterranean influence was strong in the stucco outside and tiled roof. Pink and white hydrangea ran along the curved driveway.

Two less decorative bodyguards were there in shades, white short-sleeved shirts, and black slacks. I was tempted to suggest to the Don that he might soften his image by making his bodyguards by the gate wear white shirts and pink shorts just to match the hydrangea. But I doubted he'd take me seriously. The bodyguards both carried walkie-talkies and went into action when I pulled up and stopped the car. It was like dueling walkie-talkies. One would mutter into a black box, there'd be a short burst of static, then someone would murmur something back. Then the other guard would talk. In the midst of all this, Ma started to open her car door, but when I saw a guard go for his gun, I grabbed her arm.

"Let's let the nice men open our doors for us," I told her. "And when it's time to get out, get out slowly." Even for a Mafia don, this security was excessive. I wondered if Testa had heard I was studying Aikido, or if something was going on in the world of the Mafia. I knew that in Boston, the Mafia was almost nonexistent—Whitey Bulger had disappeared and most of the second-tier people had been sent up. But I hadn't heard anything about the Providence crowd having any shake-ups.

Ma threw me a baleful stare before getting out of the car. We were escorted up the stairs and into the essence of opulence: Italian marble floors, a curved staircase, an imported crystal chandelier, and the whole house smelled of flowers. I don't know what I was expecting, but Don Testa wasn't it. Maybe I was expecting Marlon Brando with the cottonball jowls. Testa was tall and thin, still had all his hair and either had all his own teeth or had an excellent pair of choppers. He wore a pink alligator polo shirt and khaki slacks, a Movado watch, and a thick gold chain-link bracelet. On closer inspection, the bracelet was a Medic-Alert. I wondered what condition he had. Before coming here, I hadn't had time to do any research on my subject, but I planned to do plenty when I got back to Boston.

"Rosetta! It's so good to see you." He moved in to kiss Ma's cheek lightly and I noticed that she flushed. "You haven't changed much."

Wow, was that laying it on thick. I kept a straight face.

"It's been a long time, Don Testa," she replied. I felt like a schoolkid with Ma at mass on Sunday, waiting for the chance to be introduced to the new priest.

"Please, call me Giovanni." He still held her hands in

his. "We are old friends, aren't we?" He turned to me. "And this is one of your lovely daughters, Sophia?"

"This is Angela, my second oldest girl."

"Ah, the private investigator." I could tell that he knew that already, but wanted me to know that he was too busy to remember something as trivial as the name of a daughter of an old friend.

I was surprised that he had given so much information away. He knew who I was and had deliberately gotten my name wrong, the old goat. I smiled pleasantly and held out my hand, forcing him to detach his hands from Ma's hands. His handshake was firm and so was his gaze.

"She is a lovely young woman. I'm sure all your daughters are as charming, Rosetta." Putting me in my place—children should be seen and not heard. If you don't speak directly to the person, she'll be intimidated. He seemed to have forgotten that I was in my late twenties, not twelve.

"Nice to meet you, Mr. Testa. I've heard so much about you."

He didn't reply directly. "Let us repair to the dining table. Since the weather has been so good lately, I had our table set outside so we can enjoy the sun and the ocean view." We followed him through the house, passing through the middle, which made it seem as if the house was smaller than it really was. But I was able to catch glimpses of hallways on either side of the living area before we went onto the deck—hallways that most likely led to room after room. Testa practically lived in a hotel.

The spread turned out to be mostly breakfast items. Testa had employed a chef with his own little grill area where he could prepare just about anything you wanted: eggs Benedict, French toast, waffles, pancakes, omelets, eggs any way you like, bacon, sausage, ham, toast, hash browns. The table was laden with real maple syrup, fresh strawberry and

raspberry jams, fresh squeezed orange juice, Champagne
(for those who liked a little fizz in their morning juice),
and, of course, Italian roast coffee. I felt as if I were at a
really good restaurant brunch. Hell, it was probably all ca-
tered anyway.

Ma and the Don chatted about old times over large
breakfasts consisting of ham and Swiss omelets, hash
browns, bacon, rye toast, and coffee. I managed to get by
with a pecan waffle with maple syrup and fresh Virginia
ham on the side.

When the Don delicately pushed his empty plate away
and dabbed at his mouth with a linen napkin, it was clear
that we were about to get down to business. Ma had
stopped eating a while ago, and I was still wiping up the
last bit of syrup with the last bit of waffle.

Don Testa gestured to have our coffee cups refilled.
While one of the bodyguards doubled as our waiter, the
Don turned serious. "I understand that there are other con-
cerns that have brought you here today." He leaned back
in his wrought iron chair and steepled his fingers together
in front of us. Looking directly at me, he added, "Your
daughter, Rosetta, has impeccable manners, but I can tell
that she is impatient to get on with business. This younger
generation does not have the patience that we learned so
long ago. But I am happy to see that she honors her mother
by keeping with the old traditions."

"Thank you, Giovanni," Ma replied. She sipped her coffee.

I let the goon/waiter pour more coffee into my cup. The
ocean breeze was intoxicating and if I wasn't in the presence of Giovanni Testa, I would have gotten up and sat
closer to the edge of the balcony.

Don Testa turned his attention to me. "Angela, your
mother tells me that Albert has disappeared."

"That's correct, Don Testa. He never fails to call her on Friday evening. Except he didn't call her this past Friday."

Don Testa gestured for one of his goons to come over. The goon leaned down and Testa whispered something in his ear. The goon looked over at me and I felt shards of ice shoot down my spine. He seemed to lose interest and muttered something to Testa before retreating to his usual station. I could only assume that his usual job involved blending into the background, perhaps imitating one of the Grecian pillars that graced his boss's Mediterranean-style mansion until his services were needed again. For all I know, Testa just whispered that he had to piss and the goon replied that he would piss for him. But I had a feeling they were talking about me, or Ma, or Albert, or all three of us.

"Angela. As you know, your brother worked for me in some small capacity. I can understand your concern, and I must say that I am also very concerned about his safety." He paused, looked at his goon, and nodded. The goon turned away and entered the house. I wondered if he was gathering the items needed to send me to the bottom of the ocean, or buried in Fenway Park. I knew I was being needlessly paranoid—modern-day mobsters didn't kill people for asking a few questions. They were more likely to sue you for slander, tying you up in the court system until you ended up declaring bankruptcy and your last address was underneath the bridge of an expressway, while you cradled a bottle of cheap wine.

Testa continued, "My associate tells me that Albert was due for a meeting with one of my other employees yesterday, and he didn't show up. It has not been of great concern to my other employees because these things happen occasionally. What have you discovered?"

I was still working on the implications of the term *associate* applied to the goon who stood by Testa's side when he asked me that question. Ma answered for me, chronicling our excellent adventures in Rhode Island, at least what I had told her about Albert's apartment.

A small silence followed before Ma asked in a timid voice, "Albert is all right, isn't he, Don Testa?"

Testa frowned for a moment, then tried to paste on a reassuring smile, leaned forward and patted Ma's hand. "I can't answer that, Rosetta. But I can help your daughter in her efforts to find your son." He glanced over at me. I tried not to scowl, but I don't think I was very successful. He addressed the pillar by his left shoulder. "Marcus, why don't you take Mrs. Matelli on a tour of my rose gardens. I understand that you love roses, Rosetta."

Ma looked a little uncertain, then she nodded. She wouldn't know a gardening trowel from a lawnmower.

"Excellent. I have a prize-winning rose garden and Marcus is very knowledgeable about my flowers. He oversees the gardeners in their work."

I tried to keep visions of dead bodies being planted under beautiful rose bushes out of my mind, but I couldn't suppress the shudder that ran through my body. Dead bodies would account for prize-winning roses, wouldn't they?

Testa addressed me as Ma was led away from the terrace. "Don't worry about your mother, Angela. She is in safe hands." At least he didn't tell me she was in good hands. I would have had to argue that point. "I thought we needed to talk alone. Your mother doesn't know everything about your business, does she?"

"I guess Albert and I have something in common," I couldn't help replying.

Don Testa chuckled. "That may be the case, but I'll wager Rosetta knows more about Albert's business than she knows about yours."

I shrugged, not sure where he was going with this. But

thinking about it, he was probably right. It was hard for me to admit it, but Albert was much closer to Ma than I was.

Testa didn't keep me dangling for long. "I probably would not be far off the mark if I suggested that you don't totally believe that I had nothing to do with Albert's disappearance."

I wasn't sure if I should answer him, so I remained silent.

He waved a hand as if he expected me not to answer. "I won't presume you don't know that a portion of my money comes from, shall I say, illegal activities? But I will remind you that your brother has also been working for us. I've had you checked out and know you are loyal to your family, so I won't pretend to be something I'm not, Angela. Albert performed some very important services for me, and most of them were legitimate."

He chuckled. "I won't say there weren't times Albert didn't skirt the edge of the law, but he has been instrumental in helping me build and maintain my legitimate businesses. And that has been very important, especially in these times. With Whitey Bulger gone, and so many of my colleagues facing charges up in Boston, I want to transfer most of my energies to the legitimate side of my business. It's only a matter of time before the authorities in Providence begin to crack down on certain activities here."

Testa spoke in negatives and talked to me as if I was an equation he had already figured right. To him, I was two plus two equals four, and I was going to swallow any bullshit story he made up for me.

So I tried to read between the lines. He was telling me that he was going legit. I bought that part of the story. A lot of Mob figures had a legitimate side to their business, and most of them tried to go legitimate sooner or later. I also knew that a lot of Mob figures that tried to go legit often failed because it bored them after a while and they were used to living on the edge.

I also knew going legit meant giving up territories. It meant that the Colombian cartels and Jamaican Rastafarian and Haitian gangs were waiting in the wings to take over the business of selling meth, crack, and heroin to the ready-made junkies out on the streets. The Cosa Nostra and the Mafia might think they were ready to give up that part of their empire, but there were still gunfights and executions going on. I didn't know if Testa was serious about going legit, but I hoped he knew the odds.

"What kind of business are you planning to go in to?" I asked. It was a safe question, and if Testa were on the up and up, he wouldn't hesitate to tell me.

"I have an interest in an Italian fast-food franchise, and a series of liquor stores that specialize in wines and liqueurs of Italy."

I nodded. This sounded legitimate. "Can you tell me the names of these businesses?"

Testa named a fast-food joint I'd heard of, and had eaten at a few times. For fast-food spaghetti, I'd been impressed. There was still nothing like the real thing made from scratch, but when you needed a fast meal it beat burgers and fries, hands down. The liquor stores weren't anything I'd heard of, but he told me they were just opening up the first couple of branches in Braintree, Dorchester, and Beacon Hill.

"And Albert helped you with these businesses—how?"

Testa gestured for more coffee. "He wrote the business plans, scouted the locations, hired the managers and trained them. Albert is a jack-of-all-trades."

"He also laundered your illegally gotten money in these businesses, didn't he?"

Testa shrugged. "There are some parts of the business Albert didn't care for, but that's true with every job."

I noticed that he referred to Albert in the past tense. I hoped it wasn't a slip.

"Tell me, Don Testa, do the names Nick, Johnny, Eddie, or Sal mean anything to you?"

"I know many people by those names." It was hard to read Testa—he had schooled himself to stay impassive. Still, I thought he flinched for a fraction of a second. I only wish I'd said the names slower so I'd know which ones he was reacting to.

"Are there any that come to mind offhand?"

He seemed to think about it, then shook his head. "Sorry, nothing." I doubt he worked too hard at considering the names. Testa snapped his fingers and a checkbook, complete with pen, appeared in his hand. I didn't catch sight of the goon who gave it to him. It must have been the slimy accountant who always worked for guys like Testa.

He opened the checkbook and started to write a check. "I hope you will take this as it is given—" he ripped the check out and handed it to me "—in good faith. I know that you'll have to turn down other work to look for your brother, and it doesn't sound like it will be easy. I want to be your client."

I didn't take the check immediately, and he laid it down between us on the table, weighting it down with an empty glass. "I will answer any questions you may have for me," he said.

I turned to watch Ma being escorted down the last row of roses. Something furry brushed against my leg and I looked down into the face of a Persian cat. I always thought Persians had it bad—they had to rely on being groomed because they constantly had bad hair days. And they looked as if Mike Tyson had punched their faces in.

I decided to tell Testa the whole story about Albert's condo. It's not like he was going to call the police.

When I finished, Testa nodded, no expression on his face. "What do you want me to do?" he asked.

"Can you find out the name of the dead man found in Albert's condo? I have a feeling he's tied in with Albert's disappearance. In fact, I have a feeling that one of the names I gave you is the dead man's name."

Testa frowned. "I will talk to my associates and get back to you on that. I'm afraid I'm not as up to the minute on details as you would probably like." He smiled.

I didn't consider a dead man to be a detail, but then, I wasn't the one in charge. I shrugged and smiled back, even though it seemed to me that it wouldn't take more than a quick phone call for him to get the name. But this was his game, and I would get the name eventually.

"I'd also like to know what he was to you," I said, quickly adding, "He has to be connected to your business in some way, and I need to know how." I caught his eye. "It's important, Don Testa, that you be honest with me. If I'm going to clear this up, I can't be left in the dark."

He inclined his head and folded his hands in front of him. "I agree. You will get nothing but honesty from me, Angela. I understand that you are discreet. Is there anything else that you need? Just ask me."

I suspected he'd already lied to me—he was holding something back, and I was pretty sure he knew the name of the victim in Albert's apartment. But I kept it to myself. No reason to alienate him immediately. Or ever.

A thought occurred to me. "Don Testa, when I visited Albert's condo, he had boxes and boxes of these cat-faced dolls in his office. Do you know anything about that?"

He chuckled. "Itty Bitty Kitty. That was Albert's idea.

We tested the idea out on my granddaughters and they were wild for it.''

"It was his idea to buy into the company that manufactures the doll?''

"No, his creation. He came up with the idea and brought it to me. I became a silent partner. We bought a factory, the old gumball factory in East Boston, and started manufacturing them. Albert's done all the marketing. I originally went in with your brother because I thought it would be a fabulous tax write-off. I was sure it would fail. But Itty Bitty Kitty has become quite a hit.''

SIX

I LAUGHED ALL THE WAY out of Rhode Island. It was hard
to catch my breath long enough to tell Ma what was so
funny. But even when I managed to get the story out, Ma
didn't think it was so funny. In fact, she got a little mad at
me for taking Albert's brilliant creative streak so lightly.

"Angela," she chided me. "Your brother's missing and
you're acting like he's on a vacation. He could be lying
dead in some ditch."

I managed to gain some control over my behavior
"Sorry, Ma," I apologized.

Ma had never understood that in times of stress, many
people found release from unrelenting tension with humor
If Ma had a sense of humor, I had yet to see it. She raised
her six children with kindness and love; she was caring,
nurturing, and strict all rolled into one. She could be good-
humored, but I don't recall Ma telling one joke when we
were growing up. In fact, I seem to recall that every time
Happy Days was on, she was mystified by the six of us
rolling on the floor with laughter. "The fifties weren't really like that," she would say over the volume of the television. "If you want to know about the fifties, you talk to
me. I lived them. And believe me, they weren't that
funny."

My mother, I love her, but as I sat in the car, I wished
she could share in the irony of Albert, the wiseguy, creating
a kiddie toy.

I dropped her off at her home. Before she got out of the
car, she grabbed my wrist. "Angela, I feel your brother is

in danger, but he's not dead. Not yet. Please don't treat this like a joke.''

"Okay, Ma," I replied soberly. I didn't mention that I wouldn't have gone to see Giovanni Testa with her if I weren't going to take it seriously. I was going to check out Don Testa's other businesses and see if there were financial problems. It was a long shot, but maybe Testa had money problems and, being a partner in Itty Bitty Kitty, he wanted to keep all the profits for himself. Like I said, it was a long shot.

I gave her a hug and a kiss, then headed for my office. I had taken the check from Testa, but I didn't plan to deposit it until I felt I was making headway. It gave me a slight thrill to know I carried Don Testa's personal signature in my breast pocket. I felt a certain sense of power.

Testa hadn't given me all the information I needed. I knew he'd been holding out on me, and probably would dole out bits of information as I needed it. But he had given me the address of the former gumball factory, even though it was a landmark in East Boston and I had no need for it. But along with it came the name of the company—AMT ENTERPRISES.

Back at the office, I sat in my chair and went over the information I had learned, which wasn't much. I wondered why Albert hadn't told his family about Itty Bitty Kitty, then I pictured my macho brother creating this pink and lavender package with a cat-faced doll and three changes of clothes. That would go over big with the rest of the family.

Of course, Stephanie, who was another of Albert's test kids with Itty Bitty Kitty, would be thrilled that her uncle could think like a girl. But Ray and Vinnie would look a little askance at Albert the next time he wandered into Ma's house for dinner—if Albert was still alive.

I shook myself out of the terrifying doubt that overcame me at the thought of Albert's not being alive. I took Ma's sixth sense about her children seriously, and so far, she hadn't said anything to me about foul play. And I didn't feel it about this case, despite the lookalike corpse in Albert's condo.

I looked at the check Testa had written out to me. Much as I hated to look a gift horse in the mouth, I needed information on his "family."

My skip tracer, Skip T, had recently sent a message to me that he was taking a vacation. I took that to mean that his vacation was courtesy of the court system. He'd always struck me as some sort of hot dog—probably took one chance too many to get a piece of information that was off limits, and was caught. I thought about trying to find his identity, but it was a very large country and I had no idea what his court date was, or even if there was a court date to begin with. For all I knew, Skip T was really taking a vacation, seeing Europe or hiking in the outback Down Under.

In the meantime, I was down one skip tracer and I had it vaguely in my head that my cousin Antonia had done some hacking when she was in high school. I called her.

"H'lo?" the voice on the other end said. She sounded distracted, and I could hear her tapping away at her keyboard as she spoke.

"Antonia?" Antonia Stefano was a bigwig computer programmer who had her own company—she sold her skills as a computer nerd to some of the biggest computer companies on the East Coast.

"Angela! Haven't heard from you since Uncle Vito passed away. What's going on?"

I told her about Albert. It seemed she was about the only

person whom Ma hadn't called. "I hope your brother's okay," she replied. "What can I do for you?"

"I have some disks I got from Albert's place. Can you go through them and look for information that might seem important?"

"Sure. I have a little free time."

"I'll pay you, of course."

"Angie, you used to stick up for me when I was getting my butt kicked in the schoolyard. I think I can do this little favor."

"Well, you were asking for it, you know," I said with affection. "You were a nerd. Still are."

"Best-looking nerd on the block," she replied cheerfully. And she was. She came back to school one fall and boys wouldn't stop calling. She had done some modeling in Europe, and had had offers from famous designers to model their clothes, but she despised the fashion world. The only good thing she had to say about it was that at least during the summer she spent in Europe, she had been able to visit Italy.

"Anything else?"

"Uh, Antonia, how good are you at getting information?"

"I can do background checks, if that's what you mean." Antonia had a cautious tone when she said this.

"I don't want you to do anything illegal, but I need background checks on several people. Can you do it?"

"Then, sure. As long as it's not illegal. Who do you want to know about?"

I gave her Giovanni Testa's name. "And his family."

"Great," she replied. "A Mob guy. A don. Gee, anything else you want, Angie? Maybe I could lasso the sun for you while I'm at it."

"Just get me anything you can on the guy as anonymously as you can," I requested.

I also gave her the address of the former gumball factory, told her to try to link Albert's name to it. I had no idea if he'd incorporated or what. I also wanted her to look into ToyCo, and I listed the names that had popped up on Albert's answering machine: Rick, Nick, Johnny, Eddie, Sal, and Karen.

"Gee, no last names? You're making it real easy to do these background checks," she said sarcastically.

"Rick should be associated with Albert's business, Karen Hirsch is Albert's girlfriend, and Nick and Eddie, Johnny and Sal have to be associated with Giovanni Testa in some way."

"On the other hand," Antonia said, "Sal could be short for Sally, like in *My Gal Sal*."

"Yeah, right. Salvatore is more likely," I replied.

She promised to get back to me the next day with at least information on Testa, Albert's business, and ToyCo. I thanked her and we hung up.

I called Uncle Charlie.

"Hey, Angela. Got a name for you. Eddie Fazoli. He was a numbers runner. Small potatoes." Okay, one down, four to go.

"Thanks, Charlie."

"Say, Angie, I think I might of caused you some problems. You know, they got your name and description from the security guard in Albert's condo, and with me calling the PPD, well, I think they're gonna be contacting you. They hadn't known where you were from till I opened my big mouth and asked some questions. My friends, they gotta solve this case."

"Don't worry, Uncle. They were gonna find me sooner or later. Are they looking for Albert?"

"Yeah, they think he did it, although you're a close second. And I think whoever gets picked up first is who's gonna get the heat turned up on 'em."

I loved it when Uncle Charlie got upset—he always talked in clichés.

"Look, if you don't go back to Rhode Island, you oughta be okay."

"I can't promise that, Uncle. I gotta go talk to Sylvia—"

"She likes to go shopping up here—ask her out to lunch."

Not a bad suggestion. "That's possible, but I'm sure the police'll contact me and want me to come down there."

"Angie, I'm tellin' ya don't do it. The DA wants to try this case."

"Okay, I think I already know, but tell me anyway: Why is the DA so interested in this case?"

"'Cause if they get Albert on this murder, they can make a deal for him to turn state's evidence against his boss. Albert goes into the Witness Protection Program, assuming he lives past the trial of Giovanni Testa."

Even though I'd already guessed it, I needed to hear it. My hands were suddenly cold. "Yeah, well, we'll see about that," was all I said. Big threat. Just call me Ms. John Wayne. I thanked Uncle Charlie and we hung up.

I called Testa. He hadn't so much as had his goon speak to me about the dead guy. I got some guy who said he'd tell Mr. Testa to return my call.

"Thanks," I said cheerfully, "but I'll wait."

I waited on the phone for a good five minutes before Testa finally came to the phone.

"Angela. Good to hear from you." If I wasn't missing my guess, he didn't sound all that happy to hear from me, but he was trying valiantly not to let it show. Fortunately, I get paid the big bucks to pick up on that sort of stuff.

"Yeah, Mr. Testa, I was just wondering if you could give me some information on the dead guy found in Albert's condo."

There was a pause. "Oh, yes, I was supposed to get back to you on that. I'm sorry, Angela, really I am. I should have called." He didn't sound all that sorry. He tried again. "I apologize for taking so long." That was better.

"That's okay." I was slightly mollified.

"Um, I have to tell you, I'm starting to have second thoughts. Maybe we're moving too fast on his disappearance. I'm sure Albert will be back in a few days."

"Are you letting me go? Because if you are, I've already cashed the check. It might take a day or so to clear before I can safely write a refund check." I fingered the check in my pocket and hoped I wouldn't go to hell for this small lie.

Normally, it wouldn't have been a problem for a Mafia boss to give me an excuse to give him his money back. But Testa's reluctance to call me about something as insignificant as identifying a dead man meant that something had changed for him in the last day—he had learned something that made Albert expendable. Usually this means it's something personal. My best guess was that Testa had learned something about a family member. But I already had a family member in hot water and I wasn't about to sacrifice him for Testa's family member. I wanted to keep the pressure on him. Make him backpedal. I needed to tie him to me in some way, make him feel obligated to go through the motions.

"No, no. Definitely keep investigating," he replied in an artificially light tone.

"After all, you made it clear that you took a special interest in Albert, he's your partner in a legitimate business. And I get the feeling that he looks upon you almost as the father he never had.'' Oh, I was good. I could almost hear the Mafia boss cringing on the other end.

"Yes, I did look on Albert as a son,'' Testa said after a moment's hesitation. I noted the past tense. "Angela, don't think I don't know what you're trying to do here,'' Testa chided.

"What?'' I asked in an innocent tone.

"You're trying to make me feel guilty. You know I've been open and honest with you.''

"Really? Is that what I'm doing?'' I feigned hurt.

He didn't buy it. "Don't ever underestimate me, Angela,'' he said in a cold tone. "I don't like being played for the fool.''

"And I do?'' I asked in an equally chilly tone. "You're not being honest with me, Mr. Testa, and I don't like it.''

I pictured him signaling to his goons to head up to Boston and ice the mouthy bitch. I closed my eyes. My heart was racing.

"You're right. I'm not being honest with you.'' Which I thought was disarming of him to admit. It almost made me like the icy son-of-a-bitch. "There are some things I've learned recently that—make it impossible for me to continue my association with you.''

I pressed on. "But you can tell me about Eddie Fazoli.''

I could almost taste the relief. "So you do know his name.''

"I'm not without my resources.''

Testa's sigh hissed along the fiber optic line. "He was small-time. I didn't know him personally, but I understand that Albert and Eddie were acquainted with each other.''

"Tell me where he lived, who his family is, his friends.''

"I don't know him personally, I told you.''

I reigned in my impatience. "Tell me about Nick, Johnny, and Sal.''

"I know a lot of Nicks, a few Johnnys, and a couple of Sals. Which one?"

"Surely the three together should suggest—"

"Angela, I said I don't know." My fingers tingled at the ends, my stomach tightened. I had pushed Testa as far as he would go. This definitely had something to do with family, not necessarily the Mob kind, either. This was more personal. I was anxious to get the background checks from my cousin.

I tried a different tact. "Then tell me this: what happens to the toy factory if Albert doesn't make an appearance, or if he does turn up and ends up in prison for murder."

"You'd have to talk to my lawyer about that," Testa replied. He was being evasive again.

"And his name is—?"

"I have several."

That was helpful. I tried once more. "Don Testa, are you in personal danger as well?"

"I don't know," he said. "I really can't answer that. I must go now. I have a meeting." The phone went dead.

I sighed. I really didn't want to go down to Rhode Island again so soon, but I needed to speak to Albert's ex-wife, and his current girlfriend. And I needed to get a line on Eddie Fazoli. I called Antonia back and added Fazoli's last name to the ever-growing list.

I checked the clock—five. I knew Carla got home around three to be there for the kids, and Vinnie had an early delivery route. I dialed their number. I don't know what it is about being married, but for some reason as soon as the vows were said, both of my brothers became allergic to the phone. The wives always answered. It didn't bother me as much as it amused me. Albert had been that way when he was married to Sylvia, and Sophia usually answered, even if David was sitting right by the phone. Women are the

great communicators, so they say. Carla answered when I
called.

"What's up, Angie?"

"Um, you know Albert didn't show up for Sunday dinner."

"Yeah, that's not unusual."

I explained why it was unusual, according to Ma. I didn't
tell Carla about our little escapade in Providence, or the
dead body—I wanted to keep that to myself for the time
being. But I stressed that it was important for Ma to reach
Albert so she didn't have a coronary. "So he hasn't called
there or anything, has he?"

Carla grunted. "Not that I know of. Let me ask Vinnie."

She bellowed for Vinnie. "It's your sister. She wants to
ask you something."

A few moments later, Vinnie got on the phone. "Hey."
He still didn't know which sister, so he wasn't going to
make any wild guesses with names.

"Hey, Vinnie. Angela. Have you heard from Albert in
the last day or two?" I went into a brief version of the
story.

"He's probably okay," Vinnie said when I finished. Of
course, he hadn't shared a room with a decomposing
corpse, so what would he know?

"Do me a favor and if he calls there, tell him to get in
contact with me, okay?"

"Yeah, whatever you say, Angie. See ya Sunday."

We hung up and I thought about it for a moment. That's
one of the things I appreciated about Vinnie—he was un-
complicated. It wasn't that he didn't worry about Albert,
but he figured the Matelli women could do all the worrying
for him. Vinnie worked five days a week and came home
to Carla and the kids, and was a family man for two days,
including showing up for Ma's Sunday dinner. That was

all that was expected of him, and that was what he was comfortable giving out.

Before I got in the car, I grabbed the answering machine tape. Then I started the hour's drive to Newport, where Sylvia lived. No matter what Sophia said, I didn't want to talk to Sylvia on the phone. She had never liked me. In fact, she'd never liked anyone in our family. Sylvia was, in my eyes, the quintessential rich bitch. I thought a surprise visit was in order.

SEVEN

IT WAS CLOSE TO SEVEN by the time I got to my destination. Newport perches on the finger of land south of Providence, looking out over Narragansett Bay. I like to think of Newport as a cross between Provincetown on Cape Cod and Rodeo Drive, since lots of artisans and tons of wealthy people inhabit the seaside town.

I really wasn't ready for Sylvia, so I looked for Karen Hirsch in the phone book. Since there was no Karen, I called all the Hirsches in the phone book, figuring that someone must be a relative. There were at least a dozen of them. To conserve my cell phone, I used a pay phone in a gas station/convenience store. Under the seventh Hirsch, Richard M., I found her family home. Her mother told me that while Karen lived in Providence and attended Brown University, she happened to be home right now. She called Karen to the phone.

"Hello?"

"Hi, Karen, this is Angela Matelli, Albert's sister—"

She cut in. "Oh, my God, He's dead, isn't he?"

"What?" My stomach tightened.

"Well, he wasn't there on Friday night, and he didn't call me all weekend. I left messages and—"

"Look, Karen, would it be all right if I stopped by to ask you a few questions about Friday night? I swear, as far as I know, Albert isn't dead. But he may be in trouble."

She gave me directions to her parents' house, and it turned out that I was only a few miles away. The Hirsches lived in a more downscale neighborhood, each house still worth several hundred thousand on the market. Karen met me at the door and inside, I could tell that someone in her family was a potter, probably selling his or her wares to one of the many little stores that populated the Newport area around the waterfront. Colorful pottery nestled in nooks and crannies throughout the vestibule and living room.

Karen met me at the door. "My parents were on their way out for the evening when you called. That was fast... Some benefit dinner." She ushered me farther into her home. She was a perky blonde with delicate features and a pair of wire-rimmed glasses that gave her a winsome look. She led me into her dining room and we sat at the massive hand-carved cherrywood dining table. A chandelier of cut Austrian crystal, done in the colors of the rainbow, hung overhead. The semi-glazed pottery in vibrant colors sat in strategic places so your eye couldn't rest before coming across another delightful work of art. It was impressive.

"Thanks for seeing me on such short notice."

"Wow. So you're Al's private eye sister." Her eyes looked huge behind the glasses. She wore a too-large hand-knit sweater over a pair of blue jeans that were probably a size one.

"Actually, I'm investigating what happened to Albert. You went to his condo on Friday night. No one answered. Describe to me everything that you remember between the time you arrived to when you finally realized he wasn't there."

"Sure," she said, clearly wanting to be helpful.

"First, can you tell me how you know him?"

She blushed and pushed her glasses up on the bridge of her nose. "Well, I met Al only about a month ago. I work in my parents' gallery," she said, indicating the beautiful muted glazed pottery that decorated the living room, "and

he came in to look. We got to talking, and he asked me
out. We've been out several times. It's nothing serious yet,
but—'' Karen laughed a bit ''—I really like him. He's different.''

''You also go to Brown?''

She nodded and picked at her cuticles. ''I'm an English
major. Talk about a useless degree.''

''Oh, I don't know. I'm sure there are plenty of things
you can do with an English degree,'' I replied.

She rolled her eyes. ''Yeah, if you want to go on to law
school or take education and become an underpaid teacher.
I could go on to business school, if I want.''

''Isn't there anything you can do with just an English
degree?''

She shrugged. ''Social work, although you stay on the
lowest rungs of the ladder unless you get your master's in
social work.''

''Well, your parents seem to have done well with this
pottery they produce.''

''Oh,'' she said, waving a hand dismissively, ''they don't
produce it—they travel to third-world countries and buy it
up, then bring it back here and slap big prices on the stuff.
I just wish they'd pay more to the artists who create this
stuff.''

So much for my idea that Karen came from a pair of
Bohemians—more like a pair of exploiters. At least she
didn't approve.

''Tell me about Friday night.''

''Well, Al told me he wanted to make me a real Italian
dinner. I was supposed to come, like, at six-thirty, but I got
stuck in traffic.'' I noticed that Karen's sentences tended to
end like a question. It was really annoying and made it
hard for me to take her seriously. But I nodded for her to

continue. "Anyway, I got there at seven, and I parked on the street."

"In front of the condo?"

She thought for a minute. "Yes. Anyway, I went in the lobby and told the security guard who I was. He let me in 'cause Al had called ahead."

"What did the security guard look like?"

She frowned. "Actually, he was kind of cute, but I didn't like his personality. Blond, real muscular." Probably Biff.

"Did you see anyone on your way up to his condo?"

"There were a couple of guys waiting for the elevator when I got to Al's floor. They got on as I got off."

I leaned forward. "What did they look like?"

She must have sensed my urgency, because she blinked and tried to recall. But she shook her head. "One was short and one was tall."

"Beards? Mustaches? Goatees?"

"They both had dark hair."

Great, that eliminated the blonds and redheads. "Does anything else occur to you?"

She thought, then shook her head. "I waited about half an hour outside Al's door, then left."

"Wait. Why did you wait half an hour?"

She sighed. "Well, as I was going into the building, I saw Al's car drive out of the garage. He really burned rubber taking off down the street. I thought he'd forgotten some ingredient and had gone out for it. So when I got up to his apartment, I tried the door. I thought he might have left it unlocked for me, that he might have been in a hurry. Those doors automatically lock if you don't press the button in the door handle."

I'd gotten all I was going to get out of her. I stood up, and handed her my card. "Thanks for your time, Karen. If you think of anything else, give me a call."

"Gee, it's a thrill to meet a real private eye. I bet your work is exciting."

I smiled noncommittally. "Sometimes it is."

She saw me to the door and I thanked her one more time before finally getting out of there. Now I'd have to go visit Sylvia.

I got back in my car and started to drive to Sylvia's house. She had moved back to Newport when their five-year marriage finally disintegrated. She had always thought of our family as beneath her, yet she had stayed with Albert for all those years. The funny thing was, I remember having met her family, and even though her father and mother were obviously from Old Money, they seemed to really like Albert. And they'd been very gracious to us. So I didn't understand her attitude.

I'd gotten Sylvia's address from Ma's Christmas card list. She lived in a house that was modest by her family's standards—a two-story stucco with wrought iron flower boxes outside both the first- and second-story windows, filled with fresh flowers. It was almost eight-thirty by the time I arrived, but she still had a light on. Sylvia's sporty silver Porsche was parked out front in the driveway, as if she had just arrived home and was planning to go out again, or hadn't bothered to put the car away—she was just too busy to think about her expensive Porsche being stolen.

I rang the doorbell and it took only a few seconds for the door to open. Sylvia had changed a bit. Her hair had always been a long dark blond mane, carefully arranged and sprayed into a tousled look. Now it was short and no-nonsense. Her face was thinner and she looked healthier and happier than she had when she was married to Albert. She'd also had a nose job, thinning the septum and softening the tip. It made her lips look fuller, although I suspected collagen was helping them a bit. She smelled like citrus. Her trademark scent from the old days, jasmine, was gone. It was almost as though Sylvia had been replaced by a newer, better version of herself.

"Angela!" Smiling, she stepped away from the doorway and let me in. "What are you doing here, and why didn't you call?" I looked around for the old snobby Sylvia, the one who looked down her nose at me.

"Um, I was in the neighborhood?"

She laughed. "Of course you weren't, silly! Tell me the truth."

"You mean I couldn't be in your neighborhood?" I asked defensively.

She studied me with a serious look on her face, then nodded. "No, of course, I didn't mean any offense. I just meant that the last time I heard anything about you, it was from Al, who told me you were still living in East Boston and your private investigation practice was going well."

I blinked. "You and Albert talk about me?"

She laughed again. "I was just going to make some tea. Would you like some?"

"Sure." I followed her into the kitchen. "You seem— different. Not just the nose job, either. You look happy."

She put the kettle on to boil and took two mugs and teabags out of a cupboard. "Yes, I've gone through hell and back." She looked up at me. "You didn't know I was addicted to coke, did you?"

"Um, well." I thought back. Sylvia had always had red eyes and always seemed to have sinus problems, but she'd complained of allergies. She'd hidden her addiction fairly well. Man, I was usually able to spot addicts. There'd been plenty in the service, especially overseas where drugs were easier to come by, and where certain drugs were legal in certain countries. "Actually, you're right. I didn't know."

"I was always so mean to you, and to your family. Of

course you never seemed to notice that my allergies never went away." She sat on a kitchen stool, her hands folded in front of her. I liked this Sylvia.

"I wish I'd known you the way you are now."

"Al's the one who got me into rehab. We've been telling people that I went back to college. Even my family doesn't know."

"Is that the reason why you and Albert broke up?"

She nodded. "Partly. He couldn't handle my habit anymore. And I couldn't handle his business." She looked directly at me.

I cocked my head. "Why have you decided to tell me all this now?"

The kettle whistled. She poured the hot water into the waiting mugs and turned off the range. We went over to the kitchen table and sat in more comfortable chairs. "I'm making amends. I need to apologize to you for being such a witch."

My tea smelled fragrant with raspberry and lemon. She indicated a honeypot on the table. I poured honey into my tea and she got me a spoon to stir it.

"I accept your apology, Sylvia. I never understood where your attitude came from with my family. But now I know."

She blinked very fast and looked away, taking a sip of her tea. After she had composed herself, she turned back to me. "Now, you didn't come all the way here for the bombshell I just dropped on you."

I told her about Albert. She nodded. "Ma called you."

"Yes. The other day. I also heard about the dead body in his condo." She shuddered.

"I haven't told Ma about that part. You read it in the paper?"

She nodded. "I haven't told Ma either. But I can put two

and two together. The paper didn't mention any names or which apartment, but I don't need to be a detective to know the dead guy was found in Al's place.''

"You know Albert didn't do it." I was getting defensive.

Sylvia cocked her head and looked troubled. "I know he didn't, but something funny's going on."

"I need to ask some questions. You probably know Albert better than anyone. You were married to him, you know the ins and outs of his everyday life."

"We are still very close. In fact—" she blushed "—we've talked about getting back together." Her coy look turned to worry. "Of course, that all depends on what happens." She grabbed my free hand and leaned across the table. "If he's in trouble, please find him, Angie."

"If you can help me, I'll do my best. I want him back, too."

"What do you want to know?"

I gave her the names I knew: Rick, Nick, Johnny, Eddie, and Sal.

"Eddie was a friend. Even in my most hazy state, I liked him. He was honest, for a Mob guy. Strictly small-time, but he and Al had a lot in common. They liked to go to Red Sox games, they bowled, went to the movies, had barbecues. Eddie is the reason I'm still here." She looked sad for a moment. "I treated him like shit, and one day, he just looked at me and said, 'You know, Sylvia, you got that stick shoved up your ass so far that I'm surprised you have any room for the coke you're vacuuming up.'" She laughed.

I laughed along with her. "You must have been furious."

"My pride was hurt. Here was this guy, clearly from the wrong side of the tracks, working in a business that was built on spilled blood, and he was looking down on me, a girl born to wealth and privilege.'' Hot tears spilled over her eyelashes and she wiped them away. ''I never got a chance to thank him. And now he's dead.''

I looked around and spotted a box of tissues on a built-in desk in a corner of the kitchen. I brought the box over to her and she took a couple, dabbing her eyes and nose.

''I'm sure he understood, Sylvia. You said he and Albert were close.'' I felt hysteria nipping at my heels, but I took a deep breath and held it together. My brother was missing and the guy in his condo was a close friend. Jeez—I was definitely on a fool's errand. ''I'm sure Albert told Eddie what he did for you.''

''I wanted Eddie to be our best man, if we got married again.''

*Ooo*kay, that brought me to the tape. I wondered what she would think about perky Karen Hirsch. Maybe Sylvia killed him when she found out he was dating someone else.

''What about Nick, Johnny, or Sal?'' I help up the tape. ''Got a machine? This is his answering machine tape. Maybe one of the voices will ring a bell.''

Sylvia pulled herself together long enough to dig a tape machine out of her kitchen desk. We set it up and I played the first message.

''That sounds like someone, but I can't place the voice to a face or name. Nick, though, I think is Nick the Knife. I don't have a last name for him.'' She shuddered. ''His name sure gives me the creeps.''

''As it should,'' I said. ''What about Johnny and Sal?''

She got a far away look in her eye as she tried to dredge up names. ''Johnny. John is such a common name, but Johnny is less common. Unfortunately, more common in the Mafia. But there is a Johnny who is connected to Nick the Knife. They work together frequently. They're enforcers.''

Enforcers. A nice name for hitmen. Great. I was hoping I wouldn't be running into hitmen, even indirectly, but that's sort of like visiting Seattle and hoping it wouldn't rain. "Do you have a last name for this Johnny?"

She squeezed her face up in thought. "It's not a real last name it's something like hit or squash or mash or—Smash. Johnny Smash."

Whoa. Sounded like a punk rocker. Nick the Knife and Johnny Smash.

"And Sal?"

"Male or female?"

I shrugged.

She thought for a moment, then shook her head. "It doesn't ring a bell. No one in Al's personal life, anyway."

"Anyone named Sal who you recognize from his business?"

She shook her head again. "I didn't have much to do with his business. At least, not the business he was in up until a few weeks ago, other than taking phone calls for him and occasionally meeting one of these guys walking out of our house as I was walking in."

"Did he act in an unusual manner lately?"

"He seemed preoccupied, but I assumed that was because of his toy factory and Itty Bitty Kitty." She almost glowed, and she sat up straighter when she talked about Albert's new business.

"You do know that Giovanni Testa is a silent partner?"

She seemed startled by the information. "No, I—didn't know." She looked into her empty mug. "I guess Al was afraid to tell me. I was trying to encourage him to strike out on his own. But he and Testa were —are close. He knew I wouldn't approve."

"Testa tells me that it's a legitimate business, and there are no strings attached."

She squeezed her eyes shut. "You've talked to Testa?"

I sighed. "Yes, he was very helpful at first, but since this morning, he seems to have withdrawn his support. He won't talk about anything or give me any useful information. I might as well be talking to the ocean."

Sylvia opened her eyes. "I guess Al's still full of surprises."

"So is Testa. I think he really meant it, about going legit, I mean." My tea had grown cold. I switched topics to take her mind off the shock of having Testa still in Albert's life. I had another shock for her, and I didn't want to be responsible for sending the new Sylvia back to coke. "Okay, can you tell me who Rick is." I played the message.

She nodded. "That one's easy. Rick Ng. Graduated MIT last year. Al was lucky to find him. He's the research and development department of the factory that makes Itty Bitty Kitty."

I made a note of Rick's name and a question mark after it. What kind of stuff could he research, given the fact that Itty Bitty Kitty was already designed?

"What's the name of Albert's company?"

She thought about that one for a moment. "AMT Enterprises. I always thought the letters stood for Albert Matelli. Now I know the T stands for Testa."

"The silent partner," I added. "Sylvia, I—"

I hesitated. I was afraid to say anything. This new fragile Sylvia might not be able to handle Albert's betrayal, his dating another woman.

"Go on, Angela, what were you going to ask?" She looked at me patiently, but I could see that curiosity had gotten the better of her.

I took a deep breath and played the first message from Karen. Sylvia didn't bat an eyelash. I fast-forwarded and played the second message. I thought I detected a smile.

She nodded when it was done. "We agreed to date other people. You know, we want to make sure we're right for each other this time."

"Don't you think dating other people means that neither of you are committed?"

Sylvia shrugged. "I knew about Karen. She's at Brown. Nice girl. But I don't think she's serious about him. In fact, I think she thinks of dating Albert as slumming." Sylvia gave me an ironic smile. Coming from a wealthy family as Sylvia did, wasn't she slumming? "Albert and I didn't start talking about getting together until about two weeks ago. I think he started dating her before that."

I got up. "Well, if there's nothing you can think of to add, I'd better get home. I have a lot to think about."

She walked me to the door. I turned. "You'll be okay? You're not going to—"

Sylvia smiled. "Do anything stupid? I don't think so, but I'll be sure to call you if I do."

We laughed.

"Seriously, call me if you need to talk," I offered. I gave her my cell phone number.

"Or if I can think of anything else." The hug was awkward, but I thought better of Sylvia now than I had when she was married to Albert.

I thought it was funny how good things could come from bad circumstances. For instance, Sylvia hadn't been a nice person on coke—I knew that for a fact. But having been through her coke habit and a bad marriage, Sylvia had become someone I could stand to be around, someone I even liked and could respect someday. And it was all thanks to Albert's leaving her, and Eddie, the dead guy, telling her what an awful prig she was.

IT WAS VERY LATE when I got back home, and I was too tired to think about what I had learned. I wanted to hit the sheets the moment I got in the door, but I noticed the answering machine light blinking. I played back the one message.

"Angela? Albert. Look, I can't talk long. I wanted you to know I'm all right. I've been keeping one step ahead of Sal. I think I can handle him on my own, but I need you to investigate the factory. Something funny's going on. I don't trust anyone else, and until now, I wasn't able to contact anyone. But I wanted you and Ma to know that I was all right. Gotta go. I'm on the move." Click.

I called Ma to let her know I'd heard from Albert.

"I've been praying for this," Ma said. I could almost see her crossing herself.

"Look, Ma, it means he's all right for the moment. It sounds as if he's in serious trouble, but he didn't tell me what exactly it was. All we can do is keep hoping he comes in from the cold. In the meantime, I'll keep investigating my leads."

"Just be careful. Maybe I should come down there."

"No, Ma!" I said it fast and a bit too loud. "What I mean to say is, I appreciate the fact that you want to come down and help, but Ma, I need you there, waiting for Albert to call, or for someone to call you and tell you where he is. He may try. Besides, if this turns out to be dangerous, I don't want you getting hurt. You'll have to be there to pick up the pieces."

"Okay," replied a reluctant Ma. "Get some sleep, Angela. You sound exhausted."

"Yeah, Ma, I will." We hung up.

I turned to no one in particular and asked, "Jesus, Albert, what have you gotten yourself into?"

I tried to sleep that night, but visions of Albert in a coffin kept intruding. Or maybe they were nightmares, I don't know. All I knew was that the stakes had gone up—Albert had been free up until tonight, hiding out, not sure where to go or whom to trust, and now he was on the run from someone or something. If I didn't find him soon, he'd be as dead to the world as Eddie Fazoli.

EIGHT

THE PHONE RANG. I looked at my clock. It was six in the morning. Feeling around on the table, I found the receiver. I grunted into the phone.

"Hey, Angela, I'm off work—you interested in breakfast?" It was Reg, the doctor I was seeing. Ma had fixed me up with him and although I dug my heels in and didn't want to go out with him, we ended up together anyway. Life is funny sometimes.

I was suddenly wide-awake. "Sure. Where and when?"

We agreed to meet at a little place where I loved to eat breakfast—Max's Deli in the financial district.

I got dressed, checked to make sure I looked presentable, and made sure Fredd had some fresh vegetables, alfalfa pellets, and water before I left. I took the Blue Line down to State Street and walked to Milk Street, where Reg was waiting for me. He'd secured a table for us and had already ordered my favorite breakfast item, the bagel with egg, mozzarella, and roasted red peppers. We shared an order of seasoned hash browns while we made small talk.

He talked mainly about the fact that his internship at Mass General was more than half over and he was trying to decide whether to stay in Boston or seek a position elsewhere. I was very fond of him, but if Reg wanted to move away, I wouldn't try to stop him.

As he was halfway through his breakfast, he mentioned it. "Got an offer yesterday from Johns Hopkins," he said casually.

"Isn't that a teaching hospital?" I asked, showing that I

had been paying attention to him when he talked doctor to me.

"Yep. Down in Maryland. But that's for an internship in neurosurgery, which doesn't thrill me. If I took it, it would be like starting all over. I'd have to take more classes, I wouldn't be in charge of anything. I like emergency services. It's more immediate."

"Mmm, but you are good with your hands." I grinned wickedly at him. He blushed and took off his glasses, ostensibly to polish the lenses.

"I also got offers from UNC in Chapel Hill, and Wahiawa General Hospital in Hawaii."

"Reg, those are good offers. You should be pleased so many hospitals want your services."

Reg took a sip of his coffee and I watched a lock of blond hair fall over his forehead. It was so endearing, I wanted to reach over and brush it back into place. Instead, I finished my bagel sandwich and took a sip of coffee.

"I was hoping—" he eyed me over the tops of his frames now that they were perched on his nose again "—that you'd consider going with me wherever I end up."

I swallowed a larger sip of scalding hot coffee and sputtered, momentarily creating a diversion so I wouldn't have to answer him immediately. He was by my side, patting my back the way only a doctor would, ready to perform the Heimlich maneuver on me. I took a sip of water from the bottle he offered me and took a deep breath before standing up.

"Are you all right?" he asked for the fourth time.

"Yeah, the coffee went down the wrong way. Look, Reg, I gotta get to the office. Can we talk about this later?" I couldn't tell him about Albert's disappearance, which was what kept me from making any further plans, and I didn't want to be too evasive, which was pretty much what I was doing right now. But Reg had plenty of time, and I knew that if Mass General saw its way clear to paying Reg for another year of internship, he'd probably stay, despite the siren call of Hawaii or Maryland.

I wasn't too worried about Johns Hopkins stealing him away. In fact, I wasn't sure how I felt about Reg leaving the state. I hadn't become as attached to him as he'd become to me, and I was more worried about hurting his feelings than anything else. I was fond of him and was comfortable with our relationship the way it was, but I had come to realize in the last few hours that I wasn't looking for a commitment yet.

We kissed, Reg went home to sleep, and I started for the office. When I got to my station, I continued on to Government Center, and took the Blue Line back to Maverick Station. I wanted to find the gumball factory and see what AMT Enterprises looked like. I went back home, got in my Bronco and drove to the factory.

The old gumball factory was located on a street that butted up against the East Boston Expressway. The building was an old, ugly faded red brick thing with an empty, trash-filled lot next door that the employees were obviously using for a parking lot. A chain-link fence, reminiscent of prison films, surrounded the lot and made the factory and the empty lot look as bleak and depressing as an early Ingmar Bergman film.

There had been a fire in the factory about fifteen years before and it was clear that not much had been done in terms of renovation. I hesitated across the street from it—visions of immigrants crammed into this building with a slavemaster at the helm popped into my head. I shook my head, then crossed the street.

The doors reminded me of my old grade-school doors—utilitarian metal double doors with safety bars inside and old safety glass—the kind embedded with honeycomb wire. The building was much different from the last time I'd been inside—my fourth-grade class had gone on a field trip to the gumball factory—no sweet smell permeating the lobby, no gumball machines decorating the walls. I remembered that the guide had given us all gumballs straight from the factory conveyor belt, all the colors of the rainbow. It was back when individuals, not corporations, owned factories, and the bottom line didn't mean every individual gumball was counted as an asset. I remembered the small, brightly colored spheres of red, yellow, green, pink, orange, and blue.

Of course, the last time I saw the factory from the outside was after the fire: the scorched red brick, the melted gumball machine that had been rescued from inside, the scent of burnt gumballs. The red brick was still black on the outside, but when I stepped inside, I noticed that the building had been gutted and rebuilt. It was nothing fancy—a windowed section with cubicles divided the offices from the factory area. I was in the factory area—the offices were through another door. Voices shouted above the hum of machinery, telephones rang, and bells clanged. I counted about fifteen people working in the factory. No one paid me the slightest attention. I walked straight through to the door and when the door shut behind me, the noise became muffled, but it wasn't completely gone.

A woman was answering one phone call after another. She was about forty years old, with sharp features, dark hair flecked with gray, and an East Boston accent. Her nameplate told me that her name was Lorraine Garafalo-Garcia. I wondered if she was any relation to Janeane, the actress. When she saw me, she held up a finger that told me to wait, she'd get to me.

"Yes. Uh-huh. You want fifteen hundred Itty Bitty Kittys sent to your Houston warehouse? Okay. We can do that.'' She frantically shuffled through papers and came to the one she wanted. After a momentary pause, she added, ''We can ship it in two segments—one thousand tomorrow and another five hundred by next Friday.'' She waited again, her head cocked at a curious angle. ''Yes. Okay, one thousand will be on their way to you by tomorrow, five hundred by next Wednesday. Thank you for your business.'' She hung up carefully, then let out a whoop. A young Asian guy came out wearing wire-rim glasses. He seemed right out of college. He wore a white lab coat with a pocket protector. I guessed that this was Rick Ng.

''Rick! Hot damn! Fifteen hundred of the little suckers were just sold to some big toy chain, Busbee's Toyland, headquartered down in Texas. They have franchises in Louisiana, Mississippi, Oklahoma, and Kansas and wanted to make sure they had enough Itty Bittys in stock for the Christmas rush.''

Rick came over, picked her up and hugged her. ''Good going, Lorraine. We're in business.'' They seemed to remember that I was there about the time Lorraine's feet touched the floor again.

She cleared her throat. ''Um, I'm sorry. Can I help you?''

I smiled. ''I'm Angela Matelli, Albert's sister. You don't happen to know where he is, do you?''

They both gawked at me, apparently at a loss of words.

Five minutes later, after I'd shown them some identification, they led me to Rick's R & D lab, a small sealed room where I was comfortably ensconced in a beanbag armchair with a mug of coffee in one hand. Pastries from a local bakery were on a plate that sat on a small coffee table. Rick sat in his office chair on the other side of me, and Lorraine fluttered around me like a nervous butterfly.

"We haven't heard from Al since Friday," Rick told me. "We thought it was odd because he usually calls in several times a week to find out how the sales of Itty Bitty Kitty are going." His black hair hung boyishly over his forehead. If he were a little older, I could very easily go for this MIT grad.

I told them what I knew of his disappearance. I mentioned the tape with Rick's message on it. "Who are these clients and what type of meeting was this?"

Rick and Lorraine exchanged a look. "I'm not sure if we can divulge that information at this time," Rick said. It was as if he were reading it from a cue card.

I got up from the beanbag chair—make that, I struggled to get up from the beanbag chair—and paced. "I found an empty ToyCo envelope in Albert's home office wastebasket. There was also an empty file folder with ToyCo's name on it. Does ToyCo have anything to do with this meeting?"

"Angela, do you mind if we talk in private? We need to discuss how much we can divulge."

I shrugged. "Okay by me, but if this has anything to do with Albert's disappearance, and I believe it does, then you might prefer to tell me rather than the police." I strolled out of the room. I was back two minutes later. The discussion had been brief and they looked willing enough to talk.

Rick nodded. "Al owns the factory, he came up with the Itty Bitty Kitty idea, but we're partners." I wondered how many partners Albert had in this business. And did they know about each other? I'd damn well find out in a few minutes. "I'm the designer," Rick continued, "and Marty, who works in the factory, is in charge of production." He turned to Lorraine and said, "I just thought. We'd better tell Marty we need five hundred more dolls ready by next Wednesday."

She nodded and left the room. Rick turned back to me.

"How long has Al been missing?" He had a worried, thoughtful expression on his face.

"He didn't call Ma on Friday night like he always does. She came to my office on Monday, and that's how I ended up here. Your message was recorded on Saturday night. So were several others. Did you know that Albert has a silent partner?" I sat back down in the beanbag chair.

"I'd suspected as much. He's paid for things I didn't think someone in his position could have gotten. It's not unusual to have an angel in this business." Rick was frowning now. He was starting to look more attractive—sort of a young Asian David Duchovny, from the *X-Files*. I wondered why he wore the lab coat. Designing Itty Bitty Kitty dolls and accessories didn't seem to be messy sort of research and development that required lab coats. He probably just enjoyed wearing them.

"What do you mean by 'someone in his position'?" I asked.

Rick had the grace to look embarrassed. "Well, uh, you know about his work, don't you?"

I didn't want to give away Albert's secret life if I didn't have to, but I needed to know how much Rick, and Lorraine and Marty, knew. "Yes, but why don't you tell me about it?"

"What do you mean?"

"Tell me what you understand about Albert's work." I sank back into the beanbag chair.

"He works for the Providence Mob, doesn't he?" He said it with such innocence, I was wondering if I'd have to explain that the Mob didn't have a stock symbol on the New York Stock Exchange.

"*Ooo*okay, I guess you're aware of my brother's unsavory business dealings. Do you have any idea what he does for them?"

"For the Mob?" For an MIT grad, Rick was a little slow on the uptake. "He used to front for them. He told me about that."

So Albert can talk to a younger MIT grad he's known for a little over a year, and not discuss it with his family? To be fair, when would be a good time to bring up what he does for a living—during dinner at Ma's? "Hey, a funny thing happened to me the other day when I was laundering a hundred grand through Rigaletto's, that Italian fast-food place I use as a front down in the North End..." Nope. Not a good time. But he could have brought it up privately, when he and I would go out together or when we were watching the Celtics squash the Lakers at my place.

"Yeah, he's not a soldier or a numbers runner. He fronts for them. Businesses—a chicken take-out place one year, a funeral home the next year, a dry-cleaning place the year after that. He crunches numbers and prepares a second set of books, figures out how to launder money for his bosses."

Rick nodded. "Yeah, I know about that stuff. I read about it in a class—"

I interrupted him. "Rick, what are you running here?" I shifted in my beanbag chair—these things were not designed to be sat in for longer than ten minutes. I had a desire to get up and stretch, but I was afraid that I would look so ridiculous again, struggling to get up, that it would send Rick into gales of laughter and I wouldn't get the information I needed.

"A business."

"With my brother, a launderer. Work with me here, Rick."

He put his glasses back on as if he'd just seen the light. "Oh, I see. You think Albert may be laundering money through here for the Mob. But he can't do it. The feds ran the Boston Mafia out of here a couple of years ago. I read about the case of Whitey Bulger.''

Some people are just born naive. Jeez. Should I destroy his illusion that the good guy always wins? "Look, Rick, I'm not saying that this business isn't legit, I'm just saying we both know you're in it with a guy, a blood relation of mine, who launders money for a living. For the Mob. And now he's disappeared. Even though I've been assured that this is a legitimate business, let's just say that I don't trust my source. So let's take a look at the books.''

He nodded slowly. "Lorraine can get them together for you.''

"Both sets. If you find a second one.'' Hey, he's my brother, but no one said he was perfect. On the one hand, I hoped there was a second set of books so I'd have something to go on, some lead to investigate. At the moment, I had a bunch of wild theories about what was happening.

On the other hand, I hoped there wasn't a second set because then it meant he'd either hidden the second set so well that no one would find it, or he was actually, truly going legit.

"Can you think of anyone who might want to harm Albert or who has a grudge against him?''

Rick gave me an amused smile. "You probably know Al better than I do. At least you know him enough to call him Albert without having your teeth knocked out.'' I must have looked surprised because he explained. "He doesn't like his name, Albert. He insists on Al. In fact, he once tried to get us to call him some nickname—Skip or Chip, I think it was. None of us could remember it.''

I chuckled at the thought of my brother being so vain he'd rather be called Skip or Chip than Albert. It sort of sounded like him. I had always thought Albert and I were close, closer than I was to my other two brothers, Vinnie and Ray. I guess I didn't know Albert as well as I thought I did. "So you met him through work here? He hired you, I mean?"

Rick took his glasses off to reveal lovely deep brown eyes. He rubbed his left eye, then his right one. "No, we met at a benefit dinner for the Cancer Society two years ago. He was with his wife then, Sylvia. I was right out of MIT and was accompanying my mother to the dinner because my father was away on business. Al and I sat across the table from each other and started talking. He asked me about my plans now that I was a graduate. We got to talking about starting a business, really it was just fantasy, as far as I was concerned, but by the end of the evening, we'd exchanged cards and he told me he'd call." Rick shrugged and smiled. "He's been very generous to me, considering that I came into the business with a certain amount of knowledge and practically no money. I own ten percent of the business."

"And Albert owns the rest?"

Rick shook his head. "He owns the majority stock, but I think Marty has a deal with him, and Lorraine gets a certain percentage of the stock for every year she works here, along with a raise."

I was still amused by the news that my brother not only owned a business, but also had framed up the idea of the doll. No wonder he was so shy about his business.

"Rick, how well do you know Albert, I mean, Al?"

"We've gone out to dinner together, a few basketball games, but it's not like I'm his best friend or anything."

"Tell me about the meeting." I raised three fingers. "I promise I won't divulge the information. But Albert's life could depend on it."

He rubbed the back of his neck. I wanted to rub it for him, but I had to be good. "ToyCo wants to buy us. It's a good deal. A great deal. The clients who came here on Monday were muck-a-mucks at ToyCo.''

The door burst open and a heavyset man with a graying bristlecut strode in. ''Rick, what's this I hear about needing five hundred more dolls by next Wednesday? That's crazy. It can't be done.''

Lorraine followed behind, wearing a worried expression.

''What do you mean it can't be done? You told me that you could manufacture two hundred dolls a day. We have the rest of the week, hell, we have the weekend and several more days before we need to send the shipment off.''

''You pseudo-intellectual Harvard boys think you know it all,'' Marty blustered before storming out of the office.

Lorraine and Rick didn't seem put out by Marty's behavior. Rick didn't even bother to correct Marty that he'd gone to MIT, not Harvard. To Marty, it was probably all one and the same. Lorraine must have noticed my expression. She waved a hand at me. ''Oh, don't pay any attention to him. He has to puff himself up like a male peacock in order to make himself feel better. We've all gotten used to it.''

''Low self-esteem,'' I replied.

She laughed. ''Yeah, something like that. He likes to be in control. Frankly, the only person who can control him is Al.'' She stopped smiling and looked at me. ''So you think he's been abducted or is in hiding?''

I nodded. ''Probably the latter.'' I didn't fill her in on his phone call. I wasn't sure who was on which side of this game. Hell, I didn't even know the rules of the game.

Instead, I asked her some questions. ''When was the last time you saw him or heard from him?''

''Al checked in with us every day up until last Friday. He comes into the office at least once a week.'' Lorraine indicated a cubicle toward the back of the office. ''Natu-

rally, we were a little more than concerned when he didn't
pick up our clients on Monday, and he didn't show up to
our meeting. It was very important. Fortunately, Al's disappearing act didn't seem to put off the clients."

"Rick told me," I assured her. "I hope it happens."

Her eyes got bright. "Wouldn't it be great? They'd want
us to keep the factory, keep making the dolls, and they'd
keep us on as staff. But with their money, we could get
better equipment, make this into a real factory, a real office."

"What's your story, Lorraine?"

"I went to business school. Nothing fancy like MIT. It
was a little place back on the West Coast. I worked at a
major toy company for many years in marketing, and when
I met Al and heard about his plans, I had to get in on the
ground floor."

"I'll bet it was a dream come true," I said.

She nodded enthusiastically. "Especially for someone
like me who had been out of the business for a few years.
I stopped working to raise my kids. But when they went to
school, I wanted to find something to do. This just fell into
my lap. And Al's a dream to work with. He lets me have
run of everything." She surveyed her desk, her cubicle, and
the factory beyond. "This is gonna be the biggest thing to
hit the toy market since the Cabbage Patch doll."

"Can you show me his desk? Maybe I can find out something from where he worked when he was here."

"It's not much. He spent most of his time on the phone
or on the computer—you know, that little notebook thing
he carries around." Lorraine led me back to a neat desk
with a phone and a Rolodex. I sat down and started to go
through the Rolodex, copying names and numbers into a
small notebook I kept in my purse. It didn't take me very
long because there weren't many cards in the Rolodex. Al-

bert had only just started this business and hadn't built up the list it takes years to acquire.

Lorraine looked over my shoulder and made comments like, "That guy's a distributor" and "Oh, yeah, that's the woman from the advertising firm we hired."

When I was done, I turned to her. "I'm just trolling here, but what would happen if Albert didn't come back to the company, if he's disappeared for good?" A knot tightened in my stomach as I said this and a vision of Giovanni Testa shouldered its way into my mind. It's one thing when it's someone else's family member, quite another when it's your own beloved brother.

Lorraine frowned as if it hadn't even occurred to her until now, which it very well may not have done. "I'm not sure about this, but I think Marty and Rick have their own deals with Al, same as me, although Al holds the majority share. With no wife in the picture, I suppose his share would go to your mother, right?"

"So the partners don't have an agreement that if one of them dies, the others split his share?"

She shook her head. "Honestly, I don't know. I get shares in the company, but they're B shares, not the A shares. I'm a stockholder, but not a partner."

I nodded. "Can you find out exactly what happens?"

She agreed but before she turned back to her work, she hesitated. "You're serious about this, aren't you?"

"About what?" I asked, not quite understanding what she meant.

"About Al disappearing. You're acting like he's in some kind of trouble, not just off on some jaunt to Europe or something like that."

I sighed. I didn't want to tell her what I knew, I didn't know if she was involved in his disappearance or if she'd unwittingly give something away to someone if I told her.

But I needed to keep this friendly, I needed her as an ally. "I am closer to Albert than to my other brothers. We're closer in age, for one thing, and I guess we have the same outlook on life and about our family. So when Ma called to say he hadn't called her last Friday like usual, I got a feeling that something wasn't right. He's always been reliable, even with all the mystery that surrounds him."

"Mystery?" she asked blankly, as if Albert was an open book to her.

I paused, then said, "Yeah, about his job and all."

"You mean that he works for the Mob?"

Did everyone in Boston know this or what? Did they all talk about it as openly as Lorraine and Rick? Jeez. "Look, Lorraine, a little advice. I wouldn't talk about the Mob in such a cavalier manner. Yeah, my brother worked as a front for the Mob. *Worked* is the operative word, according to some people."

She looked puzzled by my advice. "That's funny, because Al was pretty open about it when he talked to us. He said your family was pretty hush-hush about the whole thing."

I was getting a little annoyed. "He said that, huh? Well, we might not have been as hush-hush about it if he hadn't been so damn mysterious about what he did for a living."

Ma was the one who didn't like to talk about it, so we didn't talk about it in deference to her. She loved her children fiercely, but any of their faults or anything she disapproved of was moved to the back burner. After a while, I mused, we just didn't bring up any of the things Ma didn't want to hear about. I guess I couldn't blame Albert for his mysterious behavior regarding his work. Ma's force field must have kept him from talking about it even when she wasn't around.

Lorraine went from bemused to amused. "He's talked

about his family to me so many times I almost feel as if I know you and Ma, Sophia, and Rosa, Ray and Vinnie.'' She'd rattled off the names with such familiarity that I was tempted to start quizzing her on whether Helene was married to Ray or Vinnie, how many kids did Vinnie have and how many were his and his first wife's, how many did he and Carla have.

Instead, I laughed. She joined me. ''Yeah, we're pretty tight-knit for such a dysfunctional family.''

''Your mother sounds like a pistol.''

I nodded, my eyes misting at the thought of how much I really loved her, even though she could drive me to distraction and was constantly surprising me. ''Ma loves us all.'' I focused back on Lorraine and added, ''And that's why I gotta find Albert. For Ma.''

NINE

I SAID GOODBYE TO LORRAINE, who promised to get the books and any other information that might be helpful to me as soon as possible. Rick had made himself scarce, and Marty even scarcer. I wanted to talk to Marty. He might have some useful information, but I doubted that this was the time to talk to him. As I walked out via the open factory area, I could hear Marty and Rick yelling at each other.

"You told me just last week that we could produce two hundred dolls a day easy. Now you're telling me that the order won't be ready for next Wednesday," Rick was shouting above the noise of the machines.

Marty was leaning into the slightly built Rick. He looked like a pitbull about to take a bite out of a frightened child. "The packaging machine is broke. I told you that yesterday before we left. What am I supposed to do, wave a magic wand over it and it's fixed? The service guy told me they couldn't get parts for that machine anymore. I'm telling you, Albert bought an old machine and we need a new one."

Rick turned away from Marty and paced. I didn't like Marty's sly look when Rick's back was turned. I wonder if my brother, who wasn't here to defend himself, would have really bought the machine without consulting Marty. Well, there was nothing to do but take the pitbull by the horns. I cleared my throat. Loudly. They didn't pay any attention to me. I moved closer and said, "Excuse me." Rick jumped and Marty looked at me, narrowing his eyes in assessment.

Rick looked as if he was working on a headache, and he was trying to be nice under pressure. "Yeah, Angela, what can I do for you?"

"Oh, no, it's what I can do for you, Rick. You need someone to fix the packaging machine? Since Albert's not here, I'm the person to talk to."

Marty took a cigarette from his shirt pocket. I glanced at the No Smoking sign and wondered if I should say something, but decided against it. That was Rick's department. It looked as if these two men were going to lock horns until Albert's return. *If he returned.* I knew he was alive, he'd called me the other day, and I just needed to find him and help him out of whatever situation he had gotten himself into. In the meantime, if I could smooth over whatever problem Rick and Marty were having, maybe I could stay on Rick's good side and win Marty's approval so he would talk to me.

"So you're saying you can fix the machine?" Rick asked, slightly skeptical.

I crossed my arms casually. "Not me, my cousin Joey. He can fix anything. Not a machine alive that can't be fixed, is his motto."

Rick's expression was worried. "He must be expensive."

I hesitated for the first time. "Actually, no, he's not. He just got out of prison and is looking for work. If he does a good job, maybe you'll give him some recommendations, call him when any of your machines need maintenance."

"Hell, as soon as we're on our feet, we'll hire him full-time to look after our factory if he's as good as you say," Rick replied enthusiastically.

Marty took a deep drag on his cigarette and regarded me appraisingly. "So you're Al's sister, the private eye." At least he hadn't said "private dick." "You're an ex-marine?"

I smiled. "No such thing as an ex-marine." He nodded. I couldn't tell if he'd been a marine or navy. That usually meant he'd probably been a Navy Seal or something like that. They tended to have the same attitude as marines, but you'd never catch a marine admitting that there was any similarity. Marty did have the requisite tattoos on his forearms, something I had managed to avoid.

I went back into the office and called Joey.

"Hey, Angie, my favorite cousin. How you been? I didn't think you'd want to talk to an ex-con like me." Joey was about twenty-two years old. He was the gentlest of souls so I found it weird that he'd just gotten out of prison.

"Aw, Joey, you know I love you, no matter what you've done." Rick and Marty and even Lorraine were trying hard to appear as if they weren't listening to my end of the conversation.

"That's nice to hear, Ange." Joey pronounced "that's" the Brooklynese way, "dat's." "You're one tough bean and I wouldn't do nothin' to cross you."

"That's good, Joey, 'cause I got a job for you."

"Private eye work?" His voice was so eager, I hated to disillusion him. Besides, he might come in handy here at the factory, overhearing parts of conversations and stuff.

"Maybe," I hedged. I couldn't exactly tell him all this over the phone with the people I wanted him to watch standing over me. "Right now, there's this machine that needs fixing."

"Oh, yeah, a machine." His voice lacked the energy of a moment ago.

"I'm standing here with these people right now. I told them about your ability to fix any machine."

"Oh, I see. You can't talk about the real job with them there, is that right?" His voice had perked up.

"Yeah, that's right." I gave him the address and told him they were expecting him tomorrow morning. "Meanwhile, why don't you stop over tonight for dinner? Long time, no see." Originally, I'd thought it would be a good deed, fixing Joey up with a job, and helping my brother with his business in a time of crisis. But it wasn't such a bad idea, having Joey be my eyes and ears at AMT.

"Sounds good. See you about six."

After I'd hung up, Rick thanked me and shook my hand. "Anything you want, you got it, Angie."

Marty didn't look so sure. He'd finished his cigarette long ago and no one had mentioned that he'd ground the butt into the carpet. Lorraine probably just figured he was an owner and she'd just have to vacuum it up at the end of the day.

"You say this guy's been in prison? What for?" Marty asked.

"He's paid his dues and if he feels like telling you, he will. It's nothing you have to be worried about," I said firmly, not wanting to tell them that Joey had been in the pokey for beating a man's head in. The fact that the man had been a pimp who had bragged about turning Joey's sister into a crack whore made Joey a hero in a lot of people's minds. That the man had survived Joey's attack with little more than losing an eye and some nerve damage in one hand was the only reason Joey wasn't in prison for life. The jury and judge had been sympathetic, and there had been plenty of witnesses outside the bar where it had happened.

I looked at my watch and realized it was almost eleven. I said my goodbyes again, finally got out of the factory, and drove back to my apartment for an early lunch. The apartment building lay empty and I felt vulnerable with no one to watch my backside while Rosa was in Italy, getting her backside pinched. While she was soaking up the museums and sidewalk cafés, I was pounding the streets, looking for our brother.

A slight resentment welled up inside me and I pushed it down as quickly as it had appeared. It wasn't Rosa's fault that Albert had gone underground. It would have been nice to count on her help with this case, considering that the client was Ma. Still, what could Rosa do that I couldn't? Aside from answering phones and getting some of the scut work done for me while I concentrated on looking for Albert, Rosa was my cheering section. Okay, I admit it—I was egotistical enough to need someone shouting encouragement to me from the sidelines. Raina would do, but I couldn't involve her in something that could turn out to be dangerous. Rosa would have been involved already, being that she was family. I thought that sounded really selfish and I willed myself to be grateful that Rosa was out of harm's way. On second thought, she was in Italy, home of the Mafia—and if this all turned out to involve the Family, Rosa could find herself in more danger there than she would if she were here with her own family.

Before I rooted around in the refrigerator for something to eat, I called Antonia and left a message, adding Lorraine and Marty to my list of background information. I needed to know where they came from, what they were doing now, and what kind of secrets they might have from their pasts. Antonia had promised to get me something by tonight, tomorrow morning at the latest.

I thought about all the facts I'd learned, and all the things that had happened lately. It was time to visit Biff down at the condo. If I left immediately, I'd be able to interview him and get back up here for dinner with Joey at six. I got back in my Bronco and headed for Rhode Island. Ma called me halfway there.

"Angela?"

"Yeah, Ma. What's up?"

"I was reading in the Providence paper—you know I get it sometimes—and I read about a murder in the same building as where Albert lives. But they don't mention which apartment or Albert's name. Angela. Was there a dead body in Albert's apartment?"

I admit, I panicked. I turned the radio up real loud to static—no station, and shouted, "What did you say, Ma? I can't hear you. My cell phone's breaking up. I'm on the road. Call you when I get back to the office."

I could hear frustration in her tone. "I would have gone with you, if you'd asked me. Angela? Are you still there?"

The traffic started to slow down. I was entering Providence. "Have to go. Talk to you soon." I hung up.

It was twelve-thirty when I arrived at my exit. I would usually turn left to go to Albert's condo, but I turned the other way and looked for a place for lunch. I stopped at a take-out Middle Eastern place for falafel on pita bread and a coffee.

By the time I was done with lunch, it had gotten colder and I wished I'd remembered to bring gloves. There was always a list of things I intended to store in my Bronco, but I never got around to doing it. I resolved once again that as soon as I found Albert, I'd stock my car with all the necessities—cables, a blanket, a jug of water, an extra coat, gloves and shoes, et cetera. By the time I was finished, my car would look as if I was on a permanent vacation.

I drove to the condo, parked, and walked in the lobby. Biff was there, wearing a light blue polo shirt that had two buttons artfully left open to show his hairy chest. His khaki shorts were more appropriate for Bermuda, but maybe he was the sort of guy who dressed for his surroundings. The two artificial palm trees and sand-colored walls probably were the closest he was going to get to Bermuda or Jamaica right now.

He showed me his smile again, the one he reserved for everyone and everybody. He even made eye contact, gazing at me a little too intently.

"What can I do for you?"

I realized he didn't recognize me from the other day, probably because Ma is a force to be reckoned with.

"Biff, huh? Say, Biff, I just moved into the neighborhood and I heard about the murder here in this building. I'm wondering if it was such a smart idea to move here. Does this sort of thing occur a lot?" I fluttered my eyelashes for emphasis. I'm not too bad to look at myself.

Biff puffed his chest up, not that he really needed to—he probably rivaled Pamela Lee's chest size already. "Well, uh—"

"Anne," I supplied. It was the first syllable in my given name.

"Anne, I wouldn't worry about it too much. This is the first violent death to happen here."

"Did you know the victim?" I asked, my eyes wide.

"He wasn't the tenant, if that's what you mean." Biff was resting his elbows on the desk, leaning closer to me as if to get a closer look. Maybe it was the fact that I'd unbuttoned the top three buttons on my blouse. Or it could have been my sparkling personality. "But he was a friend of the tenant's. He used to come here a lot."

"Were you working here that night? Were you the last person to see him? I'll bet you're an important witness." I sighed and ran my fingers through my hair.

He cleared his throat importantly. "I was questioned closely by the police."

I leaned over farther, gave him my most vivacious smile. "Ooh, that must have been exciting."

"Well, I was told that I shouldn't talk about it after talking to them," he replied slyly.

I pouted. I hate pouting, but on guys like Biff, it usually works. "I see. Of course you can't. I might be the killer." I reached out and traced a random pattern lightly on one of his hands. I gave him a sultry smile.

"But I can tell you that three guys entered the building last Friday night. And two left. The dead man was one of the three that entered, and the tenant didn't leave with the other two."

"I bet they weren't as big as you are. And I bet that if you'd known they'd been killers, you could have handled them all by yourself." I walked two fingers up his arm as I said this, all the while giving him a simpering look.

He cleared his throat again and I realized that this was an annoying habit he had. I didn't think it possible, but Biff's chest grew another inch. "Well, they were pretty big. At least one of them was. The other guy was small."

"I heard it was a Mob hit."

"Where did you hear that?" he asked, slightly suspicious that a feather-brained girl would have heard it.

"Oh, my uncle works at City Hall and hears stuff. I heard the guy whose apartment it is, is connected. And he's missing."

"They're looking for him," Biff assured me. He was breathing rapidly. "Where did you say you lived?"

"Down the block, four houses down on the left," I lied.

"I could tell you the rest tonight after dinner," he suggested.

"Oh, that would be wonderful," I breathed, then caught myself and frowned prettily. "Oh, darn. I have to have dinner with my cousin. He just moved to town. My mother insists.''

At the mention of my mother, Biff's look changed from interested to surprised, then angry. ''Hey! You don't live around here. You were here the other day. With your mother. You're Albert Matelli's sister, the guy the police are looking for in that murder.''

''The boy gets a gold star,'' I replied. I'd dropped the act and was heading out the door just as two plainclothes cops were coming inside. Biff ran around the security desk to let them in, effectively stopping me from leaving.

''Hey, Lieutenant, she's Matelli's sister. She was here the other day.''

While the two cops eyed me the way they'd eye a medium-rare sirloin steak, I turned to Biff.

''Biff, you are a man among weasels,'' I said.

TEN

MANN WAS SHORT, THICK, and had bushy eyebrows to make up for the lack of hair on his head. His second-in-command, Mike Parducci, was a whippet-thin blond with freckles sprinkled across his nose. His eyes were a pale gray. The effect was disconcerting. I imagined that he played bad cop to Mann's good cop.

They insisted on driving me to the police station. "Your car will be fine outside this condo." Mann turned to Biff. "Won't it, Mr. Sandy?"

I would have laughed at Biff's last name if I weren't so furious with him. Biff assured me he'd keep an eye on it while I was enjoying the company of Rhode Island's finest. I was tempted to stick out my tongue at him as we left, but I had too much dignity.

I was bundled into the backseat of their unmarked Chevy and we made record time, I'm sure, getting to the station. I tried to make conversation with them, but they said very little.

"So, why do I feel as if I'll never see the light of day again?" I asked.

Neither partner replied.

"Look, guys, you're making me nervous. We're really going to the station, aren't we? I mean, you're not sizing me up for concrete shoes, right?"

Parducci gave me a sardonic look. "I don't think they do the concrete shoe thing anymore, Ms. Matelli."

"Oh, thank you, that makes me feel so much better about

being in a car with two strangers who say they're with PPD.'' Neither guy laughed.

At the precinct, Parducci showed me to an interview room and left me alone. Like good little detectives, they kept me waiting an extra twenty minutes for my trouble. The interview room had the same decorator that the Boston stationhouses' interview rooms had—peeling beige paint, old radiators that knock and ping and hiss, and a cage in the back to hold those suspects who might get a little rowdy. If their intent was to make me uneasy, they were doing a damn good job of it.

But I took advantage of my time in the place. I noted the time, a quarter to two in the afternoon, and I got up to inspect the place. After establishing that there were no two-way mirrors—in fact, no mirrors in the room at all—and no hidden microphones to the best of my knowledge, I thought it would be prudent to call someone before being interviewed, someone like a lawyer. Unfortunately, I didn't know any lawyers here in Providence and the detectives hadn't thoughtfully provided me with a Yellow Pages.

So I called Ma. She was the only one I knew for sure was home.

"What are you doing back in Providence, Angela? Has Albert come home?"

"No, Ma, he hasn't." I debated how to tell her. I didn't want her to panic, but there wasn't anything to do but tell her. "Um, I'm at the Providence police station."

"To file a missing persons report on Albert, right?"

"Weelll, not exactly. Actually, I was interviewing the security guard at Albert's condo and the detectives came back, presumably to have another look at the scene of the crime.''

"And?"

"And they sort of insisted that I come along with them.

They want to interview me, and there are reasons why I need a lawyer, and fast. Could you get me a lawyer?" There was silence. "Ma? Are you still there? I can't afford for you to have a heart attack right now, Ma."

"Angela, why didn't you tell me about the dead man in Albert's condo?"

I covered my cell phone receiver and groaned. Then I got back on the phone. "We can talk about that later, Ma. Right now, I need a lawyer, and I don't have much time left. These goons will be back any minute."

"You must think your mother is extremely stupid."

"No, Ma, I just wanted to protect you. I meant to tell you by now, but it's taken me this long to find out the dead guy's name and his relationship to Albert. Now about the lawyer?" I could hear voices outside the room. "Ma, I have to hang up soon. They're right outside the door."

"I'm thinking. We don't have any lawyer relatives in Rhode Island. I'll have to make a few calls."

"I don't care who you get, Ma. In fact, maybe you should call Helene. She might know of someone good here in Rhode Island. Oh, yeah, and let Joey know I won't be back in time for dinner tonight. Tell him I'll call him when I get back to Boston."

"Joey, that jailbird?"

"Ma, he's gonna do a job for me. And Joey had reason to bash that guy's head in. Don't forget his sister."

"Ruby is a slut."

"Ma!" I held the cell phone away from my ear and stared at it. Okay, the whole family knew she was a slut, but jeez, whatever happened to family loyalty? I got back on the phone.

"I still don't understand why you're in jail, Angela."

I sighed. "I'm not in jail, Ma, I'm in the stationhouse, and these two detectives are preparing to interrogate me

about what I was doing there the other day. Now I have to
go. They're coming back in." I reassured Ma that I was
fine, but the sooner she got a lawyer to get me out of here,
the better.

Ma told me she'd do what she could, and I should be
seeing someone soon. I gave her Benny the Bond's number
as well. Maybe he knew a lawyer down here. Why couldn't
Albert have lived in Boston, nice, cozy Boston, where I
knew people and they knew me?

We hung up none too soon. The gruesome twosome entered and Parducci did what cops in bad movies do: he
hitched up his pants, then spun a chair around and straddled
it, his arms resting on the back. I looked around for the
interrogation spotlight—the one that makes the victim
sweat profusely and shake uncontrollably and say things
like, "I—I didn't do it! I swear it. I got nothin' more to
say."

Every bad film about women in prison flashed through
my head. Soon, I'd be wearing something gray and drab,
sculpting guns out of bars of soap with my fingernails, and
hiding a spoon from my meal tray to sharpen into a stiletto
for the big noon fight down in the laundry room.

Mann did most of the talking, Parducci just perched on
his chair, looking like Sylvester after he swallowed Tweety
Bird and right before Granny whacks him with her um-
brella.

"Thank you for coming in, Ms. Matelli." Mann shuffled
some papers around while Parducci crossed his arms.

Like I had a choice? I swallowed the response and nodded curtly.

"How is your brother?"

"I have three. Which one?" I resisted the impulse to
cross my arms. It would make me look defensive, like I
had something to hide.

Parducci shot me a disgusted look. Mann smiled humor-lessly. "Albert, of course. He's the only one who lives in Providence."

"I'm not sure," I said cautiously. "I haven't seen him in a few weeks." This was the truth. I was going to be playing fast and loose with the truth, but I was going to be a stickler for detail. I didn't have to tell them that Albert had disappeared. They already knew he was gone. The difference is that they were probably looking for him for murder, and they assumed he'd disappeared of his own free will. I wasn't sure they would believe me if I told them I thought my brother was in trouble.

Mann glanced at Parducci, who nodded slightly. "Look, Ms. Matelli, a dead man was found in your brother's condo."

My eyebrows shot up and I leaned forward. All those plays in the high school drama club were paying off. "Really? Have you identified him yet? Oh, God, you're not gonna tell me it's Albert, are you? This'll kill Ma."

Mann glanced at Parducci. I could tell they weren't buying the act. So much for my Oscar nomination. "He's already been identified, and it isn't your brother."

I went ahead and slumped back in my chair, resisting the urge to dramatically wipe my brow—which would have just been overacting. I was curious as hell about what they knew about the dead man, but I couldn't let on that I was interested. I settled for looking relieved, then perplexed.

"If it's not Albert, where is my brother?" I paused, then added, "Is he in jail?"

"No," Mann said, clearly ready to continue.

I interrupted him with another rhetorical question. "Do you know where my brother is? With a dead body in his apartment, he could be somewhere else, dead or hurt or something. Who is the dead guy anyway—a friend of Albert's? A stranger? Maybe a repairman?''

Parducci looked as if he wanted to shut me up. He wasn't buying my act, but he wasn't calling me on it, either. Which meant they wanted information from me and didn't want to lean on me too hard. I probably wouldn't end up in jail. Yet.

"Hold on. We have a couple of questions for you," Mann said. "Then maybe we can answer some of your questions."

"Shoot." I was pretty confident they didn't have anything on me. And I doubted they could answer any of my questions, because if they could, Albert would be behind bars right now.

"We understand you were in your brother's unit to pick something up." Biff, the security weasel, must have told them what he suspected.

"But Biff, the guy at the security desk, wouldn't let me in," I replied. How could they fail to see the logic in that?

Parducci took the opportunity to lean in, his face almost right up against mine. He must have been waiting for this moment, probably played it up in his mind a thousand times. "A witness places you at the side door a few minutes later."

I happen to know that wasn't true—the only person who had seen me perform my "break-in" had been Ma, and she wasn't talking. I'd hidden well behind the Dumpster so the guy taking out the trash wouldn't see me, and he didn't look back when I followed him to the side door and slipped the credit card in the lock. Parducci was on a fishing trip and I told him so.

"I don't know what you're fishing for, but there aren't any bass in this lake." Parducci gave me a weird look. Good. Parducci had been hoping I'd say something like, "that guy couldn't possibly have seen me when I tiptoed up to the door and slipped my credit card across the lock." I wasn't that stupid.

"Your fingerprints are all over the place."

"All over what place?" I asked.

"A couple were lifted off the Dumpster itself," Mann said casually.

"So? I had some trash in my car and I wanted to get rid of it before the drive back home."

Mann raised his eyebrows.

"It was a lot of trash," I added curtly. Okay, maybe I was slightly defensive, but who wouldn't be?

Parducci stuck his face in front of mine—invading a suspect's space is supposed to make him or her feel threatened and they are supposed to break down and confess. "What about the fingerprints on the side door handle?"

I dug into my purse, trying to maintain my confidence and failing fast. I stuck a roll of mints in between him and me, giving me a chance to scoot my chair back a bit. I smiled. "Mint?"

Parducci had perfected the snarl, I do have to say. He must have spent a lot of time practicing in front of a mirror so he could intimidate suspects. I got the feeling that Parducci spent a *lot* of time in front of a mirror, practicing how to look like a cop.

He backed off and turned away. I offered a mint to Mann, who took it. He was so calm, I figured he was the one to watch out for. I stuck a mint in my mouth and sucked on it.

I shrugged. "So? Okay, I got in the back door and used the facilities."

"Fingerprints all over your brother's condo turned out to be yours," Mann said in a conversational tone. "It's as if you were looking for something."

I shrugged. "Those fingerprints could have been there from some other time. I've been down to visit my brother before. Besides—" I leaned forward, thinking I had something here "—how did you get permission to enter my brother's condo in the first place?"

"We got an anonymous call that there was a dead man in his apartment. We were obligated to check it out." Mann smiled humorlessly. "Back to you breaking into your brother's place. He'd just moved in a couple of months ago. We checked the records and asked the security guards about visitors. You haven't signed in as a guest at his condo since he moved in."

I gripped the edges of my chair and wondered if I should have brought Testa's private number with me in case the detectives decided to throw me in the pokey. Then I decided I was being paranoid for no reason. "Couldn't I have entered my brother's apartment through his garage? He could have driven me back to his place. Don't you have to get the owner of the condo to press charges before questioning someone on her reasons for entering her brother's condo? He's my brother, for God's sake. He's not gonna begrudge me the use of his bathroom or a little nap on his couch while I'm visiting Providence." I leaned forward, tired of the game we were playing. "Look, guys, what do you want from me? You gonna hold me here? Am I a suspect in this murder?"

Mann smiled and shook his head. "No, but it does seem strange that your brother made himself scarce after Friday night, then suddenly you show up, try to get in the front door, and when that doesn't succeed, you go in the back door."

Okay, it now dawned on me why they're so suspicious. I was too close to the situation to take all sides into account. "I see. You think I went in there to get stuff for Albert to

take to him in his secret hiding place." I laughed and re-
laxed, crossing my legs at the knees. I decided to explain
as much as I could without hanging myself. "You've got
it all wrong. I'm looking for him, too."

Parducci and Mann glanced at each other, clearly not
sure what to make of my sudden transformation from wary
suspect to confiding peer. "Why don't you tell us about
it," Mann said, folding his hands on the scarred table in
front of him.

I gave them a version of the truth, bringing Ma into the
picture a bit, but leaving Testa out of it altogether. I brought
up the doll factory in East Boston, but only in passing and
to let the detectives know that Albert was an upstanding
citizen, as far as I knew.

By the time I'd finished, Parducci and Mann were eyeing
each other uncomfortably. I kept a hopeful, expectant look
on my face—maybe I wasn't so bad at this acting thing.

"Um, Ms. Matelli," Mann asked in a soft tone, "um,
are you aware of what your brother does for a living?"

I nodded brightly. "Yeah, he's an entrepreneur. This Itty
Bitty Kitty thing has really taken off and it's going block-
busters."

"We know your brother belongs to the Mafia." Mann
didn't look at me. It was almost as though he was ashamed
of what he'd originally thought of me. Parducci looked as
if he weren't buying my innocent act. I had to give him
credit for that one.

I waved the proffered speculation away. "Nah, not Albert. Maybe he has a friend or two in the Mob, but—"

I had the two detectives a little off balance until the door
opened and a drab woman entered with an official-looking
file. She handed it to Mann.

Mann read the sheet of paper. Looked up at me as if
comparing me to the Ten Most Wanted, then handed the

paper to Parducci. The two of them moved to a corner of the room, conferring in low voices, one of them glancing back at me occasionally. I felt like the pariah of the school-yard and I had a feeling my acting days were numbered.

Finally, they turned back to me and Mann spoke again. "Ms. Matelli, we have a report here that says that you were spotted at Giovanni Testa's on Tuesday morning."

Great. They had surveillance on Testa. Of course they did. And they caught my license plate number and ran it.

"He's an old friend of Ma's." I looked at them. They weren't buying it. "They went to school together—I just drove her down there!"

Mann closed his eyes briefly and opened them again. He looked hurt that I would deceive him. "You're a private investigator. Now, Ms. Matelli, please tell us the truth."

I opened my arms and shrugged, "Hey, so I'm a private detective. I'm also Albert's sister and I'm worried about him. And you can check out the fact that my mother went to school with Testa."

Parducci smirked. "But you and your mother didn't go there to talk over old times with Testa."

I sighed. "Okay, I know my brother is involved with the Mob. Testa agreed to see us. He didn't have anything to offer regarding Albert's disappearance. In fact, he seemed just as puzzled and worried as we are."

"Yeah, I'm sure Albert is like a son to him," Parducci said sarcastically. "Cut the shit, Matelli, and give us everything you have."

I threw him a cool look. "What, you're gonna threaten to beat it out of me?"

Parducci's hands became fists and he started for me. I half-stood. Mann put an arm out to stop his partner. "Watch out, Mike, she's a BAM. She'll beat the crap out of you."

BAM stood for Big-Ass Marine, a derogatory name for female marines. It was designed to piss off women marines, and it did, a fact that was backed up by thousands of black eyes—most of them male marines. But once a woman left the military, at least as far as I was concerned, it meant nothing. I smiled, even laughed.

"Yeah, Parducci, you better watch your narrow ass." I stood up. "I think we're done here, gentlemen. I'm out of here."

Mann grabbed my arm—not roughly, but with a firm "don't-mess-with-me" force. "I don't think so. We have the right to hold you for twenty-four hours if we think you're a material witness."

Parducci chuckled. "Yeah, we have to protect you. I think you witnessed some illegal stuff at Testa's and his men are after you."

"Huh?" I was stunned. I yanked my arm out from his grip a little too forcefully and felt a muscle pull in my shoulder. But to my credit, I didn't wince. "You can't do this to me."

He shrugged. "Actually, we can."

Parducci was grinning like the Joker. "We got you for twenty-four hours. Enjoy your stay."

"Shit," I said. My witty repartee never let me down. "Hey, I got a dinner date tonight. Shit." I said again, thinking of Joey and the time he did.

"You could just cooperate," Mann said.

"I've told you nothing but the truth."

As they led me to the elevators, I shouted to no one in particular, "I want to talk to my lawyer."

ELEVEN

MANN GRINNED. "Hey, you're a material witness, and we don't have to give you lawyer privileges. We're doing this for your own good." He pressed the Up button at the elevators.

The doors opened after an eternity, and standing on the other side was a tall, thin man who wore a George Hamilton tan that told me he spent more time on the islands than here in Rhode Island. He had the sort of chiseled features you can get out of a catalog at a plastic surgeon's office. An aluminum briefcase dangled from his left hand.

"Ms. Matelli, I presume?" Hey, a lawyer with a sense of humor was a plus. Especially when the laugh was on two cops who were giving me a hard time.

"That's me," I managed to squeak from between Mann and Parducci. I felt like Moses parting the Red Sea, the way those two detectives stepped quickly away from me.

The tall, elegant attorney held out his hand. "Frederick Langley. I'm your lawyer." He looked over at Lt. Mann. "May I have a private word with my client?"

Parducci was giving Langley a dark look. The attorney was clearly aware of the younger detective, but he studiously ignored him. He zeroed in, instead, on Lt. Mann. The older cop appeared to take this in stride, but it was clear to me that Langley bothered him. It was probably the fact that I was slipping through their fingers. Mann indicated a nearby room.

Langley stepped in, then immediately stepped back out and addressed Lt. Mann again. "I said a private room. This room has a two-way mirror. I know all the tricks. I've had several clients here before.''

"I've seen you around," Mann admitted with distaste. We followed him back to the other room. Mann closed the door.

I told Langley what had transpired. He frowned when I gave him an idea of my conversation with the two detectives. "You should know better, Ms. Matelli. Talking, even if you think you know what you're saying, can be dangerous.''

I shrugged. "I'm Italian. It's hard to shut me up sometimes. I just dazzled 'em with some bullshit.''

Langley seemed amused. "So basically, your brother's missing, and you came here looking for someone to help you find him.''

"Yeah, that's right.''

"And they treated you like a suspect instead of the caring sister that you are. Well," he said, standing up and gathering his briefcase, "I don't see any reason for them to hold you. The threat of incarceration is just their way of letting you know who's in charge." His hand on the door, his smile slightly sardonic, he added, "Fortunately, I know bigger fish that could chew them up and spit them out. A very unpleasant experience.''

The way he said it, I believed him. The fish he knew must be some very big piranhas, probably very high up the ladder, to mix a metaphor.

Outside, Parducci was pacing, looking as if he wanted to gnaw on someone's leg. Mann was leaning up against a wall, arms casually crossed. He was definitely the guy I would approach in a crisis. I was wishing that we could part on good terms, but under the circumstances, that was a lot to wish for.

Langley took a pair of glasses out of the breast pocket

of his gray suit—no doubt some extremely expensive Italian designer made the suit. "I just discussed the situation with my client and she told me something about taking away her civil rights? Something about a jail cell and twenty-four hours." Oh, he was good. Out of the corner of my eye, I could see Parducci blanch.

It was clear to me that Mann was having a tough time keeping his temper. "I think she misunderstood the situation. We just thought it would be best if we kept her in protective custody."

Langley took a cell phone out of his pocket and hit the redial button. At least, I assume that's what it was because he only pushed one button, and I could hear it ringing. Then he held the phone up to his ear and spoke to someone in a low voice. A moment later, he held the phone out to Lt. Mann.

"Judge Gilbert wants to talk to you."

Mann looked at Parducci. If Parducci's mood had a weather forecast to go with it, there would be thunderstorms heading our way right now.

Mann gingerly took the cell phone. "Hello?" He looked a bit surprised and a bit angry at the same time. He caught me looking at him, a half smile on my face, and he turned his back to me. "Yeah, that's right. Well, Your Honor, I think Ms. Matelli's been holding out on us. We have evidence that she's been in Albert Matelli's apartment."

Mann listened for a moment, then held the phone out a few inches so everyone could hear Judge Gilbert say loudly, "She's his sister, fer Christ's sake. What're you gonna do, hold the whole family in protective custody?"

Mann got back on the phone. "Uh-uh. Not the whole family, sir. only Ms. Matelli. There were fingerprints, sir, and a witness who places her at the scene—" He took a deep breath and let it out, listening for about half a minute before getting another word in edgewise. "Uh-huh. Yes, Your Honor, I know about civil rights. That's right. You have a good evening, too, sir." He looked at the phone as if it would change its mind, then handed it back to Langley, who dropped it casually in his pocket.

"She's free to go," Mann said unhappily. "We had every right to hold her for twenty-four hours. She could be in danger."

"Where were you planning to hold her?"

"We were going to put her in a nice cell across the street."

Personally, I thought the term "nice cell" was an oxymoron.

"I think holding her overnight would entail putting her somewhere safe," Langley replied imperiously, "not in the over-night tank where you hold the prostitutes, drunks, and drug cases."

Mann got defensive. "We were going to give her a cell of her own." Just call me Virginia Woolf. "The city's cutting back on manpower and on renting hotel rooms. She would have been safe."

"But you were doing this against her will," Langley pointed out. "And I believe she said something about her brother being missing. Shouldn't you take a report?"

Parducci chimed in. "We're not Missing Persons. Those losers are down the hall from us."

It was time for me to say something. I gave Parducci a sweet smile. "I'm sure they'll be happy to know what you think of them, Detective." Langley touched my arm and we started to walk away.

Mann came after us, his demeanor clearly at war with hostility and bootlicking. "Wait, why don't we take a report for you. I know someone in Missing and I can get it through faster than if you go there now."

Mann jotted down the information I gave him—the physical description and when Albert was last seen—in a small notebook.

"It's not much," he said, staring at what he'd scribbled down.

"I can get a photo of him for you." I wanted to be helpful.

Mann smiled, but it wasn't a friendly smile. In fact, I could swear that he wanted to wrap his hands around my neck. "Oh, don't worry. We should have a nice photo of him around here somewhere."

"I doubt it's recent," I replied icily.

"We'll be in touch." Parducci said this, his lips barely moving, his face immobile.

Langley led me out of the station. Outside, the sun was going down and it had turned cold. My light jacket wasn't enough.

"Thank you for rescuing me."

Langley made a stiff little bow. It looked funny with his aluminum briefcase at his side. He took his glasses off and put them away. "Are you parked out in the lot?" he asked.

I shook my head. "No. I'm parked by my brother's condo. The detectives were kind enough to drive an out-of-stater to their doorstep." Hey, no one can ever say I'm bitter.

"I'll drive you back there while I tell you what's happening." He led me out to a sedate gray BMW sports car. I got in. Heated leather seats, my own directional climate control panel, all I needed was a steering wheel, accelerator, and brake, and I'd be in business.

He started up the car.

"Do I need to pay you now?" I asked as I dug my checkbook out of my jacket pocket.

He shook his head. "My fee has already been paid. Your

rights were violated and I was hired to defend you. I play golf with Judge Gilbert and know that he hates it when a citizen's rights are being violated. It didn't take me long to get him on the phone. He also hates police officers who strong-arm citizens. Bad for reelection. I have a feeling your detectives are going to be called on the carpet tomorrow morning.''

"Look Mr. Langley, I'd better pay you right now," I said as we pulled up to my beloved Bronco. ''Ma shouldn't have to pay for this.''

He looked at me as I opened the door and smiled. ''Your mother didn't hire me, Ms. Matelli. Giovanni Testa did. I believe she called him about your predicament.'' While I was at a loss for words, he added, ''Please call me if you need anything else.'' He handed me his card. He hesitated, then said, ''If you want my advice, Ms. Matelli, for what it's worth, you should drop whatever investigation you're on. I've met your brother and he's very resourceful and smart. I doubt he's in any danger, but you very well may be if you continue to ask questions.''

I must have gotten a dark look on my face, because he added, ''I'm not saying this as a threat, but because I'm a good judge of character, and even though we've just met, I like you. Do your brother a favor and step away before you get hurt. I work for some very powerful people.'' He smiled as I got out of the car, still at a loss for anything to say to that.

As I watched him drive away, I tried to figure out what exactly Langley meant. His attitude was almost fatherly when he was giving advice, but how could I not believe that he was really trying to warn me to back off?

No wonder Mann got that sour look on his face when Langley came in with his big guns blazing. Great. Now Mann and Parducci probably think I'm connected to Testa.

In a way, I am. I got in my car and opened my purse. The check was still where I'd left it. I was tempted to tear it in half, but something stopped me. It was still leverage, or something. Evidence, maybe?

I started the car and pointed toward home.

Halfway there, my cell phone rang. I knew who it was. "Ma!"

"Good. You got out."

"Ma, what were you thinking, calling Testa like that?"

"I was thinking about getting you out of jail," she replied. "Helene wasn't home, and I didn't know who else to call down there. Giovanni was very nice about it."

"Yeah, and now he probably thinks he owns me." I was going to insist on paying my legal expenses to him. Or maybe I could include it in my expense account. I wasn't thinking straight right now. The whole situation seemed unreal to me. "Anyway, thanks for getting me out. I was almost stuck there for the night."

"You can thank me by finding Albert and straightening out this whole mess," Ma said before hanging up.

IT WAS NEARLY SEVEN O'CLOCK when I got back to my apartment. I was exhausted. Sitting on the stoop outside my place was Joey. I parked and got out of the car.

"Joey!"

He stood and came toward me. "Hey, Cuz."

"What are you doing here? Wasn't Ma able to reach you about me being detained in Providence?" I'd forgotten to ask her if she'd reached him.

He grinned. He was a large man, dark and handsome, looked like a bodybuilder. His shaggy dark brown hair was combed back, one or two strands having broken free to hang over his forehead. I noticed he had a couple of prison tattoos on his left forearm, and one diamond stud in his left earlobe winked back at me. "Yeah, I had to come down here and see if you were all right. She called a second time to tell me you'd gotten out of jail. Now we have two jail-birds in the family." His grin was lopsided, adding to his charm. I could imagine what a nonrelative female would be thinking when confronted with this gorgeous man.

"I wasn't technically in jail, Joey, but I came pretty close."

I realized that I hadn't eaten anything since noon and it was now seven in the evening. I punched him lightly in the arm and suggested that we go to Santarpio's to talk and eat, not necessarily in that order.

TWELVE

WE SPLIT A LARGE Italian sausage pizza and had glasses of cold red table wine with our meal. Joey put away a good deal of the pizza while we caught up on family stuff—his twenty-three year-old sister, Ruby, was now dating Jim, a divorced construction worker—a far cry from when she was sixteen and living with a local drug dealer. Joey told me Ruby and Jim were serious.

"That's good," I replied. "I'd hate to see you beat in another guy's head."

Joey's face darkened. "Juice told me my sister was a crack whore. Then he laughed in my face." He made one of his hamlike hands into a fist.

I stopped, pizza slice in mid-air, mouth open, and stared at my cousin's expression. I suddenly knew how Juice must have felt right before Joey's fist went practically through his face. When I was growing up, Joey had been easy-going, and to some extent, he still was. But I could tell that prison had taken its toll. Aside from the tattoos and the prison pallor, Joey had a couple of scars—one that cut across his right eyebrow, and one near his collarbone that looked as if someone had slipped a shiv into him.

Their father had died of cancer when Joey was thirteen and Ruby was fourteen. Joey had promised his dying father that he would look after his sister and mother, a big weight to bear for a young boy. Especially since Ruby, his sister, was an impetuous and headstrong girl.

Two years later, it was more difficult for Joey to keep the promise he'd made to his father. His mother was working two jobs and Joey maintained a B average while Ruby's grades dropped from Bs to Ds and Fs. When she turned sixteen, she dropped out and ran with a drug crowd. Ruby and their mother fought incessantly, and eventually Ruby moved in with the drug dealer she was seeing.

Joey became the messenger between his mother and Ruby for the next year and a half. One night, he met Ruby and her man, Juice, in front of a bar. Joey was fifteen at the time, sixteen in a week, but he was pumping iron even back then, and looked bigger and older than his age.

That night, Ruby was clearly high on crack, and Juice sent her to "get them some money" in front of Joey. It took a lot to make Joey mad, but with all that weight on his shoulders, he had gone from an easy-going preteen to a dark, brooding time bomb. Juice, also high at the time, confided in Joey that his sister was one fine piece of ass, and would do anything for crack. That's when Joey hit him. Juice wasn't much for fist fighting. He was a weakling who relied on a .38 that he carried in his jacket pocket. That night, he didn't have a chance to draw it once Joey started pummeling him. Although several people from the bar eventually drifted out to watch the fight, Juice was well known and hated by the decent people of the community, so no one tried to stop the fight—not until the police arrived.

Joey was tried as an adult, got five years, and served three. If he hadn't maimed and blinded Juice, he might have gotten off with a suspended sentence. Even with our family's numerous contacts in government and law enforcement, Joey still went away, much to everyone's regret— even the prosecutor and the judge were reluctant to pass the sentence, but an election year was an election year.

To Joey's credit, he made the best of his situation—he got his GED in Walpole, and took classes in machine main-

tenance while serving his sentence. The warden and all the
guards had regretted Joey's release. He had a talent for
fixing anything electrical or electronic. The warden told
Joey's mother that Walpole had never run smoother and
probably never would again.

I looked across the table at Joey, the kid who had so
much promise a few years ago. He stopped before he
brought his fist down on the table, caught my look, and
laughed. "Sorry, Cuz. Prison'll do that to you. You should
know."

I smiled back and took a bite out of my pizza as if he'd
never turned into Mr. Hyde. "What are you talking about?
I'm sure my cellmates wouldn't have tried to maul me—
they'd just give me beauty tips."

He laughed again. "Don't count on it. Women cons are
worse than the men."

The way he said it made me shudder. He turned serious.
"So what's goin' on?"

"Albert's disappeared."

He blinked. "Oh, come on. You gotta be kidding. He's
just gone on a little vacation or something. Forgot to tell
anyone, right?"

I shrugged. "I wish that were true." I told Joey most of
what was going on, leaving out the part about my meeting
with Don Testa and anything else that might make him an
accessory to whatever legal hellhole I might have fallen
into. I didn't want to make Joey an accessory after the fact.
He had enough trouble as it was.

"Albert's missing," he repeated when I was finished.
"Wow. I mean, we all knew he was working for—" he
looked around the room before lowering his voice "—the
Mob, but I guess I never thought this would happen."

I agreed. "It's not something we think about much with
him. He's always been so mysterious and—" I searched

for the right word "—resilient. But things have changed around here, in Boston."

He nodded, his eyes straying toward the last piece of pizza. I pushed the pie plate toward him.

"I kept up with the outside world these last few years," he replied around the slice. "I know what's going on here in Boston with the Mob." He shook his head. "So Albert's the one who came up with Itty Bitty Kitty, this year's Cabbage Patch Kid. If it wasn't so successful, it would almost be a joke. I didn't think the guy liked kids *that* much."

I laughed. "I know what you mean."

"So you want me to keep an eye on this place." He looked eagerly at me.

I nodded. "Yeah. If he's able to, he might try to contact someone there. I'd think it would be difficult for him to stay away from business. If anyone is holding Albert hostage or knows where he is, having you there would be a good thing. Also, you'd know if anything strange happens, you know, illegal. You probably got a nose for that sort of thing now." I was referring to the time he spent in the joint. He probably got quite an education there.

"Yeah, I know a lot about unlawful things these days. But I want to keep my nose clean."

I nodded. "That's why I told you only stuff that won't get you into trouble, and you're on a need-to-know basis." I paused, then added, "I thought of you, Joey, because you're handy. They'll keep you around, and you can report back to me. You get their packaging machine going, and keep your ears open. I'll pay you, and you should get paid by them as well." I looked him straight in the eye. "You know, if this works out well, I could hire you again for things that need to be done. It's good work, honest work, although sometimes you have to get your morals a little dirty to make something right for your client."

I gave him capsule descriptions of the people who worked there, lingering a bit on the moody and volatile Marty. Joey took it all in, eager to be part of an investigation, even if he didn't know all the facts. I knew Joey was quick on the uptake, and I knew he liked to keep busy. I gave him my cell phone number.

"Don't use it while you're there—call me from your house, or from a pay phone," I instructed. "If there's anything funny going on, make an excuse to leave—you have to get a part or something—and get out of there. Go to a pay phone and call me immediately." I paid the bill and as we walked out of Santarpio's, I turned to my cousin. "Don't go doing anything stupid, Joey. Your mother would never forgive me if anything happened to you."

He gave me a hug. "I'll be good."

"Hey, at the worst, you'll fix their packaging machine and help Albert make another million or so."

AT HOME, THERE WERE several messages for me: Reg had called, wanting to get together tomorrow night: Sylvia had called to see how I was coming on the investigation; Ma had called—big surprise; and Antonia. Probably my most disturbing message was from Albert.

"Angie? Me again. I wish I could tell you where I was, but it's not important. In a little while, I'll be out of reach of those who are trying to find me. In the meantime, I have something I want you to do for me. Something's not right at AMT. I've been thinking about it. Someone at the factory—" There was some noise in the background, tires screeching, the phone being dropped, Albert saying, "Shit!" then a long silence until someone came up to the phone. "We got him," a man said before hanging up.

I listened to his message over and over again, trying to pick up something recognizable in the background, but it didn't work in real life. I didn't hear a foghorn, no railroad warning, nothing. It was well after midnight when I fell into bed, fully clothed, and slept fitfully.

I GOT UP EARLY the next morning, showered and dressed, then dug around in the freezer for a pumpernickel bagel to toast. I noticed an envelope had been slipped under my door. I picked it up. The envelope was from Antonia and contained the background information on every name that I'd requested the other day. Antonia's cover note explained that she'd been called out on another consultation this morning and she wanted to drop the files off now rather than wait until her job was done. I munched on my bagel and sipped coffee and grapefruit juice while I read through the files.

I started with Don Testa—it was the thickest file and had everything from newspaper clippings to bank statements to FBI files. I didn't want to know where or how Antonia had obtained the federal files, I hadn't expected it of her, but maybe once her fingers started walking the keyboard, she couldn't stop herself.

Testa was worth millions of dollars, as expected, and the money was diversified. I scanned a lot of the financial stuff, enough to make sense of most of it before putting it aside. His family was of more interest to me. Testa had three sons and two daughters, all by the same long-suffering woman named Francesca who came over to America from Italy back in the 1940s. According to the photos in the older clippings, Francesca was a doe-eyed Italian beauty with a generous mouth—very Sophia Loren. In later society clippings, she had turned into a formidable matriarch with hard eyes and a smile that told of life's disappointments. I didn't sense any scandal there. Testa was probably as faithful to

her as he was to the Mafia. She didn't look like a woman
who would take news of a mistress very well.

The society clippings mentioned Francesca Testa's fond-
ness for causes. She donated to just about every worthy and
unworthy cause, in order to get her name in the paper, and
finally went to her well-deserved rest in 1989.

The children led mainly uninteresting lives of quiet desperation—it appeared from the background checks that the
two daughters, Sonia and Sofia, married right out of high
school to successful businessman.

There were twin brothers, Vito and Tito, who attended
Harvard and Princeton respectively, both graduating with
degrees in business. Vito went on to law school, then
worked for his dad, supposedly on legitimizing the old man.
Tito lived in Italy, having married a fashion designer from
Milan, and worked for his wife. He appeared to be completely out of the Mafia business, but Italy wasn't the place
to get away from the Family if you wanted to run. I was
pretty sure Tito was still doing a few things for his father
over there.

The youngest brother, Salvatore, better known as Sal,
graduated from high school and seemed to have disappeared from the newspaper clippings. While Testa's first
four children excelled in school, Sal barely graduated. He
didn't go on to college like his brothers, and he didn't show
up in the papers under the society column. But he did show
up in numerous clippings from police records. He was troubled, getting into fights, selling drugs, carrying firearms.
His father always managed to bail Sal out of jail (probably
bought off the judge) but Sal was definitely not a chip off
the old block. He didn't have the wiles that his father had.
He blundered into situations and, according to the files, if
he didn't get his way, he called Daddy, who came to his
aid every time.

I wondered if there would be an end to Daddy's protection. What would Sal do when Testa died? It didn't look like his brothers or sisters would come running. And was Sal working in the Mafia, or was he just a spoiled, troubled brat?

I noted that most of Sal's troubles lately had taken place in Boston. He was making Boston his home for now. I filed away the information for later on.

Meanwhile, I read about Rick, Lorraine, and Marty. Rick Ng was second-generation American—his parents had come over from Thailand, and he'd worked his way through high school, graduated with a 4.0 average, and although he'd gotten a four year scholarship to MIT, he owed lots of money for student loans. There was nothing in his records about tongs or other mob-types. He was single, but was involved with another MIT grad, and he liked to collect comic book art and was a *Star Wars* fan, attending science fiction conventions. His favorite website was anything to do with *Star Wars*. The guy was as all-American and squeaky clean as they come.

Lorraine Garafalo-Garcia was married to a man named Raoul Garcia, but she had grown up in Wellesley, a wealthy suburb of Boston. She was in her mid-forties, and had gone to Radcliffe in the early seventies. She had been thrown in jail overnight a few times for sit-ins and demonstration, mostly about the Vietnam War. That was where she met Raoul. She had two kids, both in college, and her husband was a biostatistician currently working on an epidemiological study with Harvard School of Public Health near Brigham and Women's Hospital.

Lorraine was probably picking up the extra money because of her kids' education. There didn't seem to be anything funny or unusual about her past or present, although I did note that there were several police reports for domestic violence over the last few years. I wondered if she was picking up the extra money to save for getting away from an abusive husband.

Marty Greer, as I had predicted, had been a Navy Seal. After ten years with the Seals and no promotions, he had gone civilian and gotten a job with a factory that made boxes, working his way up the ladder to foreman, then floor manager, and finally, supervisor.

There were several black marks against his record—he had a tendency to get involved or start bar fights and had had overnight jail stays. I surmised that he was an alcoholic. He also liked to gamble at the racetrack—Suffolk Downs. Hmm. I wondered if he'd run into my father.

Antonia wrote a note that she couldn't get anything on the names Nick the Knife or Johnny. I would have to call Raina and ask her to run the names through the police computer, maybe check the Rhode Island police computer as well. I also wanted to find out more about Salvatore Testa.

I called Raina and asked her what she was doing for lunch. "Having lunch with you," she promptly replied.

We agreed to meet at a little place not far from the station. "And by the way," I said, "are you on a secure line?"

There was a pause, then she said, "Let me call you back. Are you at home?"

I said I was, then we hung up. A few minutes later, the phone rang.

"What's up?" she asked. "I took a break and I'm on a pay phone across the street from the station, I promised to make a run for doughnuts, so make it snappy."

"Okay, I can't tell you everything that's been going on, at least not in this phone call, but would it be possible for you to run a couple of names for me?"

"Jeez, Angie, that's the only reason you stay my friend," she griped.

"You need a bribe," I said. "How about a tall, handsome twenty-two-year-old guy? My cousin's been away for a while and he needs to learn how to date all over again." Raina liked younger men, and I was pretty sure Joey would like Raina. At the very least, it would be a fun date for both of them.

"Where's he been?" she asked with a giggle. "Europe? Antarctica? Some space station?"

"Walpole."

"Angie, that's not even funny."

"I'm not joking. He wouldn't have gone to prison for his crime except that it was an election year. I'll give you the dope on him later." I gave her the names.

"Gee, thanks," she replied sarcastically. "Do I look under K for Knife? Testa won't be a problem, but this other guy, all you know is Johnny?"

"Actually, it's Johnny Smash."

Raina groaned. "Knife was bad enough—now I have a Smash? What kind of people are you hanging out with, Angie?"

"I'm willing to bet that you'll find a Johnny Smash when you start digging into Sal's sordid past. Nick the Knife, too."

Raina told me she'd look into it, we agreed on noon at Mama Cavini's restaurant, and then we hung up.

THIRTEEN

I'D RECENTLY FOUND that music sometimes kept me from distraction when I had some heavy thinking to do. Sometimes music helped me free-associate. I slipped a CD into my portable player, the Starlight Drifters, a rock-a-billy band with a sense of humor.

As the first song, "Don't Mess Up My Hair," played, I went over the meager information I had accumulated: Albert had created Itty Bitty Kitty, a cat-faced doll, and it was a big hit. So big, in fact, that he had leased the old gumball factory and outfitted it with tool and die machines to manufacture the dolls, then had taken on several other partners. Albert had also talked to Don Testa, who had agreed to let Albert leave the Family to strike out on his own as an entrepreneur. Albert had agreed to bring Testa on board as a silent partner in his now-legitimate, successful enterprise.

I saw nothing so far that screamed motive, unless Testa was being less than honest with me. I couldn't forget the fact that Testa had gone from partially cooperative to evasive with me overnight, and that my brother had been a money launderer for the Testa family in Rhode Island.

Now a couple of goons named Johnny Smash and Nick the Knife were after Albert for his factory. They had killed a lowly numbers runner named Eddie, a friend of Albert's to ensure my brother's cooperation. But to what end? Add to this the fact that there was a Sal Testa, and I had bubkes, and I knew it.

I drummed my fingers on the desktop for a minute, then leaned back to listen to the song, "Johnny Dynamite," which pays tribute to a fifties private-eye character from an obscure comic book. Shivers ran down my spine as the singer described how the gumshoe lost an eye in a Mob gunfight.

I tried to picture myself with a patch on my eye. Angie Dynamite? I don't think so. I was having enough trouble figuring out an ordinary human-type case here without encountering zombies from outer space, as Mr. Dynamite apparently did in some of his adventures. In the last verse, Dynamite encounters the Devil. I had a devil of my own to encounter. I knew he was out here but at the moment, he was faceless.

I took a deep breath and focused my mind on what I'd originally started to do. I went back over the facts. Factories. Why would someone want to take over Albert's factory? I thought about various activities that the authorities frowned upon—drugs, gunrunning, and illegal immigrants—and the only thing that made sense about trying to bully Albert was the location. The factory was in East Boston, which was an island unto itself, surrounded by water. It's a perfect place for smuggling in anything you could think of that's illegal.

Illegal plus Testa's odd behavior equaled something. I put those facts together on a blank piece of paper, then wrote ''Bulger'' and ''Boston'' and ''Mafia.'' With the fact that Whitey Bulger was out of the picture and his cronies were being indicted, could someone in Testa's family, his blood relations, not the other kind, be thinking of starting up a Family here in Boston? Maybe someone wanted to take over some of the activities Whitey Bulger had been involved in. Law enforcement was currently resting on its laurels having all these crooks behind bars right now.

Okay, so maybe I didn't have bubkes, but it would be a

difficult thing to prove. And it was a stretch. But it did make some sense.

I picked up the phone and called my police friend, Lee Randolph. Lee had recently been offered a step up, as lieutenant commander of the patrol room. I know he missed Homicide and being able to get out of the stationhouse. He talked about it constantly when we got together for dinner—which amounted to about once every two weeks—and at poker once a month. Actually, Lee didn't gripe the way women do. He talked around the subject when we were at poker. Like, when one of our poker buddies would ask me about a case I'd had that had gotten some publicity, before I could get a word in, Lee would be off and running about some case that he'd been reminded of that had happened years ago.

Most police officers have a choice when they enter the force—they can move up, or they can stay on patrol. Lee had chosen to move up the ladder, and when he found something he was really good at, they bumped him up to moving paperwork around on a desk, and overseeing a hundred patrol officers. He was good at what he did now and was well liked by the men and women who served under him, but he missed the action in his old stomping grounds. On the bright side, he was a lot easier to reach when I needed a favor.

"Hey, Angela, how are you? You want to go to lunch today? I'm just sitting at my desk," Lee said, "looking out at the bright sun and wondering what to do with the rest of my day." I could hear his chair creak as he turned around to look out of his window.

I looked out my home office window. It was a day that could fool a person into thinking it was almost spring. The sun was bright but the light from it was brittle and weak. I looked at the clock. It was ten, so I could do it, but I had plans with Raina for lunch. "Um, I'm booked today, Lee. How about another time? Actually, I called to ask you about something."

"Shoot."

"What's the word on the street about the Mafia? I know Boston has made a big deal over the fact that Whitey Bulger is being prosecuted in absentia and his captains are being indicted on numerous counts, but what's the real story? Is the Mafia dead in Boston?"

Lee paused. "It depends on who you're speaking to. The politicians like to brag about how clean Boston is right now."

"Yeah, but I asked for the word on the street. Is anyone trying to take over or start a new Family in Boston?"

"Do you know something I don't know?" Lee asked.

"It's just something I'm working on right now," I replied. I hated being evasive with Lee, but it was the best I could do now. Everything I had was speculation, as fabricated as zombies in outer space. "But if something comes of it, you know you're the first one I'll call." And I meant it. I'd rather he got the credit for anything as major as new Mafia activity being uncovered in Boston.

He sighed. "Okay. I'm gonna have to put the word out to my officers," Lee replied. "I think this calls for a famous Matelli dinner. Do you think your mother would let me come to dinner on Sunday?"

I thought about it. Lee was a friend, but he was also a police officer. I wasn't letting the information leak that Albert was gone, and I wasn't so sure Albert would be back this Sunday. On the other hand, if I didn't have a lead by then, I could use all the help I could get. Besides, there would be an empty place at the table if my brother was still missing, and I knew Ma wouldn't cancel Sunday dinner—she'd just be upset through the whole ordeal. Having

Lee there, filling the chair, eating the food, might distract Ma a bit.

"I think we have room," I said, then amended it a bit. "Ma always has room for another at the table, Lee, and you know she likes you."

Ma had tried to get me interested in Lee as more than a friend. Even though he wasn't Italian or even Catholic, Ma had taken to Lee from the moment he took a bite of her famous pasta and sauce and closed his eyes to savor the garlic, oregano, and basil. Lee was a sucker for food, especially Italian food, and it was a wonder he didn't weigh four hundred pounds by now.

"This is a man who appreciates good food and good company, Angela," Ma had said. "Did you see the way he played with Stephanie and Michael? He would be a natural father."

"This is a man who enjoys going to strip clubs until two in the morning on Friday nights," I countered. "Lee's idea of the perfect woman involves large bazooms, long legs, and the ability to start stripping the moment she hears any ZZ Top song."

Still, Ma worked on Lee every time he came over. But it didn't put him off from going there to get the kind of meal you can't even get in a five-star restaurant. He absorbed Ma's arguments for marriage and family like Italian bread absorbs garlic butter. He was always polite, always helpful, and always firm in his convictions.

We agreed that I would pick Lee up on Sunday to go to Ma's house in Malden. Lee also agreed to call me back as soon as he heard anything from his officers on the subject of a new Mafia.

"Angie, is everything okay?" he asked. I should have known it would be difficult to keep anything from him.

"Yeah, why?"

"It's just—well, you hardly ever stay home during the week. Are you sure everything is okay?"

"Yeah, it's fine. I just felt a little under the weather and didn't feel like trekking all the way into Boston." I wasn't exactly lying—I did feel a little sick to my stomach.

My next call was to Craig Cohen, who had left the newspaper business to work as a feature editor for *Beantown* magazine, a glossy monthly that focused on the best restaurants, the best places to live, and the best places to shop in Boston. But they did have a conscience, and often their feature article was about politics or scandal in Boston. They also kept up with what was happening in organized crime. Craig was in charge of the features department, and he was having a blast.

"No more having to answer to editors, no more silly puff pieces for me," he said. "They want me to concentrate on the hard feature pieces."

He was also an ace poker player, and we found out that we enjoyed the same types of movies. We had a standing date to see anything foreign, anything arty, or anything that we knew wouldn't last. The last movie we'd seen together was *Clay Pigeons* a small-budget movie with a solid mystery plot and wonderful characters.

"Hey, Craig, how's it going?"

"Angela! Did you know that *Life Is Beautiful* is playing in Cambridge next weekend?"

"Sounds like a date to me," I replied. "But I'm actually calling about business."

"I'm your man. What do you need?"

"I'm looking into the whole Mafia business. Your magazine did several articles on Whitey and his gang. Have you heard anything about anyone trying to move in on this territory?"

"Hmm, well, you got your Haitian gangs, and your tongs

in Chinatown. Jamaica Plain and Roxbury have the black gangs."

"What about the Mob? Any movement in that direction?"

"Now, Angela," Cohen said in a coy tone, "you know what the politicians say—"

"Fuck the politicians."

"My, my, such strong language from the lady. But I agree. The Mob isn't just going to roll over and die. Not without a fight. What's going on?"

I made him swear, crossed pinkies over the phone, that he wouldn't dig into this subject until I'd investigated, then I'd give him everything. Exclusively.

"Can't argue with a deal like that."

I gave him everything I had—names, what had happened to Albert, theories that I had.

His tone grew serious when I mentioned my brother was missing. "That's not a good sign, which is an understatement. But the good news is that the Mob wants something from your brother, so they probably haven't killed him yet. It's clear that he doesn't want to give it to them, though, and that's bad."

My heart sank even further when he mentioned this. "But Testa swears up and down that he doesn't know where Albert is and this is going to sound weird, but I believe him." Even as I said it, I didn't believe it. He had to suspect where Albert was being held.

"But you also said you have a feeling he's holding something back from you."

"Yeah," I replied glumly. "I wish I knew what it was."

"You mentioned this guy, Johnny Smash. I've just dug up my notes on him while we were talking. He's not the kind of guy who would try to take over the Mob. Definitely a follower, not a leader. Same with Nick the Knife, only even more so.''

''What about Salvatore Testa, the troubled son?''

I could almost hear Craig shrug through the phone line. ''Could be him. He never struck me as leader material, but anything could happen over the last ten years.''

''What has Salvatore been up to these last few years? Maybe that would give us a clue. He's the only Sal who's come up in the last few days in my investigations. Can you find out?''

Cohen said he'd do some more digging. With all the people I now had working on obtaining information for me, if I didn't find Albert before Sunday, something was definitely wrong.

I was a few minutes early meeting Raina for lunch. She walked in a few minutes after noon and we got our orders out of the way before I asked for the information.

Raina pulled out a manila envelope from her large shoulder-bag. ''Before I show it to you, do you think you could do me the big favor of telling me why I'm getting this information for you?''

I'd hoped to skirt it, but Raina was my best friend. I just didn't want her to feel torn between her loyalty to the police department and me.

''Okay, but please don't spread it around. Albert's been missing since Friday night.''

She closed her eyes briefly. ''Okay, that explains it.''

''Explains what?''

''When I called down to Rhode Island, the detective I talked to assumed these characters were in trouble again and sent me their information so we could keep up with the records. The detective told me that if we could find some charges to stick, putting Johnny Smash, Nick, the

Knife, and Sal Testa away would be the best thing that could happen to Boston.''

''Good to hear,'' I replied in a dry tone.

''He also told me that there was a murder in Providence recently and they were looking for one Albert Matelli. They want to pull him in for questioning.'' Raina had been looking down until now. She looked straight into my eyes. ''Don't tell me if you're hiding him, Angela. I can't keep information like that from my superiors. They already know that I called Rhode Island for this information, and the only reason they're letting me give this to you is that they want me to squeeze you for the truth. They figure with enough rope, you'll hang yourself and Albert in the process. Besides, this isn't information that any public-minded citizen can't get by filling out a few papers and waiting a couple of weeks.''

I leaned forward. ''Raina, I can honestly say I don't know where he is. He disappeared on Friday night, and we haven't heard from him since.'' Okay, I lied—I had heard from him several times, but it was always on my answering machine and the only information I had was that he was still alive—at least as of last night.

But I was back to square one: I didn't know if he was alive or dead today. The only thing I knew was that I had to follow every lead and get every bit of information I could from anyone who could help me.

She studied me for a moment, then nodded. ''Okay, I believe you.'' She turned to the envelope and pulled out a photo and a rap sheet. ''Nick 'the Knife' Aquino has been arrested at least once a month for being suspected of stabbing someone. He's been in jail three times for killing, always manslaughter, always the lightest sentences possible, and always with time off for good behavior. Not a pretty character.'' She was right. He had mean little eyes

and mean little lines around his mouth as if he frowned a
lot. He was about my age, according to the vitals, but he
looked ten years older. He was small for a man, five-four,
and had long, thick sideburns and slicked-back hair. I mem-
orized his face.

"That's right, Angie, get a good look at him because if
you are looking into his past, you might find him in your
present, and he doesn't mind using the pig sticker on
women. In fact, I don't think he even likes women." She
took the photo back and handed me a second one. "Johnny
'Smash' Pirelli. Tall dude, a schemer. Thinks he's brighter
than he really is. He's been picked up on numerous occasions, but has a good lawyer. He's never been to jail. Used
to live in Rhode Island, but has recently moved here."

"At least I know who I'm up against," I said with a
frown. Smash looked a little like Quentin Tarantino—gan-
gly, prominent Adam's apple, tousled dark hair, a sneer on
his face. His features looked as if someone hadn't put them
together quite right—more of an approximation: the nose
goes about here, the eyes up here somewhere, the mouth
about there.

"It gets better." She pulled one more photo out of her
purse and handed it to me. "Salvatore Testa. What's he
been doing these last few years? He's been out of the country, that much I was able to determine. That's why his
police record just stopped as of 1996. He's back and hasn't
been in as much trouble as before. But he's definitely no
angel. And I'm not sure it's such a good thing that Sal
Testa hasn't been in trouble. It just means, to me anyway,
that he's saving it up for a whole lotta trouble."

I studied Sal Testa's photo. A wide face, deep lines on
either side of his mouth, heavy-lidded eyes, and thick lips.
I thought he had an ugly face, but some women might

consider him attractive. "Have either Johnny Smash or Nick the Knife worked for the Mafia?"

Raina shrugged. "It never says stuff like that in the records, you know that. It's what you pick up from the streets. I'd ask around, but most of the officers who know the streets well were out today on patrol or it was their day off. I'll catch a couple of them tomorrow morning after roll call."

"While you're at it, see if there's a history of Sal hanging around with Johnny Smash and Nick the Knife."

"The records don't indicate that they've been arrested or picked up at the same times for the same things, but I'll ask around."

We got our food and ate and talked about Joey. Raina was a little leery, a guy recently had burned her, but I finally convinced her that a date with Joey wasn't going to lead to marriage, and he was a nice guy who deserved a break.

"Okay, now tell me about your doctor," she said.

"He's got a couple of offers, Maryland and Hawaii want him, and he is thinking about them. But I think he wants to stay here if Mass General will renew his contract."

"Hawaii?" Raina asked incredulously. "And he wants to stay here? Hey, give me the contract. I'll learn medicine! Better yet, if you're not interested, throw me your leftovers."

We laughed and talked about guys in general, then she went back to work. I went back home. I didn't feel like going into the office today. I'd just have to turn down work if it was offered. But I did check in with my machine, and there were only two calls from lawyers about serving subpoenas and one call about a repo tonight. I returned the calls and turned down the offered work, explaining that I had some personal things to take care of in the next few days.

Ma called. "What's going on? Have you heard from him? Do you know where he is or if he's alive?"

"No, Ma, but I have some names and I'm working on it." I was tempted to ask her to come stay here with me, but I wanted her to stay home in case Albert tried to contact her. Also, she might cramp my style if I needed to go out. She'd insist on going along, like she went along to Albert's apartment, although that had turned out all right for me. I might be in the Providence Jail system right now, *not* as a protected witness, but as a guest of the system, slapped with breaking and entering.

It was late in the afternoon and I gazed out of my home-office window, thinking about the case, wondering how many ways I could torture Biff the weasel, wondering if Craig Cohen or Lee Randolph would be getting back to me any time soon. Craig beat Lee. He was busy developing ideas for future articles, which meant sitting around and throwing pencils into the ceiling until an idea struck him— or a pencil, whichever came first.

"I made some calls," he told me, "and it was pretty bleak at first. No one had heard from Sal Testa for several years—no law enforcement official and no one on the other side. The theory is that Giovanni got tired of bailing his youngest out of petty crime situations. He wanted Sal to take over the family business, but Sal didn't appear to be interested in the racketeering end of the business. He wanted to be a gangster, influenced by the Bloods and the Crips and the Kings. So from all that I've gathered, Testa sent his son overseas."

"That would explain why we haven't heard from Sal in a few years. He was probably attending the military version of a finishing school for future Mafia bosses."

"You're not far from the truth. I lucked out with one of my information sources, who has contacts overseas." He paused and I heard him tapping on his keyboard. "Sal spent most of his time in Sicily with occasional trips to Milan."

His brother lived in Milan, so that needed no explanation. But Sicily? He wasn't studying art—that was for sure. For a crazy moment, I actually began to wonder if there was a school for godfathers. Or was it like the Catholic church— to devote your life to God, men and women locked themselves up in monasteries and nunneries. Sometimes if they felt they were getting away from the point of what they were doing, they retreated to these cloisters to focus on their purpose in life. Was that what Sal did? Did his father send him to Sicily, which was like the Vatican for Mafioso, to find his purpose in life? I had a nutty vision of a Mafioso retreat that looked like an Italian restaurant, and everyone had to wear dark suits and thin ties with white shirts, shades, and they all looked paranoid and talked like Marlon Brando.

"Wow. Thanks, Craig. You've given me a lot to go on."

"You owe me, Matelli. Movie's on you."

I promised to call him when this case was done, he wished me good luck and we hung up.

Lee called back later. "No one's talking," he said.

"Great."

"Your brother's in trouble, isn't he?"

I sighed. "I never could hide anything from you, Lee."

"Wanna tell me about it?"

"Lee, you're a friend, but you're also law enforcement."

"As long as you don't tell me that you're hiding him—"

"I'm trying to find him. He hasn't contacted anyone in the family. I think he was abducted, or at least chased out of his apartment with the death of his friend."

"The guy was a friend of his?"

"That's what Sylvia told me." I gave him a brief description of what was happening between Sylvia and Albert.

"Look, the police down there told me that his car was found abandoned just now, in the college area." Brown University was a prominent Ivy League school located in the middle of Providence.

"Just now?"

"Yup, the news came in while I was on the phone with someone I know on the police force down there."

I told him some of my ordeal with Mann and Parducci. After he finished laughing, he said, "Look, Angela, I just want you to be real careful."

"Duh. You think I'm running around with a big target painted on my forehead?"

"More like on that pretty backside of yours. When it comes to the Mafia and the police, I wouldn't want to be caught in the middle. And I sure as hell am not happy about you being caught in the middle."

"So I'm supposed to go back to my nice life while my brother may be in hiding, held against his will, or—" I stopped there. My heart was trying to climb out of my body and the words choked in my throat.

"Angela, I'm sorry. But I wanted you to know how I feel about it. You're one tough broad, but you may not be tough enough for these bozos. If there's anything I can do, you know you can count on me as a friend, not a cop."

I blinked back tears and managed to thank Lee before hanging up. I had to get control of myself. Yeah, I was one tough broad. I looked in a drawer for a tissue and dabbed at my eyes. I'd been working on finding Albert for several days and it was starting to get to me. I was feeling like a hamster on a wheel—running but not getting anywhere.

I needed to be doing something. I was tempted to call

David to do a session of Aikido, but he was now almost
family, and I didn't want to talk about Albert. So I was
staying away from Aikido until this case was closed. The
gym where I occasionally kickboxed was closed for reno-
vations for the next few days. A water main broke and I'm
glad I wasn't there at the time, taking a shower or something.

I'd bought a treadmill a few months ago, and hadn't
really broken it in, so today was the day. I slipped into a
pair of shorts and a sports bra, and laced up my Reeboks.
I stretched my legs and warmed up a bit before stepping
on the treadmill and setting it for an easy pace. Ten minutes
later, I was loping along on the conveyor belt, my breathing
a little more ragged. Twenty minutes later, I was huffing
and puffing, my legs feeling like elastic that was being
stretched beyond the limits. Half an hour later, I was cool-
ing down. I did a few Aikido moves to limber up and then
I was ready for a cool shower to wash off the sweat I'd
accumulated. When I stepped out of the shower to dry off,
I felt my heartbeat returning to normal.

I went back into my home-office, glancing at the answering machine to see if anyone had called. I felt wrung
out, which was good, because then I wouldn't feel the pain
of letting Ma down. I slumped in my office chair and
watched the park across the street. I liked my bird's eye
view of the Boston skyline. I could see Commonwealth Pier
and the Industrial Park area of South Boston. It was an
unusual view and I appreciated it.

With the new park came more people, which I wasn't
crazy about. I had liked the feeling of solitude I used to get
from gazing out at the stretch of brown grass and the occasional piling sticking out of the choppy gray harbor. Now
I lived across from the new East Boston Waterfront Park,
a pastoral place for mothers to take their children to play.

One would almost think that East Boston was turning into a suburb.

The same empty car had been sitting across the street from my window most of the morning. Over the last couple of years, I'd grown accustomed to noting makes of cars that frequently visited the park, as well as my neighbors' cars. Maybe it was just a game with me, maybe it was something I carried with me from the military—that attention to detail—or maybe it was because I wanted to keep this new park drug-free. I kept an eye out to make sure the park didn't become a hangout for drug dealers and their connections.

The parked car was familiar, but not from visits to the park. I was able to see the license plate, and noted the CEDDY on it. My heart sank. Maybe it was a coincidence. Maybe Chuck Eddy, the sleaziest private eye in Boston, didn't really have me under surveillance. But I didn't think it was so.

I picked up the phone and called his office. His secretary, Edna, was a surprisingly matronly type. I had expected Eddy to hire a bimbo to file her nails rather than his cases, but he'd actually hired a respectable woman who wore smart suits to give his business some class.

"Eddy Confidential Investigations," Edna answered. She'd decided the word "confidential" attracted a higher class of client, and from the way Eddy bragged Edna had done the right thing.

"Hi, Edna, this is Angela Matelli. Is Chuck in?"

There was a pause before she answered, something Edna normally didn't do; she was very efficient and tried to eliminate pauses and hesitations from her actions—it wasted too much time. "Mr. Eddy is on his way to a dinner meeting with a big client, Ms. Matelli. Would you like me to leave a message for him?" Deception was not one of Edna's strong suits. I could tell she was dying to come clean, but I didn't want her to lose her job. I thanked her and told her I'd call him another time.

I went back to my living room and took the cell phone, something I splurged on after my last case, and I haven't regretted the purchase. Especially now. I dug around in my desk until I came up with a scrap of paper with Eddy's cell phone number on it.

Fredd eyed me curiously while he chewed on a cricket, almost as if he was asking me, "Where you going?"

"Out for a minute to take care of a complication." I had to get a life. I wasn't even thinking twice about talking to an iguana.

I changed into a sloppy T-shirt, slapped a billed cap on my head, and slipped out the back door, climbing my back-yard fence to take the long way around. I went around the block and entered the park through the former Maverick low-income projects.

I couldn't see Eddy, but I was willing to bet that he had a view of my windows. Using my cell phone, I dialed his cell phone number and listened for the ring. It was faint, but I could hear it on the other side of the park. I walked toward it.

"Hello?" Eddy's voice answered.

"Hello, Chuck?"

There was a short moment of silence. "Who is this?"

"Angela here. Listen, I just talked to Edna and she said you'd gone to a business dinner with a big client. But after I hung up, I thought, why don't I try to reach you on your cell phone. You see, I still have the number from the time I borrowed your van for surveillance." At least he hadn't used his van to keep an eye on me.

"Um, yeah, good to hear from you. But I am in the

middle of an important job for a client," he replied. "Can I call you back?"

I'd traced the call and could see him leaning up against the swing set. His back was to me. I came up behind him.

"Oh, I don't think this can wait," I said into the phone.

"Gee, Angela, my connection makes it sound as if you're right here."

"Yeah, it's almost as if we're talking face to face," I said as I used my free hand to whack Chuck on the back of the head.

"Ow," he said, dropping his cell phone. He stooped down to pick it up, one hand still covering the spot where I'd hit him. He looked up at me, then closed his eyes. Chuck Eddy was a polyester wonder. He made the Pillsbury Doughboy look well dressed. Today he was wearing shit brown slacks that were too short for him and a reddish-orange shirt accompanied by a tan jacket, well worn at the elbows.

"Gee, Chuck, you're almost well-dressed today. For someone who has as much money as you profess to make, you should spend some of it on a better wardrobe."

"Oh, man," he groaned. "I told the guy that he shouldn't hire a PI to follow a PI."

"Not this private eye," I said, slipping my cell phone into my jeans pocket. "What the hell do you think you're doing?"

"Making money," Chuck said. "And what did you do to have someone hire me to follow you?"

I crossed my arms. "Things must not be going so well at your agency if you've got to do the work yourself." Within the last two years, Chuck Eddy had hit it big with the decoy market, hiring beautiful young women and good-looking men to target and hit on the spouses and fiancées of suspicious clients. If the target reacted positively, he or she was caught on tape and the heartbroken client paid Eddy for his time. If the target rebuffed the decoy, that was also caught on tape and the happy client probably doubled Eddy's fee.

Eddy had become more of a figurehead at his office, devoting much of his time to consoling the soon-to-be-separated wives and husbands, collecting and depositing their checks after they left his office. I can safely say that the difference between Chuck Eddy's style of investigation and my style is the difference between a fast-food restaurant and a five-star restaurant.

If it sounds as though Chuck Eddy is a sleaze without a decent bone in his body, he is. For some reason he's decided to attach himself to me. When I was first starting out in private investigation, Eddy would hand me small jobs to do, but I eventually figured out that the "small jobs," like bad chili, would come back to haunt me. The funny thing is that even though I knew better, I usually ended up taking these jobs. It wasn't that Eddy was a slick talker or could win me over with his looks and confidence, it was that he always appeared to be so completely incompetent that I always ended up saying yes just to pull his fat out of the fryer.

Now I find him spying on me. I was curious how he would manage to get himself out of this one.

"So you've taken up spying on me, Chuckie."

He blinked. "Now, Angie, I have to make a living, too."

I feigned surprise. "You do? I thought you were in charge of a large stable of decoys whose job it is to flush out the four-flushers. I didn't think you would stoop to such a lowly job as surveillance."

The sweat had begun to appear on Eddy's brow. I didn't take it as a sign of nervousness—sweat was a part of Eddy the same way that breathing is. "I was doing a friend a favor, Angie. He wanted to know your moves for the next few days.''

''And you didn't think it was the least bit strange that a friend of yours was interested in me?''

Eddy grinned. ''Hey, I've asked you out on occasion—why shouldn't someone I know ask you out?''

I gaped at him. He was either sincere, or the best actor I've ever encountered. I voted for the former, which made him either the dumbest human being on the planet or the most gullible. I voted for both. Of course, he was really the guy with the largest ego I've ever seen, which probably had something to do with his gullibility. Chuck Eddy lived under the delusion that at any moment, I'd call him up and tell him I was ready to be his woman. Mighty Joe Young had a better chance with me than Chuck Eddy did. But Eddy was ever hopeful, calling me up and asking me out every few months on the off chance that I might have forgotten that he repulsed me.

''Okay, who is this great friend of yours that you would do such a favor for him?''

Eddy had the gall to look coy for a moment. ''Angie, you know about client-PI privilege.''

I took a deep breath, refraining from whacking him upside the head again, then performing some painful submission hold on him until he whimpered for his mommy. Instead, I said slowly, ''Chuck, if this guy is interested in me, don't you think I should know? This doesn't sound like a good idea in the first place.''

''Johnny's not like that, Angie. He called you a fox.''

Ooh and they say I don't have a soft side. ''Chuckie,'' I said softly, ''this wouldn't by any chance be Johnny Smash.''

The look in his eyes was brief, but I was reassured that I hadn't lost my investigative skills, unlike my colleague.

I grabbed him by the arm and walked him over to his car. "Okay, now, Chuck, we're going over this once. I want to get it through your head: Johnny Smash does not want my phone number, he doesn't want to know what I like to do on my nights off. He doesn't want to call me up and ask me out to the movies."

"He doesn't?"

"No." I reached out and straightened Eddy's eternally polyester collar. "Now you can tell me something."

Eddy's breath had gotten labored. I couldn't tell if I was having that effect on him or he'd just walked too far without the aid of a golf cart. Did I mention that he was out of shape in the same way a beanbag chair is?

"What?"

"Tell me what you know about Johnny Smash. How long have you known him?"

"So you're interested in him, huh?" Eddy grinned. I managed not to throw up on his shoes. "We went to school together in Dorchester."

"And what has he been doing for a living the past, oh, say, ten years?"

Eddy frowned on that one. "Um, well, you know, he's kinda in between jobs, Angie. Um, the company he used to work for relocated and—"

"He worked for the Mafia, huh?"

Eddy was quiet for a moment, then nodded. "I figured since your brother worked for the Mob, you wouldn't have any problem datin' a guy with that career choice."

"Do I look like I would date my own brother?"

Eddy made a face. "Angie, don't be crass." Pot calling the kettle black. On the other hand, I might get some information out of Eddy after all.

"Tell me, Chuck, why did Johnny relocate to Boston?"

Eddy drew his brows together, which wasn't much of a

stretch because he had only one brow. "I think he got a job offer, right here in Eastie."

I turned to him. "Have you heard anything about the Mafia reestablishing itself back here in Boston?"

Eddy waved a hand at me. "You hear stuff like that all the time." He was about to say something else, then came up short. "You sayin' Johnny has something to do with it?"

"Could be."

Eddy started to turn to his car, then turned back. "Then why is he havin' me follow you?" His eyes strayed down to my chest.

I leaned forward, my arms crossed so he wouldn't get any ideas. "Because he thinks I have something he wants."

Eddy agreed to keep his mouth shut and give Johnny a false report. I had no idea if I could trust him. Eddy had worked for the Mob on a job or two in his day, but I didn't think he'd be too happy about Johnny Smash lying to him and would consider falsifying a report for Smash to be justifiable. Especially if I paid him.

I escorted Eddy up to my apartment and sat him down in front of my computer. As he was typing up his report for tonight, he stopped. "You know, Angie, I don't know if this is such a good idea. If you're right about Smash's motives and he finds out I double-crossed him—"

I moved in close. "Are you telling me that a big man like yourself can't handle a little guy like Johnny Smash?"

Eddy shook his head. "Johnny's not so little. He's about six feet tall."

"But he takes orders from someone, and you don't."

"And I could get my neck broke." He started to stand up.

I pushed him back down. "And I could do a submission hold on you right here and now. Think about it. Hard."

He thought about it. "I guess I wouldn't want to cross you more than I wouldn't want to cross Smash. Still, the Mob—"

"I'll double your pay for another day. And I'll be there if Smash gets it into his head that he wants to beat the living shit out of you." I didn't mention that I'd probably be standing in line for the leftovers.

From then on, for the next hour, I talked and Eddy typed. His reports were to be handed in to Smash on a regular basis, all fantasy about where I was going and what I was doing.

It was a work of art. it was a work of fiction. It was the best we could do on short notice.

FOURTEEN

AFTER EDDY LEFT, I spent the rest of the night drinking cold red table wine and planning my strategies for the next few days. A rerun of the *X-Files* was on and I spent an hour watching Mulder and Scully run from aliens, run toward aliens, and try to figure out if there really were aliens. I found it to be a stylish show, and in some weird way, very accurate of those top-secret government agencies—all conspiracy and no substance.

For dinner, I found some pita bread, hummus, and feta cheese in the refrigerator, and made a meal out of that. Sometime after midnight, I turned in.

I WOKE UP EARLY ON WEDNESDAY and got ready to go back down to Providence. The weather had turned brittle and cold. I looked out the window and saw snowflakes drifting down. I dug out a bulky sweater and an old down vest, a pair of jeans, and my hiking boots from the closet. A soft-sided hat with a brim that I could turn up or down completed the outfit. I looked in the mirror, something I rarely did, and although I was no Itty Bitty Kitty, at least I was dressed for the weather.

The air was mildly cold, something that happens when it snows. One of the things that always amused me about Boston at the beginning of winter was how unprepared the city always was for the first snow. It was like watching a Keystone Kops routine with everyone in the public transportation department running around, wringing their hands as the first flakes fell. While the subways would stop run-

ning, or would run very slow, Boston drivers were fearless
enough to take Storrow drive's curves at fifty-five miles per
hour. Don't even get me started about the Sumner and Cal-
lahan Tunnels that run to and from East Boston. I was just
grateful that I'd be getting out of Boston for a few hours,
even if I was beginning to feel like a yo-yo—Boston one
day, Rhode Island the next.

As I stepped outside, I stuck my tongue out to catch a
couple of flakes. I noticed the flyer on my windshield. Annoyed, I grabbed it, intent on throwing it away when it
struck me that this wasn't an advertisement, but a note. It
was written in block letters in pencil:

IF YOU WANT TO SEE ALBERT ALIVE STAY
OUT OF IT.

I don't know what made me look inside the Bronco—I
was already intending to go back into my apartment to get
a few things—but a small box sat on the passenger seat. I
opened the door, which I had locked the night before, but
wasn't locked now, and picked up the box. It was the sort
of box you'd have a necklace in, but I had a feeling there
wasn't any jewelry inside it. I don't know what I expected,
but when I opened it, the thing inside was worse than I
could have imagined—it was a freshly cut off finger. A
man's pinkie, neatly severed, a little blood on the cotton
that cradled it. And there was a ring beside it—I recognized
it as Albert's high school ring. A wave of nausea came
over me and I snapped the box shut.

Crazy thoughts came to me—should I put it in the refrigerator? How long before doctors can't sew a finger back
on? But I knew the answer—it would be too late by the
time I found Albert.

I stared at it and wondered if I should give up, let this

thing play out. But I'd already gone to Don Testa and it was clear that something was up, that he knew something that made it impossible for him to interfere. And I thought I knew what it was. And I got mad as hell. Who the hell would do this to my brother and why? I already suspected whom, and I sort of knew why, but I didn't know where— where Sal Testa was holding Albert, and what he expected to gain by chopping off fingers. One thing this warning told me was that I was close to where Albert might be hidden. I didn't think Sal Testa would go to the trouble of giving me this warning if he was holding Albert in Providence.

I thought about going to Mann and Parducci with the flyer and finger, but I was afraid that they'd just dismiss it as something I cooked up to take their attention away from Albert as a suspect in Eddie Fazoli's murder. Now if I had left on good terms, maybe they would have considered this evidence, but not as things stood.

I stomped back up the stairs to my apartment and got to the bathroom in time to throw up for real. After I cleaned up, I got a tape recorder, made sure the batteries were fresh, and the tape worked. The tape recorder went into my purse. I put some ice into a baggie, not that it would do much good, and put the box and the baggie with ice into a small thermal pack. Then I got back in my Bronco, threw my purse, the note, and the thermal pack down on the empty seat beside me and headed out for Providence.

An hour and a half later, I pulled up in front of Albert's condo, the tires of my Bronco squealing to a stop. I grabbed the box out of the thermal pack, got out of the car, and stalked into the front lobby. Biff was seated behind the desk, and he looked up, surprised by my appearance. A low desk separated him and me. I reached across it grabbed his powder blue polo shirt front and hauled him up from his seat until his nose was an inch from my nose.

"Wha—?" Biff asked. His arms flailed around help-lessly. I tightened my grip and he said, "Aaack!"

"Hi to you, too, Biff, " I responded conversationally. "Now, we're going to have a little talk about the night of Albert's disappearance. The stakes just got higher. I want to know everything about that night." I wanted to know if he'd told me everything earlier, or if he'd been trying to impress me when he didn't realize who I was.

"You can't do this," he said in a strangled tone. Maybe it was because I was holding his collar tight around his thick neck. I loosened it a tad without letting go of my grip. Okay, it wasn't a submission hold, but it was working.

"I seem to be doing it just fine. Now, about that night?"

"Screw you!" Big words from such a little man.

I gathered Biff's collar in one hand long enough to pull out the box with the finger in it, open it and shove it in his face. The finger and the ring rolled around and Biff's eyes grew wide. His Adam's apple moved up and down.

"Well, screw you, too," I said. "This is what they've done to Albert Matelli and if you don't start talking, you are gonna be as responsible for his death as if you held a gun to his head. Now tell me what you know or we call the detectives and have them deal with you."

"Okay, okay," he said. "Just let me go. And get that thing away from me."

I opened my hand and he fell backward, not quite into his chair before sliding onto the floor. "Ow!"

He got to his knees. I put a foot out and pushed him back down onto the floor.

"Tell me."

"Okay, okay," he said again. "I was working for Todd that night. He had a hot date and I agreed to sub for him if he took one of my days." He rubbed his shoulder and

looked up at me. "You don't have to be so rough." He
tried to get up again. I pushed him back down.

"So what happened that night?"

"Why don't you ask the police? I told them everything."
He tried to get up again. I pushed him again with my foot
and held him down with a little pressure on his sore shoulder. "Hey! That hurts."

"I'm asking you, not the police. I want to get it straight
from the weasel's mouth."

"Your brother's friend came in, the dead man. He'd been
here before, so I called Albert and got permission to let his
friend up. That's all. I never saw Albert come down, I never
saw anything else."

I curled my lip. "You're lying. You told me earlier that
two men were with him. You were paid to turn a blind eye
to the other men who came in with Eddie. And when I
prove that you were lying, I will tell the police and they
will come after you."

Biff made a show of bravado. "I'm dead if I talk to the
police. I'll just tell them you're lying to save your brother."

I reached down and he grabbed my wrist reluctantly.
Then he tried to get me off balance, but I'd planted my feet
securely and bent my knees. He pulled himself up, not letting go of my wrist. I performed *nikkyo,* trapping his hand
with my free hand, the blade of my other hand overlapping
his wrist as I leaned into his center. It hits a nerve in the
attacker's arm that disables him.

"Aaarrgh!" Biff said, sinking back down to his knees.

I said very quietly, "You may not care now, but when
I tell Testa that you were paid off to let Albert take the rap
for a murder he didn't commit, he'll have your balls hanging on his wall by the end of the day. Albert is like a son
to him."

"Huh! A lot you know," Biff was fairly bursting to talk.

"It was Testa's son who came in here with those two goons."

It wasn't a surprise at this point. It confirmed my suspicions. I let go and stepped away from Biff. He got up with all the vigor of an old and arthritic man, rubbing his wrist and looking ruefully at me.

I reached out and patted his cheek. Biff flinched. I favored him with cold smile. "That's a good boy, Biff."

He glared at me, his bravado beginning to return,. "I should call the police and charge you with assault."

My smile grew colder. "Why don't you do that, Biff? I got quite cozy with them yesterday. I'm sure they'd be interested in what I have to say about the way you make your extra money. You might even be charged as an accessory to murder."

He held my eyes as his hand reached for the phone, hesitated, then dropped. He looked away. I'd won many a staring contest in my day. Good thing it came in handy this time. "Maybe we should just forget this ever happened."

"Yes, I think that's best." I started for the front door, then turned around. "Oh, and Biff? Just for future reference, if my brother comes out of this alive and I come visiting again, you won't give me any trouble, right?"

I left without waiting for his answer.

MY NEXT STOP was Testa's residence. I drove to his gate and rolled my window down. I depressed the button on the monitor and a few moments later, a tinny voice asked who was calling.

"Tell Don Testa that Angela Matelli is stopping by to give him an update."

I sat in my car for a full five minutes before someone came back on. "I'm sorry, Ms. Matelli, Mr. Testa cannot

ee you at this time. He asks that you call him before com-
ng by next time.''

I got out of the car and walked up to the monitor. ''Lis-
en, buddy, I came all the way down here from Boston, and
want to see Testa right now. I have information that can't
wait. If he doesn't reconsider, I'll ram my Bronco into your
gate and make a scene. I'm sure the police will be interested to hear what I have to say.''

Voices could be heard over the monitor—someone had
orgotten to mute the microphone.

''I don't want to see her now, Dom. Can't you get rid
of her?''

''Sir, she said she was going to ram the gate to get in if
ou refused to see her. I think she meant it, sir.''

''Well, call the police.''

''Sir, do you think that would be a very good idea?''

''We must have some friends on the force.''

''It would take longer to try to explain this to your
riends than to just let her in and—''

''Oh, okay. This is very inconvenient.'' It was nice to
know I was an inconvenience.

''Ms. Matelli?''

''Yeah.''

''Please get back in your vehicle and drive through after
he gates have opened.''

I thought his tone was a bit sarcastic, but I complied.
While I drove up to the front door, I took advantage of my
ime alone to reach into my purse and turn my tape player
on record. A few minutes later, I parked and got out of my
Bronco. I stalked up to the front door before the guards
had gotten into place.

A young man, darkly handsome with a long chin, greeted
me at the door. He was trying to look sober, but I could
ell by the look in his eyes that he was slightly amused. I

suspected that he was the one whom I had threatened with damaging the gate. I looked around and didn't see any of the bodyguards that had been loitering around Testa's property a few days ago. Maybe they were all taking a break in the Mob Soldier Break Room. Although Dom looked more intelligent than the run-of-the-mill soldier/bodyguard he looked like he could handle himself in a pinch.

"Ms. Matelli?"

I gave a curt nod.

"Don Testa will receive you in the library." Ahh. Dom came from the British School of Polite Mafia Leg Breakers. He showed me the way and waited until I was seated. The library was straight out of someone's stereotypical imagination of what a mansion's library ought to look like, right down to the leather-bound books that covered the wall from ceiling to floor, the dark leather easy chair, and the antique mahogany writing desk. There was a mahogany bar with Baccarat crystal decanters and a sterling silver cocktail shaker and ice bucket standing on one side of the doors. On the other side, there were two sterling silver urns with all the amenities: a creamer, several kinds of tea bags, sugar and honey, cups ready to fill with coffee or hot water. It reminded me of a really good restaurant—not a home.

"Would you like a cup of tea or coffee?" He indicated the urns. "Perhaps I could get you something stronger? Wine? Beer? A gin and tonic?"

I was tempted to order a pecan waffle with real maple syrup and Virginia ham, but instead, I shook my head. "You could get me Don Testa."

He raised his eyebrows slightly. "You are single minded, aren't you?"

I crossed my arms. "You must be Dom."

He turned to rearrange the tea bags and wipe down the

rns. "I noticed I left the microphone on, I didn't let Mr.
'esta know that." He turned back to me with a smile.

"It'll be our little secret," I said, returning his smile with
ne of my own. "I was here a few days ago, having break-
ast with Don Testa. Why didn't I meet you then?"

Dom looked thoughtful. I didn't think Mafia goons
ought at all. This one was different. If he wasn't a soldier
 Testa's little army, I might have gone for this guy. "Was
at Tuesday? I was sent on an errand."

"You don't appear to be a bodyguard," I said. "What
o you do around here?"

"Mostly I do secretarial work, go over the accounts, do
e stuff that no one else does," he replied, folding his arms
cross his chest.

"Since the normal jobs around here involve leg breaking
nd killing, I suppose you more or less supervise the run-
ing of this place."

He nodded, clearly amused. "I suppose so."

"But back to this errand you ran on Tuesday, I don't
uppose it had anything to do with Don Testa's youngest,
alvatore." I casually took the box out of my purse, and
nowed him the finger. "I found this in my car this morn-
g." I closed the box.

Dom hesitated, looking a little shaken. He looked as if
e was going to answer me, but another voice spoke.
Thank you, Dom. That will be all."

Dom jumped, inclined his head once in my direction, and
ft the room. Giovanni Testa stood there, clearly uncom-
ortable. It was quite a feat to inconvenience a Mafia boss.
lways willing to take advantage of a situation, I smiled
nd gestured toward the leather easy chair. "Please, sit
own."

Testa smiled back, clearly not amused that I was trying

to reverse roles. He walked across the room and sat in the chair.

"You took me away from some business, Angela."

"I'm sorry, Don Testa, but this couldn't wait." I tossed the box to Testa and, surprised, he caught it.

"What is this?" he asked.

"Open it."

He complied, then quickly closed it and looked up at me angrily. "Is this some kind of joke?"

"Why don't you ask your son Salvatore that question? I'd like to know. I certainly hope so," I replied.

He stood up and thrust the box at me, anxious to get rid of it. I took it back and stuck it in my purse. "Kind of poor taste," I said. "That is my brother's high school ring and the thing next to it is supposed to be Albert's pinkie. What do you think, Don Testa? Do you suppose it's made of rubber? Maybe this note is a joke, too." I handed the note to him.

He made a show of examining it, looked up at me and shrugged, extending the note to me. I took it, and slipped it back in my purse.

"Anyone could have written this. What do you want?"

"I noticed that you haven't asked about Albert at all, Don Testa." I was overusing Testa's name and title. But I wouldn't have it any other way. I was making a show of how pissed I was—in a polite way. It was the Angela Matelli School of Etiquette.

He gestured with his hand. "An oversight. How is the search coming?"

"I think you already know. I have a strong suspicion that Salvatore has something to do with the finger in the box." I still stood, my arms clasped behind my back. I wanted to move, I wanted to find Albert, but the best could do was to walk over to the bar and indicate the decanters.

"Brandy," Testa said, adding, "The bottle on the left."

I poured a generous amount in a snifter and handed it to him. Another rule of the Angela Matelli School of Etiquette: Always get your enemy drunk before you accuse them of being less than honest with you.

Testa swirled the amber liquid around in the glass, concentrating on it in order to avoid eye contact with me.

"Tell me what's going on, Don Testa. I want my brother back. You've known for some time that Salvatore was at the bottom of Albert's disappearance."

He shook his head. "I was told what was going on after our meeting. You and your mother had already left."

"Why didn't you order Salvatore to release Albert?"

"I don't interfere with my children's affairs, Angela. And Albert doesn't work for me anymore."

"But Albert is your partner in business, Don Testa. Aren't you concerned for his welfare? Don't you think you should have said something to Salvatore?"

Don Testa shrugged and sipped his brandy. "I talked to Salvatore. My son explained his reasons to me. It is not my policy to interfere." Yeah, him and Captain Kirk—the Prime Directive.

"I should go to the police with this information." As soon as the words were out of my mouth, I wondered, What was I thinking, to threaten Testa with the police. I'm sure he was shaking in his custom-made Italian shoes.

He smiled. There was no warmth in his expression. "Do what you think is right, Angela. But you shall have your brother back, as soon as Salvatore gets what he wants." But whether Albert would be alive or dead, missing more than a finger—Testa gave me no guarantee, no words of comfort. I had to push away a vision of Albert with a patch over his eye, a souvenir of a Mob gunfight.

"Tell me what Salvatore wants."

"Control of the factory." He finally looked up at me. "He wants Albert to work for him, to continue running the business, but Salvatore wants to own AMT Enterprises and the factory."

"Don Testa, you're a silent partner. Why are you allowing this?"

Testa closed his eyes briefly and took a sip of brandy. "He's my son. He's trying to make a name for himself. He wants to fill a space that's now open in the Boston market."

"By filling an open space, you mean Whitey Bulger and his crew."

Testa nodded briefly. "Salvatore wants to start up his own business in Boston, start a Family up there." I knew Testa didn't mean a wife and little ones, but he beamed with all the pride of a grandpapa.

"And Albert doesn't want to help him." Shame on Albert.

"Your brother is a stubborn man. Angela. I put your brother through college, and he doesn't want to help my son." Testa closed his eyes and tilted his head back in the chair.

"Albert worked for you for six years. That's long enough. Your son seems to be bringing back the old ways of the Mob, the days when sadism was rampant, and you just sit here and let it happen—to someone you professed to like. Your son wants to take everything Albert has done to legitimize himself, and make it his through brute force." I was outraged. It was hard to keep a lid on my fury. I wanted to start throwing stuff, the crystal and silver and leather-bound books.

Testa didn't seem to notice. He was practically beaming

with pride. "Ever since Salvatore came back from Sicily, he's been working on this, waiting for a time to seize the opportunity. When Bulger and his lieutenants were indicted, Salvatore waited a year or two for it to cool down, then started up his business in Boston. The time is ripe. Salvatore wants to move now. The Justice Department boys are patting themselves on the back. They are not as vigilant now as they once were."

"Why Albert? Why the factory? Why not some other place in Boston?"

Testa go up and paced a bit, then turned to me. "Don't you see? It's the perfect place. East Boston is isolated, and there's the harbor. Albert has done this sort of thing before, he's good at it and Salvatore needs his help. Albert will come around. He's just being stubborn. Salvatore is smart." Salvatore sounded a lot like a sociopath to me. I'd heard that sociopaths were usually brilliant.

Testa had taken his seat again to sip away at his brandy. I walked up to his chair and leaned in on him, boxing him in by putting a hand on each chair arm. I brought my face up close to him. "How many fingers stubborn? Is my brother dead?"

Testa shook his head. "No. At least, that's what Salvatore says. But Albert is resisting."

I tried to appeal to his desire for legitimacy. "He wants to go legit, same as you, Don Testa. You have to know that ToyCo has made a generous offer. Albert wants to take it. It would work in your favor to let Albert take the ToyCo deal and talk Salvatore into moving his operation somewhere else. Albert's factory can't be the only place in Boston that your son can set up operations from." I moved back, allowing some space for Testa.

He got up from his chair and walked over to the window. "Do you see what I already have? What is one more deal?"

"I understand it's a generous deal, worth potentially millions."

Testa shrugged. "What is money to me? You have read my financial statements, I am sure. I won't be able to spend it all before I die. But my son, I can do something for him."

Testa was pissing me off, whether he was a Mafia boss or not. I was beginning to think he was slightly nuts. He'd have to be to turn down a potential of millions in order to make nicey-nice with a scumbag like his son. "You're willing to screw over my brother, whom you once thought of as a son, for the sake of your real son, a guy who's a chronic screw-up?"

Testa shook his head and walked over to me. "Albert is not being reasonable."

"*Albert* isn't being reasonable?"

"Salvatore, well, he is my youngest. We had some trouble with him, but I am finally getting to know him better. He values my opinion now. Blood is thicker." Testa sighed and reached a hand out to stroke my hair. "Ah, Angela, how little you know of someone like me."

An image flashed through my head of Don Testa's bloodied hand, and I moved out of his reach. "What do you mean by that?"

He dropped his hand, put his snifter down and steepled his fingers. "I mean that I want to become legitimate, but the time isn't right. I need to continue doing things the way they have always been done. For now. For Salvatore's sake."

"Don Testa, we both know that your son committed a murder, or ordered a murder committed, in Albert's condo. Even if he turns Albert out in the street, my brother will, in all likelihood, do time for a crime he probably didn't commit."

Testa looked sad. "Ah, but he did commit the crime. At

least technically, he did.'' He stood. ''Angela, please go. Your brother is on his own, I'm afraid. Salvatore is my blood. I cannot go against him, even if I wanted to.''

His son was turning my whole world inside out and Don Testa wanted me to leave? ''Don Testa, you are part owner of AMT Enterprises. I'm asking you once again: Why can't you order your son to leave the business and Albert alone?''

Testa strolled over to the window and looked out on his estate. ''Yesterday, I signed over my ownership. Albert now has a new silent partner.''

''Salvatore?''

He turned and looked at me. I hated the sight of the pity in his eyes. He nodded. My brother's life was now worth squat. Testa didn't even have an interest in seeing Albert live. Are a man's hands so tied by blood that he can't do the right thing?

''Why is your son doing all of this? What changed him? Please excuse me for saying this, Don Testa, but from what I know of his life, Salvatore was nothing more than a petty thief and hellraiser a few years ago.''

Testa turned back to his view of the garden. ''When I sent Salvatore to Sicily to live with my uncle's family, my son had an opportunity to learn things, to change his life, the way he lived it.'' Testa rubbed at an invisible spot on a pane of glass. ''He embraced his new lifestyle, and I cannot discourage him.''

''Don't you think his bullying tactics might be a little too—'' I searched for the right word ''—harsh?''

Testa looked at the empty doorway. ''I think I have said all there is to say, Angela. You must leave now.''

Like a magician's assistant, Dom suddenly appeared. He must have been listening from somewhere. Maybe he left another microphone on. I was escorted out of the library, but I abruptly turned and marched back in. Testa was pouring himself another brandy and several bodyguards had appeared out of nowhere. They had been caught off guard and one of them strode over to the door to keep me out. I spoke up. "You know I'll continue to look for my brother. When I find him, your son might get in the way. If that happens, will you come after me?"

Testa waved the guard away. His smile was somewhat patronizing. "I do not think it would be wise for you to go after Salvatore. But if you did, and you get your brother back, it is out of my hands."

I gripped my purse. "Will you go after Albert?"

Don Testa walked up to me, standing a few feet away from me. "You have my solemn word, Angela, that as long as you don't personally harm my son, I have no fight with you." A shiver ran through me and I realized that like Johnny Dynamite, I was fighting the devil.

I reached into my pocket, where I had been carrying Don Testa's check, held it up, then placed it on a nearby end table, all the while holding Don Testa's gaze. "Then our business is completed. I still owe you for the lawyer."

Testa shook his head. "No, I owed your mother for something a long time ago. We are now even."

Dom escorted me to the door. "That's some boss you have," I said.

He turned to look at me. "He may not be liked by a lot of people, but he keeps his word."

"That's a relief," I muttered. Despite Dom's encouraging words, I didn't trust Testa any further than I could throw my Bronco.

Dom watched me get into my car and drive away. He didn't leave his post until I was through the gates and they had closed after me. Talk about paranoid.

FIFTEEN

WHEN I LEFT PROVIDENCE, I intended to drive directly to my office. I needed to pay my rent and check my mail, and I was hoping to talk to Benny the Bond about lawyers for Albert. Benny would know the right lawyer for this situation, assuming Albert got out of this alive.

I'd been thinking about what Don Testa had said to me in his office. Hell, I didn't need to think about it, I had recorded the conversation on my trusty tape recorder for safekeeping. Testa had mentioned that Albert had committed the murder, at least, technically, he had. The only way that could have been done was if someone had made him pull the trigger. I wished I'd been able to think faster—I might have gotten a more concrete admission from Testa. It wouldn't have stood up in court because it would be considered hearsay, but it would have placed serious doubt on whether Albert had committed murder willingly.

I had just crossed into Massachusetts when my cell phone rang.

"Ange?" The voice was hoarse, almost as if the caller was in pain. "It's Joey."

"Joey? You don't sound like yourself."

"I'm at the hospital, Ange. They came and smashed stuff up at the factory."

My stomach tightened. "Are you okay?"

"Yeah, yeah. Just some minor cuts and bruises—" Someone took the phone away from him and cut in. "Minor cuts and bruises, my ass."

"Who is this?"

"Lorraine. Joey got beat up. So did Marty. Rick got slapped around some, but I don't think the guys who came into the factory thought he was much of a threat."

In the background, I could hear Rick saying, "I took tae kwon do. I could have done some serious damage if that one guy hadn't sucker-punched me."

"Huh!" Lorraine said.

"What about you? What about the other workers?"

"The other workers were scared off. I got pushed around some. But Joey has some sore ribs and a tooth knocked out. The doctor says he might have a concussion, too."

"You said Marty was hurt, too?" Before she could answer, I told her I'd be right down there. She told me they were at Mass General. "But before you come here, are you near the factory?"

"Probably closer to it than the hospital. I'm south of Boston."

"Look, I have the books you want—they're in my desk. You can get in through the back door. There's a key hidden in the drainpipe nearby."

"I can get it later. I should come see Joey now."

"Joey's okay and not going anywhere for now," Lorraine said. "I'd feel better if you went for them right away. There's also a couple of diskettes that have AMT's financial history on it. I didn't get a chance to go over them."

"Okay," I said. "I'll be down there as soon as I get the stuff."

I drove directly to the factory and parked around the corner from it. Although I was going in there on Lorraine's authority, I thought it would be circumspect to make my visit as quickly and covert as possible. Police tape surrounded the front of the building, but I wasn't going in that way anyway. I slipped around back until I found the door Lorraine had mentioned, and it was open. Great security, I thought. I'd have to talk to Albert about the way he was doing business.

Inside, it was deathly quiet. I had brought my penlight with me, and used it to find my way to the front where the offices were. The factory was a mess—boxes smashed, dolls strewn all over the place. The door to the offices was unlocked, and I went straight to Lorraine's desk, where the computer usually sat—it was currently on the floor along with upended file cabinets and broken furniture. I found the ledgers in the bottom drawer.

I couldn't resist going through them then and there, just a quick look, so I sat at her desk, turned on the desk lamp, and began reading. Although I don't know much about bookkeeping, I noticed right away that there was a discrepancy between the numbers coming in and the cash flow going out—much more was going out than what should have been. I remembered Marty's comment about buying second-rate equipment when I first encountered him. I also remembered Rick's comment about how Albert was the one who bought the equipment and he only had so much money. But, I thought, Testa had been his silent partner, and he could easily have lent Albert enough money to buy new equipment, especially since it was clear that Itty Bitty Kitty was a hit.

Even if Testa wasn't willing to lend the money, Albert could have gotten a bank loan. There was no good reason top-quality equipment couldn't have been bought.

I thought about calling the accountant listed on the ledger, but what if he was aware of the fraud and wanted to cover it up? Instead, I called Bob Leone, one of my clients who owned an insurance agency, from my cell phone. The office phone was definitely not working. Someone had taken a baseball bat to it.

"Angela, are you looking for work?" he asked in a hearty voice.

"Usually, but I'm actually calling you for advice on accounting. Bob, you know something about bookkeeping, don't you?"

"Sure. I was an accountant before I got my own insurance business." He paused, then said, "Hey, wait a minute, you don't want me to help you with your books, do you, Angie?"

"No. But I'd like you to take a look at some books from a business and tell me, if you could, if they've been cooked."

"Sure, just drop by. My afternoon's pretty freed up right now."

I thanked him and hung up.

I'd just turned out the lamp when I heard the front door open and close. Unlike in the movies where the heroine, alone in a deserted factory with a crazed killer on the loose, calls out, "Brian? Is that you? Mom? Dad? Aaaaghh," providing a road map for the killer to her location, I held my breath. The intruder was more likely to be someone official like the police or an employee. Either way, I didn't want to be discovered here, and have to explain my presence to anyone.

The intruder stopped for a moment then started to walk again within the factory. I hoped he or she would head toward the back, but the footsteps came toward the offices.

I picked up the ledger and crept into Rick's R & D room, quietly closing the door just as the outer office door opened.

I looked around, but his room held nothing but the bean-bag chair, a file cabinet, and a desk. There were no closets, no other exits, no cubbyholes to crawl into. The intruder was opening Lorraine's desk drawers, looking for something. The one plus was that the prowler hadn't turned any lights on. He or she was using a flashlight. I figured that if he came in here, I could hide behind the door until he left.

But much to my relief, he didn't come in here. After going through Lorraine's desk, then the file cabinets, I heard a drawer slam shut.

"Shit," he said—the voice sounded as if it could be a man or maybe a woman with a low voice—then the foot-steps began to retreat. My brain went into overdrive and a moment later, my feet followed as I ran through the offices, out into the factory and tried the front door. It was locked. Whoever had come in here had a key. Why not turn on the lights?

I retraced my steps to the back door and burst through it into the weak winter sunlight. I ran around the building, hoping to catch sight of the intruder. I looked up the street, then down it, but I couldn't determine where he or she had gone.

I walked back to my Bronco and, intent on going to the hospital and my office, stopped on the way to drop the books off at Bob Leone's agency. He greeted me with a smile. "So what's in it for me?"

"I do the next investigation for free?" I asked.

He nodded. "Sounds good to me."

"But if it involves expenses, you pick them up."

He frowned. "Gas money and one free meal."

I nodded. "You drive a hard bargain, Mr. Leone." We shook on it and grinned.

"So what am I looking for?"

"Discrepancies in incoming money and outgoing ex-penses. Anything that looks a little strange. I can give you a starting point—AMT bought used equipment when they started up."

I remembered the tape recorder and cassette in my purse. I didn't want to leave the cassette at my office or home. It was evidence, and although Testa didn't know I'd recorded our conversation, I didn't think it would be a good idea to leave it at either location. "By the way, is there a chance that I could leave something here with you?"

"Yeah, go ahead."

"You have a safe, right?" I took out the tape cassette and handed it to him. Bob took it, examined it, and nodded.

"Sure. I'll put it in a sealed envelope with your name on it." He got an envelope out and did just that. A minute later, the cassette was in the safe, locked up. I felt better.

"Thanks, Bob."

He nodded, apparently understanding, and bent over the books as if I wasn't there. A few moments later, I wasn't —instead, I was driving through the Sumner Tunnel to Boston proper to Mass General.

Lorraine was in the waiting room. "Angela, thank goodness." She came up to me and grabbed my hand. "I would never have forgiven myself if anything had happened to your cousin. But without him there, I don't know if Marty would have been able to fight off the men who came in."

"What happened? Wait. Let me see Joey first. Is he okay?"

"He's getting a nasty cut on his hand superglued right now," she said. "Why don't we go back and check on him?"

As we walked back through the emergency room doors, I asked, "Where's Rick?"

"He wanted to go home, he told me he wasn't feeling too well after everything that had happened today," Lorraine replied. "He left a little after Joey and I talked to you on the phone."

"So tell me your version of what happened." I wanted to keep her talking. She was clearly upset and it would be better for her to go over the details again soon after the incident.

"It was awful," she said. "I was just working at my desk when these goons came barging into the factory, looking around as if they owned the place."

"What did they look like?"

"One was short, a scrunched-up face, and he kept playing with a knife as if he wanted to scare me. He kept looking at me out of the corner of his eye. Another guy was taller, heavier, and younger. They both carried baseball bats. The short one called him Johnny. They started breaking stuff up. My computer was the first thing to go in the office, and when I got up to say something, the short one pushed me back down. I reached for the phone and he snatched it away from me."

She was starting to shake and I spied an empty chair in the hallway and led her to it. Several people stared at us, including one guy who seemed to be bleeding profusely from a cut on his arm. He was holding a bloody towel to it, patiently waiting to be seen in the emergency room. A pool of blood had already accumulated on the floor.

I focused back on Lorraine. "Tell me more."

She took a deep breath and continued. "I asked them what they wanted, and they just sneered. Then Rick came out of his office and wanted to know what was going on. The guys just shoved him out of the way and walked into the factory. I followed them, and Marty came over to tell them to leave me alone. The little one hit him in the shoulder with the bat." There was indignation in her voice now. "Just hit him without any warning. Marty yelled some obscenity, then Joey came up. There was a scuffle between Joey and Marty and the two guys, and Rick had the presence of mind to go to a phone. The tall one noticed and ran over, smashed the phone out of Rick's hand."

She was starting to breathe faster. I lightly rubbed the middle of her back. "Take it slow. It's over."

She turned to me. "But, Angela, don't you see? It isn't over. The men told us they were coming back."

"Was there more? Tell me anything else that might have happened."

She shook her head. "They yelled at the workers to leave before someone else got hurt, and not to come back again. Then they punched Joey a couple more times because he mouthed off to them, and Marty got another hit in the leg. Then they left."

She started crying. "I don't know if I can work in an atmosphere like this, Angela. I didn't think Mob guys were so bad. I mean, you see 'em on the screen, and they seem all nice, a little bad." She sobbed. I got a tissue out of my purse and while she dried her eyes, I waited for her to calm down.

"Joey's in that room over there," she said, pointing to a room down the hallway. "You should go see him. I'll be all right. I'll stay right here."

Joey received me like a prizefighter receives his press after a good bout in the ring. He was almost jaunty: a black eye, a cut on his hand, his ribs taped. "Hey, Cuz, you missed all the action." A nurse was marking something down on a chart. She looked up at me briefly before going back to her work.

"Oh, I'm sure you got more than your share. Your mother is gonna kill me for sending you into a dangerous situation." I crossed my arms and leaned against the wall. "You okay?"

He shrugged, then winced. "I've had worse fights in prison. And don't worry about Mom. She's in Vegas for a week. I won't tell if you won't."

I nodded. "I'm just glad you're all right," I said, my voice soft. "Jeez, Joey, I'm sorry."

"Hey, you didn't know, did you?"

"You should've let them do whatever they wanted, Joey. You shouldn't've mouthed off to them."

He laughed until he remembered that his ribs hurt, then said, "And you would've stood by? You wouldn't've mouthed off? Ange, it runs in our family."

I nodded and pushed myself off the wall to stand closer to him.

The nurse spoke. "Mr. Marcella?" Joey looked over. "The doctor will be with you shortly to make sure you understand your aftercare. You can't be left alone." She gave us a professional smile and left the room.

"Okay, this is the version Lorraine told me." When I was finished, Joey nodded.

"That's pretty much what happened. They came in out of the blue."

"Are you going to be all right?" I asked. "Do you need me to stay with you tonight? You can have the extra bedroom at my place."

He shook his head. "I got a place to stay. I met this girl—" He flushed. Ah, well, so much for getting him together with Raina. "I called her and she wants me to stay the night."

"That's great, Joey. Give me the number where you can be reached. Should I go with you?"

"Naw, you go on. But be careful, Ange. These guys aren't to fool around with."

I kissed his forehead and left.

I stepped out into the hall and almost ran into Marty, who was in a wheelchair. His right arm was in a sling and he had a crutch laid across his lap. "Hey, Angela, I wanted to thank you for recommending Joey."

"Yeah," I said ruefully, "I got him beat up."

"Hey, without him there, I would have been killed by those two guys. Lorraine, well, she's a woman and they didn't do much to her, but Rick was almost useless. He's a guy with education, and he didn't want to get his hands dirty. But Joey there, he didn't think twice about jumping in when he saw me gettin' beat up." He stuck his left hand out.

I took it and we shook awkwardly, but I was beginning to have a new respect for the man. "Well, I'm glad I was able to help. Did he fix the packaging machine?"

"What a mechanic. Walpole sure lost a good thing when he was let out." Marty grinned enthusiastically. But he lost his grin soon after. "I dunno what's gonna happen to AMT. I was counting on it being a big company, or merging with ToyCo."

"What's your deal with Albert?" I asked.

"I get five percent. I put some money into the company, but the way things have been going, I don't know if this was such a hot idea." He gave me a guilty look. "No offense, but Albert has connections, and those connections don't seem to be too happy that he's trying to go legitimate."

I nodded. "Yeah, that seems to be the case. But I'm working on it."

"Are you any closer to finding Albert?"

I shook my head. "No, but I still have a few leads. Thanks for the encouraging word. Keep me informed on what's happening at the plant."

"Yeah, that sounds good. Appreciate your doin' it." He stood up slowly, hopped a bit and flinched. "They got my knee good. Doc says it's not broken, though."

I nodded, held out a hand and said, "I'm glad."

As I turned to leave, Marty laughed. "It's funny, 'cause

when those guys first came in, I thought they were here to break Rick's legs.''

Marty had gotten my interest. I turned around. "Why?"

"Rick's always down at the track, placing bets. He owes so much in student loans and stuff, he justifies it by saying he only needs one good win to pay it all back."

Before I left the hospital, I stopped by the waiting room. Lorraine was there in one of the chairs. There were other people sitting there: a couple with a baby: a young gang member who was clutching his arm, accompanied by a girl-friend; an elderly man with a woman who looked like his daughter by his side. All of them had something in common, they all wore worried expressions, all were concerned about their own welfare, or that of a loved one.

"You said Rick went home?" I asked.

She smiled. "Yes, over an hour ago. He didn't get hurt as bad as these other two, but he was really shaken up."

"What do you know about Rick's gambling?"

Lorraine smiled and smoothed her short, dark hair. "I sometimes see racing forms in his office. He thinks he has a system and he's gonna win some big amount of money to pay off his outstanding student loans."

I told her about the person who came into AMT while I was there. She frowned. "I can't imagine who would have done that. We didn't give the police a key, and we didn't tell them about the back door being open."

"I don't think the police would have gone to such lengths to avoid turning on lights just to go through your desk. This was definitely someone who knew what you were up to, and was looking for something in your desk. He didn't find it, though."

She looked distracted. The lines around her eyes had deepened even since I'd been with Joey. "The only thing different was the books. I put the ledgers in the bottom drawer.''

I nodded. "I'm sure that's probably what he was looking for. Tell me, Lorraine, did anyone try to go back into the building once the ambulance arrived? Did anyone step away?''

"Marty wanted to go after them, but he was too hurt. Joey was down for the count. None of the workers stuck around long enough to help us. Rick wanted to go back in the office to make the nine-one-one call, but I pointed out that there was a phone in the factory. He seemed reluctant to use it, seemed to want to go back in, but I told him I wanted us to stick together. I was afraid. He stayed put.''

"What about you? Shouldn't you go home?''

"I'm waiting for my husband to get off shift and pick me up. I also want to make sure the other two are taken care of before I leave. I know Joey has someone coming to pick him up, but Marty lives alone. I know he's an old grump sometimes, but he cares about AMT and what happens to it.'' She looked worried. "I'm sorry I didn't get those books to you sooner, Angela. I'd been meaning to, and I knew it was important, but things have been hectic without Albert around.'' She shook her head. "I know it's no excuse.''

I patted her shoulder. "Don't worry about it.'' Before I left, I asked her one last thing. "Can you give me Rick's address and phone number? I want to ask him his version of the events.''

She gave me his address, which was in East Boston, near Suffolk Downs. I also got her phone number, just in case.

As I left, I reflected that Rick's gambling habit hadn't been in the report Antonia had provided me. I wondered where he got the money to place bets. Marty had made it sound as if Rick gambled a lot. Lorraine didn't seem to have any idea how much Rick gambled. I wondered how Rick was doing his gambling. His financial statements hadn't given me any clue that there was something wrong. Whose money was he using? I was starting to form an idea, and I didn't like it one bit. But confronting Rick wasn't as important as getting Albert back.

I drove to the North End. I needed to get to my office and pay my rent. It was close to two-thirty and all the heavy traffic was going the other way, so I lucked out. I knew I wouldn't be so lucky on my way back to East Boston.

Whenever I drove into Boston, I parked my Bronco at a garage owned by a cousin who let me park it there for free. But he wouldn't like it if I took advantage of his generosity too often. I usually used public transportation to get to my office. When he saw me this time, he waved me through.

If I thought my office looked a little like Mattel had decorated it with the green and pink couch and the lavender paint job, it now looked as it Mattel had decorated it, didn't like it, and had crushed it with a giant Monty Python foot. The pebbled glass door with my name stenciled on it, something I was proud of and that had made me feel like a female version of Mike Hammer, was smashed inward. The desk had been overturned, drawers emptied and smashed, as if the intruder had taken a sledgehammer to everything. Papers were thrown everywhere and the phone had been ripped out of the wall. That in itself wasn't bad, because I just had to step through the trashed room and plug it back in. The reality of what had happened to my office hit me suddenly and I sat down in the midst of pebbled glass and broken desk drawers. Shock might have set in if I wasn't so worried about who might have done this and why.

I called the super to tell him what had happened. He was grumpy but promised to be up to my office within half an hour.

I needed to get out of my office for a few minutes, so I went down the hall to visit with Benny the Bond. His work didn't really start until after five some nights—especially Friday and Saturday nights when all the drunks got arrested.

He was a fireplug of a man who was sitting behind his desk, screaming at someone over the phone as I walked in. "Don't threaten me, you asshole. You owe me money and I want you to walk it by here tomorrow morning by nine or I can't be responsible for what happens to you." He banged the phone in the receiver so hard I thought it would shatter. Then he looked up and smiled at me.

"Client?"

He shook his head. "Nah, my bookie. Keeps trying to screw me outta my winnings."

I shook my head sympathetically.

"Say, Angie, what's with your place? You redecorating again?" There was a twinkle in his eye, curtailed by concern.

"Nope. Got an intruder. But I may have to leave before the super gets here. Can you have him board up my window?"

"Sure, kid. Say, you wouldn't know someone who wants to do some bounty hunting. I got a couple of guys who skipped."

"My cousin Joey is looking for work."

"No hurry. These guys aren't real bad. Couple a nineteen-year-olds who knocked over a liquor store with a note, no gun."

I thought of Ma—she'd straighten 'em out in a hurry, but I didn't think Benny would go for it. Besides, if I didn't get Albert back to her in one piece, she might kill me and then she'd be in prison. I was thinking crazy thoughts.

I went back to my office and zoned out while I swept

up broken glass and checked my files and my computer. I was so jumpy that when the phone rang, I let out an involuntary yell. I picked up the receiver.

"Hello?"

There was someone on the other end, and he was breathing into the phone.

"Hello? Who is this?"

Whoever was on the other end hung up and I got a dial tone. I dialed star 69 and the phone number was read back to me. It was my home phone number. I called Raina. She was just getting ready to leave work.

"Get someone over to my place right away." I told her what happened.

"No shit," she said. I heard her talking to someone, telling him or her to send a squad car over there. She got back to me. "You want them to go up to your place or should they cruise around until you get back?"

"Do you have your set of keys to my place?"

I heard her digging around in her purse. I heard a noise behind me and turned around. The super had arrived and was surveying the mess. He had a piece of plywood, a hammer and some nails. He gave me a cold nod. He didn't approve of a private investigator in the building and had voiced his objections many times to the owners, but to no avail. The owners were my unofficial godparents, and would never eject me from the building on his say so. Frankly, I think he didn't like me because I was a woman. He'd told me a couple of times that women should stay home barefoot and pregnant.

"Raina? I gotta go. The super's here, and if I get moving now, I can be in East Boston within the hour. It's rush hour, so it may be a while."

"I can't find my set of keys."

"That's okay. Just have 'em sit outside the building, if that's okay. If anyone comes out, they'll know."

"Whoever it is could easily go out the back of the building," she pointed out.

"Yeah, but he'll be seen by my neighbors."

"Oh, yeah," she said with a giggle before hanging up. Raina knew I had the nosiest neighbors in the world, God love 'em. They leaned out of their windows all day long, while they were cooking dinner or diapering babies, and they talked to each other. Loudly. There was always someone calling to someone from a window, and they kept an unofficial eye on my building.

Things were moving along, and the super was putting up a piece of plywood. He shook his head when he saw me. "The way you're going, you'll be out of this building before the end of the year," he said, referring to the number of times my office had been broken into.

"Have I always paid the rent on time?"

"Yes."

"And has anyone else's office been broken into?"

He jingled some nails in his pocket. "Not that I recall."

"And my uncle owns the building, so what's the problem? I always pay for the glass that's broken, and I hardly ever complain about the leaky corner of my ceiling. As far as I'm concerned, I'm the perfect renter." I gave him my rent check and scrammed before he could think of a comeback.

SIXTEEN

THE DRIVE HOME TOOK LONGER than the thirty minutes I'd hoped it would take, but I was driving down Marginal Street toward my apartment building within forty-five minutes. I spotted the cruiser sitting out front of my place. The cops were drinking coffee from styrofoam cups and eating sandwiches. I pulled up behind them, parked, got out and approached their car. After I showed them my identification, I explained the situation in as few words as possible.

One of the guys was my age. He was a big guy, like a teddy bear, with a moon face and a shock of dark hair that hung over his forehead. "No one has gone in or come out of your building since we got here, ma'am. Raina couldn't find her set of keys to your place and we didn't want to break in without your permission." He brightened. "Hey, didn't we go to high school together? Your name rings some bells with me."

I shrugged. "What's your name?"

"Andy Famulari."

It sounded familiar.

"Class of eighty-three."

"Same year as me." I'd have to get out my old yearbook. "You on the football team?"

"Yeah, I was defense."

Andy was a good guy to get to know in my line of business. I smiled at him. The other guy was younger and wiry with a shock of faded red hair and pale skin. "Hey, Andy, we goin' in there with the lady?"

"What about it, Angela? You're a tough PI now, why do you need any help?"

I was a little irritated by Andy's condescending attitude, but I wasn't about to go into my apartment and confront some goons without a couple of East Boston's finest escorting me there. I know those loner private eyes in fictional situations would go to their apartment alone after their office was broken into, but I'm not that brave or that stupid. If a couple of thugs named Johnny Smash and Nick the Knife showed up at my apartment, I wanted to make sure that they saw a police car cruising up and down outside the building. They could still get in and out the back way, but it would be more risky with cops right around the corner.

Besides, if anything happened to me, Ma would kill me.

Famulari and his partner, who was introduced to me as Lance Healy, walked me to my door on the third floor. If there were any burglars in my apartment, I wondered if I'd have to fight them off anyway. Healy was probably just under one hundred and fifty and looked as if Ma could whip him in a fight. By the time we'd climbed the two flights of stairs, Famulari was huffing and puffing from the exertion. His extra pounds overlapped his belt—he looked like a heart attack waiting to happen. I just didn't want him to collapse in my apartment.

The door was slightly ajar—the lock was broken. I let Healy enter first—he had his big gun out and he shouldered the door open, sliding in the way they do on all the cop shows. I went in next, giving Famulari a chance to catch his breath.

I peeked around the corner of the front door. "How's it going?" I asked.

Healy returned, his gun drawn, his chest puffed out, the

lack of color in his face returning after being the first one into a possible danger zone.

"Your place has been tossed like a Caesar salad," he said.

Famulari rolled his eyes. "He's always wanted to say that."

While Healy and Famulari called it in, I shoved past them to see if Fredd was all right.

"Don't touch anything until the fingerprint crew gets here," Healy warned me. Like my fingerprints weren't already all over the place. Still, I knew what he meant and I took care to keep from touching anything.

Fredd's glass enclosure was still intact, and the fluorescent bulb was still on. I thought he looked a little put out by all the excitement, but it was probably just my imagination.

Famulari took my report while we waited for the fingerprint unit to be dispatched. Raina had already left, but the dispatcher recognized my address, and it didn't take more than fifteen minutes before the unit arrived. By that time, the officers were ready to go. I didn't have much to tell them, I certainly wasn't going to let them in on my brother's disappearance. You never know who's in close touch with the Family, especially in law enforcement.

The officers left with the promise that they would canvass the neighborhood—maybe someone saw something suspicious. I thanked the officers for responding so promptly and made a mental note to myself to make something special for them the next time I got the urge to bake.

The fingerprint team arrived in time to powder and dust like housewives on speed, sometimes gathering at a spot in the living room or the bedroom, the two main areas that had been disturbed, oohing and aahing over this fingerprint or that smudge. My fingerprints were taken for comparison and I gave them a list of regulars at my place, my sisters, Rosa and Sophia, Sophia's kids and live-in boyfriend, Raina James, Reg Giordano, and Ma.

The sergeant in charge of the unit was anxious to get back to the precinct and play some kind of joke on Raina, something that would require using her fingerprints and my break-in. He made me give my solemn promise I wouldn't call Raina to warn her. I was so happy to know that the break-in could be used for comic relief—at least someone saw something funny about the whole situation.

After everyone packed up, I was left alone to inspect the place. I immediately went into my bathroom to check on my gun. At one point in my life, having a gun nearby was a good thing. Considering how much crime is out there these days, I didn't want to add to the problem, but being a private investigator, I still used the gun sometimes, especially when I went on car repos. Some of the people who hadn't paid for their car in six months got a little touchy when you tried to take their transportation away. I didn't much care for birdshot in my butt, or worse, so I'd taken to carrying whenever I went out on a repossession. So far, I'd always been able to talk myself out of a situation when confronted with an irate person holding a shotgun.

In my apartment, I didn't want my gun handy—yeah, there could be break-ins, but having a gun handy wasn't such a hot idea. Most gun owners have a tendency to pull the trigger a little too quickly and ask questions later. By then, Mom, Sis, or Dad is already bleeding on the carpet. Although I do have more training and probably have less of a tendency to pull the trigger before asking ''Who's there?'' I didn't want my gun to be a temptation to someone who was breaking into my place. So I hid my gun in a Tupperware container, which I'd rigged to the inside of the toilet tank. Not a real handy place in an emergency, but in this case, I'd had plenty of warning.

I took my gun out of its hiding place and checked to make sure all the parts worked properly. Then I loaded the clip. I kept the bullets in my dirty laundry. Two places thieves usually won't look—the toilet tank and the dirty laundry.

I checked my windows to make sure they were locked, and all my closets to make sure no one was hiding inside, even though I'd just had a group of policemen in my apartment. I noted that the box of Itty Bitty Kittys was still in the storage space behind my desk.

Then I took stock of my apartment. I'd had my office broken into before, but never my apartment, and I didn't like the feeling of violation that went with it. I noted that the phrase "the place had been tossed like a salad" described to a T what my living room looked like. On a happier note, it was clear to me that the thief had been interrupted when he started on my bedroom. Only two of my dresser drawers had been spilled out across the room. In fact, the fingerprint powder was more of an annoyance to clean up than the clothes, books, and CDs that had been recklessly thrown around.

Antonia called. "I tried your office first."

"Yeah, well, my apartment was broken into."

"That's terrible!"

"Yeah, especially since it happened right after my office was broken into."

Antonia groaned. "You know, Angela, I think there's a nice security director's position for you at one of my clients' companies."

I sighed. "Thanks for the offer, but this is personal. You got anything?"

"Look, I hadn't finished up the background checks, as I

mentioned in my note." Actually, her note hadn't mentioned it, but I didn't bring this up. "And I have more
information on Salvatore."

"That's great. Do you have his current address?"

I heard papers shuffling in the background. "Yes, right
here." She gave it to me. Sal Testa didn't live too far away
from where I lived.

"And what about any buildings he might have purchased
or that his family might own in the vicinity?" I was going
to start searching for Albert, and I wasn't coming home
until I had him in my Bronco and we were driving back to
East Boston.

"There are a few properties listed."

"Great. Give them to me right now."

"Now?"

"Now," I replied. I was tired. I wanted a confrontation,
and I wanted it now. But I didn't want them to see me until
it was too late.

Antonia repeated the addresses over the phone. I instructed her to drop what she had at my apartment or my
office tomorrow, whichever was most convenient for her.
Then I thanked her and hung up. A moment later, she called
back. "Angie?"

"Yeah?"

"Are you okay?"

"Yeah, I'm fine."

"You sound strange," she said.

"Well, I just had my apartment and my office broken
into on the same day. Wouldn't you sound strange, too?"
I hoped I didn't sound snippy, but Antonia was getting too
close to the truth—I was going to kick some butt tonight
and I needed to do some reconnaissance work.

"Yeah, I guess so. Just do me a favor and don't do
anything stupid, okay?"

We said a few pleasantries, then rang off again.

I took a map out and plotted in what order I was reconnoitering Sal Testa's properties. He owned an Italian eatery in the North End, a dry cleaners here in East Boston, and his home was also here in East Boston, on Lewis Street, which was near my apartment building on Marginal. In fact, he had a better view of the Boston skyline than I did, but I guess that only made sense since he made money the old-fashioned way—he inherited it.

Before I left my apartment, I fed Fredd, stuffed my set of lockpicks in my pocket and a small penlight in case I needed them. My gun was still stuck in my waistband at the small of my back, my jacket concealing it well enough for me to feel comfortable going out in public.

The fall weather was playing tricks with those of us who lived in Boston. Yesterday, it had been snowing, today, it was sunny and warm, almost balmy. The snow was melting.

I started with the North End eatery, taking the subway there to case the joint and determine if it might have some area that would hold a prisoner. It took me twenty minutes to get to North Station, then I caught a cab to Hanover Avenue. The place was called Sal's and was basically a cappuccino café. The décor was done in red, green, and white, the colors of the flag of Italy, and the tables and chairs were spindly white wrought-iron open lacework, which left curlicue imprints on the customers' legs and butts if they sat longer than ten minutes. But it didn't seem to bother anyone who was there. It was a popular place, most of the tables already occupied with young couples sharing a pastry and lattes in the late afternoon, and businessmen discussing big deals over an early dinner of minestrone and sandwiches.

I took a seat at one of the two empty tables left, and

looked at the menu. A waiter came up to me and took my order, bracciole with dark roast coffee, and I watched the comings and goings of the customers until my meal was served. Their service was quick, which was a blessing because I didn't want to stay too long. I noted that the kitchen area was open with a counter in between where the waiters took the money, sort of like a pizza joint.

I didn't finish my meal, which was fair but not fabulous, but ate enough to make it look like I just had a small appetite. Which, I will be the first to admit, I don't have. I left a tip and went up to the counter where my waiter took my money and made change, wishing me a good day. I made a noncommittal remark and headed for the hallway, a woman on mission—finding the restrooms.

The hallway had five doors—one led to the kitchen area; at the end of the hall, a door led to the outside alley; and three other doors. The owner hadn't bothered to put real signs denoting the men's from the women's bathroom, just stick figures drawn on with markers, so I was able to tell which was which. That left one door, which I assumed was the office. I opened it to find a pudgy, overworked man sitting at a desk in a cramped space. He looked up and I apologized.

"Yeah, we gotta get real signs for the bathrooms," he said. "I keep telling the owner that."

Inspiration struck. "Say, I heard that there are catacombs under this block. Is that true? You know, during Prohibition, they made passageways to hide the liquor? I'm kind of a history buff."

He laughed. "I wish. We could use the room for storage. Nah, there's nothing like that. There's a small cellar underneath. We gotta get to it from the back door, though, and it's stuffed to the gills with our supplies."

"Oh," I replied. "Well, thanks."

I used the restroom, then left through the back door. The alley smelled of old garlic and onion, vinegar and tomatoes. The cellar door was wooden and looked as if it wouldn't take much to break it down. There was a padlock on it, and I was glad I'd had the presence of mind to bring along my trusty lockpicks. I was by no means adept at picking locks, but the padlock looked easy. I took out the sturdiest of the picks and moved it around inside the lock until the tumblers clicked and the padlock fell open.

I checked the area to make sure no one would see me entering, and I stepped inside. It smelled like a combination of wet dirt and concrete. I crept down the rickety stairs, the padlock in my hand so I wouldn't be locked in accidentally, and I began to probe the walls. Just as the manager had mentioned, the cellar was small and contained canned tomatoes and jars of marinated artichokes, and blocks of Parmesan and Romano. It was cool enough in the cellar to keep the cheeses cold. There were no hidden doors.

As I started back up the stairs, I could hear voices outside the door.

"What the hell happened? Where's the damn padlock? It's that stupid kid again. He never listens to me. Lock the door, I say, after you've gotten the supplies needed—" The door opened wide and I was caught. I'd had enough brains to hide the padlock. Both the manager and my waiter were standing there, staring at me as if I was an alien emerging from a spaceship.

The manager was looking at me and I probably looked as pale as I felt.

"What're you doing snooping around here?" he asked.

I marched up the step with purpose, and out into the alley, making sure the padlock dropped on the ground at the same time I slammed the cellar door shut. "I told you earlier that I'm a history buff, and I thought I'd just take a

look at the alley, see if there was anything that would tell
me about the catacombs I told you about.'' I took a big
breath and exhaled. "Imagine my surprise when I discovered that the cellar door was unlocked. You'd think you'd
have a padlock on this door. Anyway,'' I rushed on before
they could question me too closely, "I thought, What's the
harm if I sneak down there and see if there are any hidden
doors?' Imagine my disappointment when I discovered no
hidden doors, not other ways of getting to these catacombs
I've heard about." I brushed past them, heading for the
street. "Anyway, thanks for letting me take a look. I'll have
to check around at the other stores, see if any of them have
access to catacombs. Thanks again." I walked off, leaving
the two men staring at me, not saying a word.

As I got to the opening of the alley, I heard the waiter
say, "Hey, here's the padlock. I swear it wasn't there a
minute ago. I was looking on the ground for it—''

I heard footsteps coming my way. I hustled out of there
and crossed the street quickly, ducking into a Mom and
Pop pharmacy where I stood behind the newsstand, which
was filled with mostly Italian newspapers and magazines. I
leafed through a copy of *Life* in Italian and looked at the
pictures. I watched the manager come out of the alleyway,
huffing and puffing. He took a handkerchief out of his
pocket and dabbed at his sweaty forehead. It was probably
the most exercise he'd gotten recently, and he looked like
a candidate for a heart attack.

He looked up and down Hanover Avenue, then shook
his head, and turned back into the alley. The waiter had
apparently thought it would be too much trouble to go after
me. Or maybe he was guarding the cellar door in case I
wanted to make off with a case of marinated artichokes.
Which, believe me, I'd been tempted to do.

After that close call, I headed back to East Boston and

got my Bronco ready for tonight. It was close to seven-thirty when I took my car out for a little reconnaissance—the dry cleaners, which was in Orient Heights, was first. It was just closing up when I drove by. I parked, got out of the car and walked around it, looking for ways in. I noticed that there was a window slightly open in the back of the store, probably propped open most of the time to provide some relief for the cleaners in the back. It was high up, about eight or nine feet from the ground, and I made a note to bring along a stepladder when I returned. I didn't notice any alarm system installed, although the owners had put a sticker in the front door that warns trespassers off by saying there was an alarm system. That would scare off the amateurs, but not the pros.

I got back in the car and drove to Maverick Street, and kept going. Lewis Street was a short dead-end street off of Marginal that ended overlooking the Boston Inner Harbor.

I could practically walk there tonight. Sal Testa lived at the very end of Lewis, in a large house set apart from the rest of the Lewis Street community by an acre of land, a six foot wall and very decorative spikes that were designed to seriously injure anyone who tried to scale the wall. Sal definitely had a nicer view than I did—he was closer to the water and had no nearby neighbors.

I walked up to the gate and two Dobermans met me. One of them stood silently by and eyed me, drooling as if I were filet mignon. The other one barked at me and took the warning stance.

"Nice doggies," I said.

I looked up in time to notice the drapes twitching slightly in one of the upstairs windows, and I beat it out of there fast. I wasn't sure how I was going to breach the security, so I'd have to make it up as I went along. My best guess was that Albert was in there, helpless.

I drove back home to think. At eight-thirty, someone knocked on my door. Aside from Rosa and Ma, the only person with a key to the entry door was Raina.

"Angela? It's me," Raina said. I was beginning to think Someone Upstairs was intentionally trying to intervene with my plans. But I let her in anyway. It was a good thing I did because she was carrying a large white paper bag that was slightly damp from a drizzle that had begun a little while after I returned home. The delicate smell of mei fun, orange chicken, crab Rangoon, and hot and sour soup emanated from the bag, and my stomach growled in recognition of good food.

I opened the door. "What are you doing here? Don't you go home after five?" I didn't want her to stay all night, which sometimes happened. We'd get to talking, and suddenly it would be midnight, and she'd stay in the guest bedroom, which was also my office.

"When I got off, I was hungry and thought I'd bring dinner over here." She looked the place over. "Sergeant Aquino gave me a copy of the report, including my fingerprints as that of a suspicious character who had entered your apartment."

"Funny," I replied, grabbing the bag and bringing it into the kitchen. Raina followed, dropping her jacket on one of my red and gray vinyl and chrome kitchen chairs, then following suit by dropping herself into a second chair. "You want jasmine tea or plum wine with that?"

Raina blinked. "You have plum wine here?"

"No, but I thought we could pretend that my red table wine was plum wine." I took a jug of it out of the fridge and set it on the table, then brought two plates out of a cabinet and set those down in front of Raina and the chair that I would be sitting in. Two tumblers followed, and by the time I got the forks and chopsticks out, Raina had poured two healthy glasses for us. "I guess the jasmine tea is out, huh?" I asked.

She laughed. "I bet you don't even have any jasmine tea."

I tried my best to look offended, but soon gave it up. "Nah, Earl Grey is the closest I've got to Chinese tea. I really should get some for these occasions."

We'd been making small talk up till now. Raina was a good enough friend to know that I'd talk about the break-in when I was good and ready, and in the meantime, she told me about her day, asking for advice about getting back at one of her co-workers for pulling a practical joke on her. I told her that itching powder in his jock strap was always a classic, and she gave it some thought while we ate.

When the food had been eaten and we'd been through three glasses of wine each, I started to talk about it.

"Bastards!" I said.

"Sons of bitches," Raina agreed. "Have you found Albert?"

"No," I replied glumly. I felt guilty all over again—guilty and helpless. I absently touched the metal of the gun I'd stuck in the back of my jeans.

"What the hell did they expect to find—Fort Knox?" I mused. "They didn't break into Rosa's place, and the ground floor apartment is still intact."

"You have to be relieved that they didn't go into Rosa's apartment," Raina said, looking at me with curiosity. "And you know why they broke into your place. That's why you're carrying right now."

I waved a hand and looked down at my half glass of wine. "Yeah, I know why. I have something the other guy wants. And I have to do something about it. You just came by at the wrong time." I looked over all the empty take-out boxes and corrected myself, "Actually, you came by

at the right time—I was pretty hungry. But I have to go
now. I don't mean to push you out or anything—''

"What're you going to do?"

I smiled. "There are a lot of things I can confide in you,
Raina, but this is not one of them."

She half smiled. "Hmm, something illegal, huh?" Raina
stuck her lower lip out. "Damn. There are times I wish I
wasn't in law enforcement. You make private investigation
seem so sexy with that gun stuck in your waistband."

I chose to ignore the sarcastic tone. "Really?" I tried to
do a cheesecake pose, by sticking one hip out and thrusting
my chest forward. I almost fell over. She just looked disgusted.

"Call me when you grow up," she suggested briskly
while gathering up her jacket and purse. She was only angry that I wasn't taking the subject seriously, but I had to
make it sound as if I wasn't all that concerned. The last
thing I needed was some well-meaning friend tagging
along, getting herself killed for me.

I saw Raina to the door and promised to call her tomorrow. I was putting on my jacket, making sure the gun didn't
make a bulge back there when Raina stuck her head back
in. "Angie?"

"Yeah?"

"Be careful. Please be careful. Don't do anything stupid.
Even Healy and Famulari figured out that you were holding
out on them. And believe me, I got some shit for it. They
think I'm privy to your every move just because we're best
friends."

I smiled. "Well, you tell those boys that you plied me
with good Chinese take-out and wine and I still refused to
tell you a thing."

Ma called before I left. It was just as well, because it

wasn't totally dark yet, and I was pretty sure that she had a sixth sense about this sort of thing.

"Have you heard from Albert yet?" she asked dully.

"No, Ma, but I'm going out right now to check a few places out." I couldn't tell her about the finger. I'd put it in my refrigerator when I got home earlier. I was tempted to throw it out, but maybe it could still be saved. I guess I was hoping for something that wasn't going to happen. I needed to keep hoping, though. "I think I know where he is, but I have to rule out the other possibility."

"Do I need to get hold of a lawyer?"

"Not yet, but please, please, please don't call your old friend Testa again, capiche? I don't think he wants to be involved in this anymore anyway."

"Why do you say that? Giovanni and I go way back—"

"Yeah, but you're not blood," I said.

That took a moment to sink in. "Oh, a relative is involved."

"Yeah. Now do me a favor and stand by. If I don't call you by tomorrow morning at nine, get Helena involved, and Lee Randolph, too." I gave her Lee's number.

"Angela?"

"Yeah, yeah. Be careful. Don't take any chances. And find Albert if it's the last thing I do."

"I wasn't going to say all that."

"Then what?"

"I don't care if it is Giovanni's son, daughter, cousin or nephew. Get the bastard."

SEVENTEEN

TEN MINUTES LATER, I was in my Bronco, heading for the dry cleaners in Orient Heights. It was well after ten and although there were a few people on the streets, it was a weeknight and the night owl population was much sparser than on weekend nights. I parked around the corner from the dry cleaners, near the alley, got out, grabbed the step-ladder, and locked my car.

No one was around, unless there was someone watching through an apartment window. But I'd have to take my chances. I strolled down the alley, daring an assailant to take me on, but no one jumped out at me. When I got to the back of the building, I set up the ladder and climbed it. I was in luck that the window had been closed, but it was so far up that no on bothered to lock it. I pushed it open and slipped halfway in. Taking my penlight from my pocket, I swept the light across the floor to find out what I had to deal with. I discovered a utility sink almost directly below me. The window was wide enough for me to wriggle around, get my feet under me, and slither down until my toes touched the sink ledge.

Once I was inside, I prowled around. It was eerie to be in a dry-cleaning store at night—the coats and suits and dresses lined up on the rack like good soldiers, the rustle of plastic against my skin, and the hum of the exhaust fan.

I snooped around, looking for someplace where Sal might be keeping Albert, but nothing stuck out. I checked the office in the back, the broom closet, and the floor for a hidden cellar. The place was clean.

Getting out of the building presented a problem—I'd had to really stretch to reach the sink with my toes when I slipped in, so jumping from the sink to the window was a bit problematic. If I missed, I could break something vital like my leg or my arm. I'd heard of burglars who'd gotten into a building only to discover that they couldn't get out. At least one of those stories involved a naked burglar. I was glad I still had my clothes on.

I searched the joint for something that could easily be used and taken away with me. I finally found a wooden hanger that would do—I just needed a few more inches to reach the window. A few minutes later, the hanger caught on a chink on the outside of the windowsill and held, and I was able to hoist myself up and grasp the sill.

I have seen the movies where the cat burglar glides effortlessly to the ground, not making a sound when his feet hit the cement. Not so in my case. I should have just slid down, but I landed with a thud, completely missing the stepladder and bruising my tailbone in the process.

I felt foolish carrying the stepladder back to the car, but I was lucky that no one noticed me. Not until I got in my car. Then someone noticed me, and I noticed him or her by the length of sharpened steel pressed against my neck.

"Don't scream, don't make a sound," he said.

"So, we finally meet, Nick," I replied as casually as I could, under the circumstances. "Nick. Is that short for Nicholas, or is it a cute nickname. Hey! The word nick is in nickname, too. Isn't that funny?" I couldn't stop babbling.

"Shut up. I hate dames that talk too much. Start driving."

My hands were shaking, but I managed to start the car. He directed me to Lewis Street. Well, fancy that. I'd been trying to figure out how to get in, and now I had my invitation pressed against my neck.

I stayed silent until the gate opened to usher my car in. The Dobermans must have been put back in their kennel because all was silent. We got out of the car simultaneously, Nick warning me not to try to escape.

"Where am I gonna go?" I asked. "We're in an enclosed area."

"Shut up. Move." He pushed me toward the front door, but we were still a ways back. I turned around.

"Didn't your mother teach you how to treat a lady?"

This was the first time I'd gotten a good look at Nick. He was an ugly little guy with a cauliflower nose and beady black eyes sort of like a hamster. He wore a bad suit and his wristwatch hung on a slender wrist. "I know how to treat ladies, but you ain't no lady." He tried to scare me with his pigsticker, waving it in front of my face. I slapped his hand. I was scared to death, but I had to get the upper hand here.

He lunged at me, using a high forty-five degree arc with his knife, cutting down and across where I should have been. But I was ready for him and I stepped away at an angle and grabbed his knife arm with both of my hands, pulling him in the direction he was already going, except now he was off balance. I was performing *kotegaeshi* and slid my hand along his arm to switch hands without letting go, then stepped behind him and spun him around. Once he was off balance, I bent his knife hand back against his shoulder until he couldn't help but fall down. Keeping my stance wide and my knees bent low, I took the knife away in one fluid movement and rolled him onto his stomach, his arm perpendicular to my body. I knelt, cradling his arm, wrist and elbow, and applied gentle pressure across his shoulder blade.

"You stupid bitch," was all he could scream. No thank you for not killing him or breaking his arm, or cutting off his finger, which I would have done if I weren't so squeamish at the sight of blood.

Once I was sure he was properly humiliated, I let his arm go and stood up. I slid the knife into my jacket pocket, and walked toward the house, a bit more confident about being on Sal Testa's property. Still, I wasn't comfortable enough to walk around without my gun, so I pulled it out of my waistband. I was fortunate that Nick hadn't taken the time to pat me down before ordering me into the car.

I walked up to the front door and was reaching for the handle when it opened by itself. Actually, there was a man on the other side and he had a gun.

"Ms. Matelli? We seem to be at an impasse." He indicated my gun and his own. If we were going to compare gun sizes, mine was bigger, but he had the advantage of Nick coming up behind me and grabbing the gun out of my hand. Of course, Nick didn't perform *kotegaeshi* and his movements were clumsy, but I wasn't about to insult the guy who now had my gun, or the guy who had his gun pointed at me. He patted me down and found the knife, too.

Now that I was disarmed, he ushered me in, and glanced at Nick, shaking his head slightly to tell his guard dog to stop twisting my arm behind my back. Nick tightened his grip on my arm and I winced.

"Nick, stop it." The order was a sharp reprimand and I could tell that Nick was reluctant. But he let me go. My heart was trying to jump out of my throat at the moment and it was all I could do to keep breathing.

Nick gave me an unnecessary push when we got to the entryway, just to remind me what a great guy he was. The taller guy—I suspected I was looking at Johnny Smash—led the way into a large room to the right. I faced Nick and the other guy, who was a tall, heavyset man, but clearly a little younger than Nick.

"You must be Johnny Smash," I said. "Your photo doesn't do you justice." I turned to Nick. "But yours does. Did you get your photo retouched or something?"

Nick sneered and tightened his grip on the gun. Smash put out a hand to calm him down. He inclined his head. "I'm sorry we have to meet under such circumstances, but you've been trouble for everyone."

"Where's my brother?" My heart was definitely in my throat, and I was desperately trying to find my center, my *ki*. I wanted to be calm, a master of Aikido right now. There is a story about the founder of Aikido, Ueshiba Morihei, and how he could dodge bullets using his martial arts training. I would have given anything right now—even my right pinkie—to be able to dodge bullets calmly and unremittingly. But it was just a wish, and the reality was that bullets would cut through my body as quickly and easily as a chainsaw cuts down a sapling.

"When can I see my brother?"

"You shouldn't be so eager to see Al," Nick said. "You'll be joining him soon enough."

I could feel the blood drain from my head, and my hands and feet grew cold. I couldn't say it. He couldn't be dead. I had gone through all of this and I hadn't saved my little brother.

Nick had a sly smile on his face and I had a vision of literally ripping his smile off his face with both hands. I had humiliated him earlier, and now he had a gun and the knife. He kept the gun in his hand, casually down by his side. I looked around for something that was within easy reach, something that I could use for defense. A large, heavy cigarette lighter of the coffee table variety sat on an end table.

Both Smash and Nick seemed to be waiting for someone. Sal, probably. A few minutes passed before Salvatore showed himself. He was a fatter version of his father, the same coarse, wavy hair, although it was dark instead of white, the same nose and cheekbones, but his eyes and mouth were cruel. Giovanni didn't have that hard edge to his facial features. Whatever misery Don Testa had dealt out in his lifetime had not touched his features the way death and misery had affected his youngest son. I was immediately repulsed, but tried to control my expression.

Sal wore a polo shirt and slacks with a cardigan and he held a lit cigar in one hand. It smelled like death to me. He eyed me impassively. "So this is Angela Matelli. What the hell is a woman doing playing private dick? You should have stopped when you got my message."

"Would you have left one of your brothers to die?"

He shrugged. "If he wasn't being reasonable, yeah." Ah, familial loyalty at work here.

"What's so reasonable about what you're offering Albert? You want to take his business away from him, you want to force him into working for you." I tried to use a neutral tone, but my voice got tighter with every word.

"Hell, I was offering him his life. But he's a hard bastard. I gave him every chance. He just doesn't get it—I win every time. I hold all the cards. And you"—he poked the lit end of the cigar at me—"you've been nothing but a buzzing mosquito and all you've done is cause an itch that I have to scratch. You're probably more responsible than I am for both of your deaths."

"Where's Albert? Is he still alive?"

Sal chomped down on his cigar and sucked on it till a foul-smelling cloud emerged from his mouth. I wished on him a bad case of mouth cancer. "Yeah, he's still alive. Stubborn bastard." He shook his head briefly. "I have to say, he's brave in a stupid way. He didn't even cry out when I snipped that pinkie of his off.''

I lunged at him, but Smash was ready for me and put an arm out to bar my way. Nick had stepped behind me so he could yank painfully on my hair, which caused my head to snap back. I let out an involuntary yelp. Nick laughed. Sal and Smash didn't seem to get any pleasure out of my pain, but they didn't seem to mind it much either. They dealt in pain and misery and death every day, and it was as familiar to them as breathing.

"Nick, bring Albert here. Let's see this touching reunion between brother and sister." Sal grinned around his cigar and my limbs suddenly felt like jelly. I crossed my arms to keep from showing how angry and scared I was. Nick left the room.

"Gee, Daddy must be proud of you," I said, voice dripping with sarcasm. At least I hoped it was. It sounded more like a waver to me. "Stepping on the bodies of the dead to get to the top seems to be a tradition in your family."

Sal frowned. "You makin' fun of me?"

Sal was a walking poster boy for the sarcasm-impaired. I wanted to keep him talking. I asked him the same questions I'd asked his father this morning.

"Why do you need Albert's factory? Why can't you leave him alone?"

Sal took the soggy cigar from his mouth to answer. "Albert's a hell of a frontman. My father suggested him. We thought it would be easy to get him to fall in line with us. I even offered to let him keep some of his interest in the factory. He turned us down. Said he wanted out."

"We? You're talking about you, Smash, and Nick, right?"

"Nah, my father wants to help me start up my business. He's the one who's been giving me advice. You know, I never appreciated the old bastard till I came back from Italy."

Shit, Don Testa was more involved than he'd led me to believe. So much for Dom's testimony as to what a great guy Testa was and how he always kept his word. As long as his own blood isn't involved, maybe there was some validity to it.

"Even if Albert were to fall in with you," I pointed out, "how could he ever be certain that you wouldn't kill him once he'd outlived his usefulness?"

Sal shrugged. "He wouldn't ever know that, now, would he?"

"Your father had more integrity than that. What are you planning to do with the factory?"

"You're a bright girl. You should know what could be done with a place here in Eastie, near the harbor, near the airport. It's a great place to ship and receive anything I want to get into."

"A great place to get rid of dead bodies, too," I added. "So you're going to run guns, smuggle drugs, do anything that will make a profit for you."

"That's about right. Albert's right. You are smart." Sal's cigar had gone out, and he picked up a heavy ceramic lighter to light it again. The heavy smoke seemed to fill the room, sucking all the good air out.

"Sounds like you've got it all worked out. What're you going to do with the people who own a piece of AMT once you get rid of Albert?"

"He chose the hard way. If he'd just agreed to help me, I would've fronted him the money to buy them out, get them out of the business. I was able to buy at least one of 'em, although he's not real happy right now."

"Rick Ng," I said.

"Give the lady a cigar."

"Please don't. Rick was borrowing from the company."

"Seems he has a thing for the dogs. Albert noticed the discrepancies in the cash flow. Rick bought used equipment for the factory and charged Albert for new equipment. Then he turned around and lost it all at Suffolk Downs. That's when he started borrowing from me. I have a nice little loan business down at the track."

"Rick was sure he'd be able to pay you back, wasn't he?" I asked.

Sal laughed. "Yeah, but he kept losing and asking for more money. He knew I wanted to take over AMT. When Albert escaped the first time—"

"From his condo on Friday night?"

Sal nodded. "Yeah."

"Rick was the first person he called," I said, Sal confirming it with a nod. "Albert thought you'd never think to look to his employees. He didn't know about Rick's gambling problem, or that Rick called you when Albert got to his place.

"So Rick set Albert up for you," I said to Sal. They probably took him while he was on the phone with me. I'd heard the struggle. "Tell me, did you get Albert at Rick's place?"

"We almost got him there," Sal replied. "We got him in Newport. We'd been staking out his ex-wife's place, and drove past him while he was talking to someone at a phone booth down the street."

Albert must have figured out that Rick was the traitor and he was trying to call to let me know. He probably thought he'd be safe at Sylvia's. Albert didn't think they would look for him in Testa's backyard, or at his ex-wife's place.

Someone was pounding on the front door. Sal looked

sharply at Smash. "Who the hell is that? Did Nick leave the front gate open?"

I had no idea what was going to happen from one moment to the next.

Nick returned, dragging an unwilling and disheveled Albert with him. His left hand was bandaged and there was dried blood where his finger had once been. There was a swelling on his cheekbone, maybe broken, and a split lip. His face was covered with bruises and he walked hunched over. Smash and Nick had worked him over pretty well. Not that it would matter in a few minutes. We'd both be dead. "Albert!" Every nerve in my body screamed and I wondered why others couldn't hear the rush of blood in my ears. I started to go to him, but Johnny Smash stopped me.

The pounding got louder and more insistent. "For Christ's sake, Nick, answer the damn door," Sal yelled, waving his cigar, ashes fluttering in the air.

Nick scurried out of the room and I tore myself away from Smash's grip and crossed the room to where Albert was standing. Up close, he was pale, sweating, and shivering, but the house was warm. It was clear that he'd contracted a fever, probably from the amputation. I doubted they had done it in a sterile environment. God, he might even have the beginnings of blood poisoning. I didn't even want to think about it. I touched his face and realized tears were streaming down my cheeks. "I'm so sorry. I wish I'd gotten here in time."

He looked up at me. The pain in his eyes was almost more than I could bear. But he grinned. He was probably just gritting his teeth. "Hey, you did your best, Sis. I'm sorry I got you involved. It was my problem. I shouldn't have called you. I just didn't know where to turn."

"Who the hell else were you going to call? Rambo?"

He shrugged. "It would have been nice."

It would have been a funny line if we weren't standing in Sal Testa's living room, about to be killed.

Nick walked slowly back into the room, followed by Rick Ng, and interrupted our reunion. This was not the suave Rick I had first met, but a desperate version that held a .45 on Nick. Rick had my gun in his other hand.

Smash, who still held his gun, started to bring it up, but Rick clinked the safety off of his automatic. "Don't even try," he said. "Drop the gun."

Smash slowly put the gun down on a nearby end table. I noticed it was still within his reach. Rick didn't seem to notice. Sal was making sure Rick stayed focused on him.

"Rick," Sal greeted Rick as if he were a guest invited to an afternoon tea. "Why don't we all put our guns down and discuss our mutual problems. I bet we can solve all of them."

"Hah!" I couldn't help it. The word just burst from me. Sal's eyes narrowed at my intrusion. Rick didn't take his eyes off the three men, but acknowledged my presence.

"She's right. I don't think there's anything to discuss," Rick said to Sal.

"We can wipe your slate clean. You can walk away, not owing us a nickel."

"Bullshit. You'll come after me." I could see Rick wavering, wanting to believe Sal.

Sal nodded. "Fair enough. I'll throw in a day for you to disappear. We won't look for you as long as you never show your face in this town again."

"You'll let me walk out of here, owing you nothing?"

Sal nodded. Johnny nodded. Even Nick nodded. I laughed. Every head but Albert's turned to me. "Rick, you can't be so desperate that you think this fairy tale Sal's spun is for real, do you? You think the Mob would forgive a debt, especially after you've added to the insult by holding them at gunpoint?''

Sal looked sharply at me. "Don't believe anything she says. She just wants to get out of here alive, with or without her brother.''

I shrugged. "I won't argue with you, Sal, but you gotta give this guy more incentive than to disappear, and a day's head start. I think you should give him more money. After all, he lost it all betting on the dogs, didn't you, Rick?''

Rick nodded, at a loss for words. He swallowed and I could see that his hands were shaking. He wasn't used to holding up that heavy gun.

"Your best bet, Rick, is to call the police. Have them sort it all out.'' I took a step toward him. "Why don't you let me have one of those guns and I'll keep an eye on 'em while you call the police.''

"Don't listen to her, Rick,'' Sal said. He'd thrown the cigar on the floor and it was smoldering on the rug. "She gets one of those guns and you're gonna be in with the rest of us. And trust me, you won't last long in prison, even if we're not sent to the same pen. I've got friends everywhere.''

"I wouldn't feed you to these dogs, Rick,'' I said. "You haven't killed anyone yet. I bet even Albert is willing to forgive the money you took. I bet if you cooperate with the feds they'll give you immunity, a new identity, and you can be set up with a nice life.'' I could feel Albert tense up beside me. I could see Rick wavering, not sure who to trust.

By some invisible signal, Sal lunged for me and Johnny Smash and Nick tackled Rick at the same time. I heard gunshots, but I had no idea if anyone had been hit, who was alive or who was dead. I could only hope that Albert had gotten out of the way.

Sal grabbed my nearest arm and put me in front of him
like a shield. His left arm went around my neck and I sank
into *ushiro kubishime kokyu-nage*. I slid one foot off to the
left and raised my right arm up, the arm Sal had a grasp
on, until our right arms were on the left side and I was able
to spin out of his grip. Then I grabbed Sal's arm and elbow
and twisted him around onto the floor.

"Angela, get Albert out of here." Rick was struggling
with Smash. Nick was on the floor, holding his side, which
was bleeding. Sal scrambled up and ran toward the end
table with Smash's gun. I grabbed his neck and arm and
spun him away from his destination. Sal came at me again
and I used his body force to push him off in another direction. He crashed into an armchair, tipped it over with his
weight, and sent Sal sprawling. I knew it would only daze
him, but I needed to get to Albert.

Nick was crawling toward the gun on the end table, leaving a bloody trail from where he fell. I was about to make
a grab for it when Rick and Smash knocked me to the side
in their struggle. Sal had gotten back up and was heading
over to join the struggle for the gun, which was pointing
at Albert. I dove across the distance and pushed Albert out
of the way. I heard a shot and then a groan.

"Are you okay?" I asked Albert. He grunted and I took
that as a yes. I looked around—Sal had crumpled to the
floor, his hand covering the hole in his gut.

On the other side of the room, now littered with turned
over chairs and broken end tables, Smash was punching
Rick repeatedly in the face. But Rick, perhaps sensing how
desperate his situation had become, was hanging on to the
gun for dear life. Nick had given up his quest for the gun
on the end table, which was now on the floor, half under
the sofa. I couldn't tell if he was dead or alive, and I really

didn't care. It looked as if Smash was winning, and Nick was dead or close to it.

Sal stood up and removed his hand from his belly. He was definitely leaking. He stared dazedly at his bloody hand before sinking back to the floor on his knees.

Before the body count got any higher, I grabbed the gun near the sofa and shot it into the ceiling.

''Freeze,'' I bellowed and pointed it at Smash and Rick.

Smash and Rick fell apart. Rick dropped his gun. Smash tried to grab it in one last, desperate move. I pointed my gun at Smash's knee and fired another shot. I only hit his upper thigh, but I got my point across.

EIGHTEEN

WE LISTENED FOR SIRENS, some sign that a neighbor had heard the shots and called it in, but nothing happened. No police, no ambulances, no fire trucks. I was sure the shots would be heard in the neighborhood. Sal wasn't talking—he was busy conserving his energy to stay alive. I went over to Nick the Knife and felt for a pulse, but he was gone. Johnny Smash's thigh wound was superficial but he was wincing, the big baby. He cut off my brother's finger, but couldn't stand to be winged. Wimp. Now that the action was over, Rick's bravado was gone. He'd turned as pale as the first snow.

After a ten-minute wait, I assumed Sal had either paid off his neighbors to ignore his presence, or the neighbors thought the shots were cars backfiring.

Albert was holding up pretty well. Johnny Smash had given up the big baby act and now looked at me as if I was a red silk cape fluttering in the wind, and he was a bull lowering his horns. I didn't give him a chance. I kept my gun trained on him while I debated whether or not to call the police. It was clear that Sal would be dead soon without help, but Albert had been through enough without police involvement. I had an idea of how to solve the problem unofficially.

I called Giovanni Testa. Dom answered. "Angela, I don't think Mr. Testa will talk to you."

"I've got his miserable son's life hanging by a thread."

"I'll get him."

"Just a minute. I want to know if you're being straight

with me, Dom. I have a deal for Testa, one I think he'll want to hear about. Is Testa the stand-up guy you think he is or will he screw me over the first chance he gets?''

Dom paused before answering. ''He may not like the deal, but he'll honor his part of a bargain.''

''Okay, I'll talk to him.'' By ordering Dom to put his boss on the phone, I had effectively turned the tables—I was no longer the one who necessarily wanted to talk.

''Angela.'' Don Testa's tone was warm with concern. Not for me, but for his own blood.

''Don Testa. I am at your son's house and there was a little fight. Salvatore here has been shot. I was not the one who shot him nor was Albert.''

''Who, then?'' he asked.

I shrugged. ''I can't really say, there was so much pandemonium. It could have been Johnny Smash, it could have been a third party whose name I won't mention, or it could have been Nick.'' I didn't mention that Nick, in actuality, had been dead or close to death at the time Sal was shot.

''What is my son's condition?''

''He was gut shot. The bullet probably didn't hit anything vital by my judgment, but he could bleed to death or have serious problems if we don't work something out soon.''

''What is there to work out?'' Don Testa asked, his tone hard.

''I want several things, and I think you know what they are. If I don't get your word on this before I turn Sal over to you, Albert and I will take our chances with the police and the feds.''

There was a sigh. ''Tell me what you want.''

''First, Sal signs over control of the factory to Albert. He has no part in it, and neither do you.''

''I cannot answer for my son, Angela.''

"Tick-tock, Don Testa. Sal's not getting any better." I put the phone up to Sal's ear. "Say something to your old man, you son of a bitch."

"Papa?" He was breathing fast and a thin sheen of sweat layered his brow.

I took the phone away. "Well?"

"All right. You have my word."

"Your word isn't good enough. I want Nick the Knife to take the blame for killing Eddie in Albert's apartment."

Again, the pause. "I can arrange that for you. Is that all?" I think Testa was being sarcastic, but I chose to ignore the tone.

"You leave Albert, me, and the rest of the Matellis alone. Stay away from us. I was told you are an honorable man. I hope this is true. Dom reminds me a little of Albert. I think he's basically a good guy in a bad situation. Is he telling the truth?"

"I haven't gone back on my word yet."

"Just as long as you're not crossing your fingers when you say that. Also, in the event that you die and Sal inherits your role as boss, I want a codicil to this agreement."

Testa sounded weary. "Why?"

"Because he's not as honorable as you are. He might decide to go after Albert or me. I want Dom to have control of your business. I want you to start showing Dom the ropes, and keep your boy a second-in-command who has to answer to Dom."

"And if I decide not to do this? I will be in my grave and my word won't matter," he replied.

"I'm glad you brought that up, Don Testa, because I have a cassette with a conversation on it that pretty much fries Sal. And you're the star of the tape."

"That tape could be suppressed by my lawyers in any attempt to go to trial, and you know it."

"Ah, but remember, Sal abducted my brother and took him across state lines. Now it's federal and it won't go away as easily."

I could almost hear Testa's frustration across the phone lines. He finally sighed and said, "All right. I will do as you say. But I don't like it."

"Of course you don't. None of this is in your favor. But you've made a wise decision, Don Testa. Now, I'm gonna leave Smash here alive to tend to your boy. If Sal dies, it's on Smash, not me. Albert and I are walking out of here. I expect to see something in the papers tomorrow morning that the Providence police found evidence of Nick the Knife struggling with Eddie in Albert's apartment, and the gun went off. Make Albert's fingerprints disappear off that gun. I know you or your son is keeping it in a safe place." I'd figured out that was what they must have had on Albert— why Don Testa had said that Albert had "technically" killed Eddie. They'd made him hold the gun, pressing his finger on the trigger. And they kept the gun as evidence, away from the police, but always with the threat of turning it over to the law.

"I'll make it happen." Before I could hang up Testa quickly asked, "Who shot my son?"

"Who shot your son?" I repeated, locking eyes with Johnny Smash. He grimaced, whether out of pain or guilt, I didn't know. Out of the corner of my eye, Rick looked nervous. "There was so much commotion at the time, it's hard to tell, but my best guess would be Nick."

"I'll take care of him."

"He's already taken care of. He died from a bullet." I was wrapping up my talk with Testa. "And when your boy gets better, tell him to lay off Boston. Maybe he can be king of the hill somewhere else, but not on my turf. I want to see a For Sale sign on this property tomorrow morning."

"You are testing my patience, Angela," Don Testa replied.

"You tried mine a long time ago, Don Testa. I'm through talking to you. Here's Johnny." I tossed the phone to Smash, who caught it.

In a low voice, he said to me, "I can tell him who really shot Sal." He looked at Rick, who was shaking his head in disbelief.

I smiled. "Oh? Let's see. As I recall it, the both of you were struggling over the gun when it went off. If you mention Rick to Testa, I'll have to mention that you might be trying to cover up the fact that you shot your boss by accident. Then of course, Rick would be in hot water, but I doubt you'd get out of that unscathed. Think about it before you say anything stupid."

Smash looked thoughtful as he pressed the phone to his ear and turned away from me.

I looked at Albert and Rick, who got up and made their way to the front door. Smash was still listening to Testa and nodding. "Sure thing, Don Testa. It happened the way she said. Nick did it."

The three of us limped out to our cars. Rick turned to Albert and me. "Um, what happens now?"

I shrugged. "I didn't make a deal for you. You're gonna have to work it out on your own, bud. I may have gotten you out of being blamed for Sal being shot, but you betrayed Albert. Don't expect me to thank you."

"But if it wasn't for me, you'd be dead!" He was sweating.

"If it wasn't for you, we wouldn't be in this mess in the first place. It was you earlier today at the factory, wasn't it? You were looking for the ledgers."

"You were there?" Rick swallowed.

I threw him a nasty smile. "Hiding in your office. Lorraine told me that you left about the time she was on the phone with me. I just happened to get there before you. You later broke into my office and my apartment, didn't you?''

He didn't look at me.

I helped Albert into the car. "Just consider yourself out of a job as of now," Albert told him. "Get yourself some help for your gambling problem. Maybe you'll come out of this alive and stronger than before."

I turned to Albert. He looked funny. I felt his forehead—he was burning up. I got in the driver's side, started the car, and took off, tires squealing. I glanced in my rearview mirror once to see the image of Rick standing forlornly in front of Sal Testa's house.

When I got to my apartment building, only a few blocks away, helping Albert up the stairs was a struggle. He could barely walk. When we finally got into my apartment, I placed Albert on the sofa and immediately called Reg at the hospital. I was lucky, I'd caught him at a break. I told him I had an emergency and could he come over, no questions asked. "Bring your medical bag."

"Sure, Ange. You okay?" He sounded worried.

"Just get here as quick as you can."

"I get off in an hour. Is that soon enough?"

"Take a cab. I'll pay for it. Oh, and Reg? Bring drugs for pain and possible blood poisoning."

I ran a cold bath and helped Albert into it, clothes and all. His teeth were soon chattering and I hoped I was doing the right thing.

"I don't feel so well. Ma? Where's Ma?" He turned to look at me "I hurt."

"You gotta hang on, Albert. You lasted this long. Ma'll kill me if you don't get better."

Reg was over sooner than I expected. I buzzed him up

and stood sentinel on the landing, gun in head, until I could
see the top of his dark blond head. I didn't want any surprises right now, and I didn't totally trust Testa or Smash.

"Hey, Angie, what's going on?" He smiled. "One of
the other doctors is covering for me. He owes me. What's
the big emergency?" He waggled his eyebrows and I realized he thought I wanted him to come over for a medical
examination of another kind.

I stopped him at the top of the stairs. "This is pretty
grisly, and it can't be reported. Can you do that or will it
go against your medical ethics?"

He sobered finally, realizing from the look on my face
that this wasn't going to be a night of fun and games. "It
depends. Is it a gunshot wound?"

"No."

"A knife wound?"

I shook my head.

He shrugged. "You have my word that if it isn't either
of those, I'll keep my mouth shut."

I led him inside, locking the door behind us, and brought
him into the bathroom.

Reg immediately knelt at Albert's side and felt his forehead. "Jesus, Angie, what the hell happened to him?"

Albert's injured hand was draped off the side of the tub
nearest the wall. I leaned over and picked up his arm to
show the injury to Reg.

"Christ!" Reg went white on me. Everyone seemed to
be going pale on me. I shook his shoulder.

"Sorry, Angie, I see this in the emergency room a lot,
but I've never seen it outside of the hospital."

"Consider yourself baptized by fire."

Reg opened his medical bag and took out a hypodermic
and a bottle of liquid relief. "You'd better get someone
else over here to help me get Albert out of the bath. He

may not want to wake up to find that his sister helped undress him.''

I called Joey, who answered on the third ring. He was ambulatory, and best of all he could be trusted.

Two hours later, Albert was resting in my guestroom. Reg had cleaned out the stump where his pinkie had once been. I had told him about the finger in my refrigerator, and he shook his head. ''Much too late, but I'm glad you kept it in case.'' He sewed up the stump properly, making sure that Albert was shot up with plenty of antibiotics.

With Albert resting in the guestroom, I had started to make tea for everyone, but we all opted for wine or beer. Reg and I had wine; Joey had one of the Leinenkugel Reds I kept for such occasions.

I made a short call to Ma.

''Albert's here with me.''

''I'll be right over,'' she said, the anxiety in her voice almost more than I could bear.

''Ma, it's past midnight.'' The truth was that I didn't want her to see him this way. He was beat up and looked awful. She'd insist on a hospital, and that was what we wanted to avoid, at least until the shooting had been cleared up in Providence and Salvatore had had his wrist slapped by his daddy. The last thing I wanted to do was tell Ma everything that had happened. Explaining how Albert had lost his little finger was going to be as tough as climbing a mountain.

It took some convincing—Ma kept bringing up getting a cab to take her all the way into East Boston, but I finally got her to agree to wait until tomorrow.

Joey and Reg ended up spending the night, Joey on the couch and Reg with me. We took turns getting up every hour to check on Albert. I couldn't sleep past six, so I got up to check on Albert.

"Hey, Sis," he croaked as I crept into the guestroom. "I feel as if I've been hit by a sledgehammer. Did we go to the fights last night or was that my imagination?"

I helped him sit up and fluffed a couple of pillows behind him. Then I sat on the edge of the bed and felt his forehead. "It was your imagination. But we were the guests of Salvatore Testa for a short time."

Reg stumbled into the room. "Looks like our patient is awake."

"I think his fever is gone," I said. Reg took the ear thermometer from the nightstand by the bed and checked.

"Yup. Looks good. Let me check the bandage."

Albert held his hand out for Reg to work on. I averted my eyes.

"I'd better clean out the wound one more time and give you a prescription for antibiotics," Reg said.

Albert gave a weak salute. "You're the doc."

"You bet your ass he is." I grinned at Reg. He smiled back.

"Ange? Can we talk in the other room?" Reg gestured to the door.

"Sure. It'll have to be the bedroom, though. Joey's snoring up a storm in the living room."

He nodded. I leaned over and kissed Albert's forehead. "I dunno what we're going to tell Ma."

He gave me a weak grin. "Do we have to tell her? Maybe she won't notice."

I rolled my eyes and left with Reg.

When we got in the bedroom, I put my arms around Reg. "Thank you. You saved his ass."

He returned my hug and kissed the top of my head. "I don't know what you're gonna do without me here."

I moved away, looked up at him. "You're leaving?"

He nodded. "Hawaii. I thought it might tempt you. Wanna come?"

I closed my eyes and leaned my forehead against his chest. He smelled of antiseptic, but to me, it was the best smell in the world at that moment. "Reg, I—"

He put his finger to my lips. "I know. I have it all figured out. Someone has to watch over the Matelli clan. I'd never get you away from here, and if I did, it would only be a short time before you wanted to go home."

I sighed and snuggled back into his arms. "I'm sorry I'm such a homebody. I wish it could be different. You can't stay here?"

He laughed. "And say no to Hawaii? Besides, Mass General didn't renew my residency. Too many new residents want to come here. It's one of the best hospitals in the country." He stroked my hair, and his arm tightened around me. "If I send you a plane ticket, will you come visit me?"

"Are you kidding? Hawaii? How can I say no?" But I knew how this was going to end—I'd come over for a week, and that would be the end of our long-distance romance. Besides, I liked Reg, but I wasn't in love with him. He'd find some nice nurse or doctor or Island girl, settle down, and we'd be exchanging Christmas cards in two or three years and that would eventually dwindle. But I would always be grateful that he was here for me and for Albert.

A few minutes later, I showed him how grateful I was.

NINETEEN

JOEY CAME BACK WITH doughnuts and I made a gallon of hot coffee. Reg left after showering. He needed to go back to his apartment to change clothes and get ready for another long shift at the hospital.

Ma called while Joey was pouring coffee.

"I just got a call from Sylvia. She says that the news down there is that the police found the man who killed the guy in Albert's apartment. The case is closed. Can I come see Albert now?"

I looked over at Albert in the bedroom. "Uh, Ma, there's something you oughta know—"

"I'm just so glad he's all right. Angela, thank you. I'll be there in a couple of hours."

I went into Albert's room. "I got good news and bad news. Which do you want first?"

"After what I've been through," Albert said, "the bad news can't be so bad."

"The bad news is that Ma's coming here in a couple hours. You gotta figure out what you're gonna tell her."

Albert grimaced, whether from pain or the bad news, I wasn't sure. "What's the good news?"

I told him what Sylvia had told Ma about the investigation into Eddie's death being closed.

He nodded, a sadness weighing on him. He hadn't been able to grieve for Eddie since it had happened.

I sat down on the edge of the bed. "You want to talk about it?"

Joey came in right then, and Albert nodded briefly.
'Later.''

We all sat in Albert's room—I was beginning to think
of it as such—and talked about all the things that had happened over the past week.

"How did you avoid those guys for three days?" Joey
asked Albert.

"I always carry a wad of cash. Once I got away from
them on Friday night, I drove my car to a parking garage,
took a cab to the train station, and went to Hingham." After
polishing off his second jelly doughnut, Albert lay back on
his pillows and closed his eyes. He still looked pasty, but
of course, after what he'd been through, I was just grateful
my baby brother was in one piece, more or less.

Joey frowned. "Why Hingham?"

Albert grinned. "Why not? The best way to disappear is
to go where no one could possibly know where you've
gone. I'd never been there. I'd never really even thought
about going there or talked to anyone about Hingham. It
could have been Maine or California or Oklahoma, for all
they knew."

"I don't understand why you surfaced at Rick's," I said.
Actually, I kind of knew why, I just didn't understand why
someone so smart could do something so stupid.

Albert opened his eyes again. His hair was plastered
against his forehead and I knew he'd have to get in the
shower in the next day or so, if only to wash off the memory of what had happened.

"Well, I was sitting around in Hingham with nothing to
do. This is half the reason people get caught after they go
underground. They want to get in touch with someone and
they eventually think it'll be okay. I called Rick on
Wednesday morning before he went to work, and asked
him about ToyCo. He told me they weren't interested. I

hung up and thought about it, and decided to call my contact, George, at ToyCo to get more information about why they weren't interested. I didn't have anything else to do but sit around and worry about my investments. When I reached George, he told me they were very interested and didn't understand why Rick would tell me otherwise.''

''So that's why you went to see him,'' I said, the light finally dawning. Albert must have felt he had fires to put out.

He nodded. ''I had to find out why Rick had done what he'd done. He told me he was caught in a bad situation. I was looking out the front window of his place and I recognized their car as they pulled up and parked. I have to give Rick credit for showing me the back way out.''

''So they almost caught you,'' Joey said as he chewed on his fourth doughnut. I'd been keeping track.

''Johnny Smash and Nick the Knife very nearly caught me there, but I managed to give them the slip,'' he told us before turning to me. ''I wanted to get to you, but I realized I had to get out of Boston. I had rented a car and drove down to Sylvia's place. She wasn't home, and I realized it was stupid to even be in the area. But I had to talk to you and it was getting late. So I took a chance and called from a pay phone by the marina near Sylvia's place. Smash and Nick cruised by—they'd recognized the rented car from my narrow escape at Rick's''

''I got your message,'' I told him.

''So how do I tell Ma about my, um, amputation?'' Albert asked me.

Joey looked at his watch. ''I gotta go pick up my mother from Logan. She's coming back from her trip.''

I walked him to the door and gave him a hug. ''Call me later. If you're not too sore, I think I got you a gig with Benny the Bond, the guy down the hall from me. And I think Albert will probably keep you on with AMT, if you want.''

"Thanks, Ange. You're a great cousin.''

I gave him a playful sock on the arm. "So are you. See you later.''

I went back to Albert's room. His face was looking a little pale and drawn. "I think I need another pain pill. The one Reg gave me is starting to wear off.''

I doled another pill out to him and got him a glass of water. After he'd taken his medicine, he turned to me. ''You talked to Sylvia?''

"Yeah, she's like a whole new person. I like her now.''

"So do I. You know, she's the reason I got out of the whole business. I made good money at it and liked my boss, but I guess I never really thought about the impact of what I was doing. I thought I was legitimate, and yeah, some money came through that wasn't clean, but I didn't think that was my fault. Then I looked at Sylvia and her drug habit, and remembered her as she was when I met her, and realized that while I may not be on the streets selling the stuff, I wasn't as clean as I'd thought.''

"She told me how Eddie sort of woke her up to the fact that she was addicted," I said.

Albert nodded. "We were already going through the process of divorce, and one night, Sylvia and I started talking, and she broke down and cried, and that got me started. We realized we still loved each other, but we couldn't live together. That's why I remained friends with her throughout the divorce.''

"And that's why you didn't say anything to your family.''

We looked into each other's eyes.

"I was always afraid you'd see through me, Ange.

You're such a strong, self-sufficient woman. Jeez, if I had half your courage—''

I laughed. "Sal told me you didn't scream when he cut off your finger."

Albert smiled, but it wasn't a nice smile. "I'd fainted. I hope the bastard gets blood poisoning. Yeah, I was so out of it, I didn't have the strength to scream. Shit, he took a finger, for Christ's sake." He looked down at his bandaged hand as if he still couldn't believe it.

"Why didn't you give him the company?" I asked. "It's not worth your life."

"The Mob took my wife away from me and AMT was my baby."

"You mean, Itty Bitty Kitty is your baby," I teased.

He rolled his eyes. "Honestly, Ange, it came to me in a dream. And I couldn't get rid of it until I'd pursued it as far as I could go. And suddenly, it's this year's Furby."

"You wanted to stand up to the bully."

Albert sighed, ran his non-injured hand through his hair. "You want to know the truth? I kept thinking Giovanni Testa would come through for me. He'd tell Sal to lay off. And by the time Sal had cut off my finger, I was so far gone, I didn't care anymore."

The buzzer sounded. Someone was downstairs. I went out to the living room and looked out the window. Down below, I saw a silver Porsche parked out front. A little elderly lady with black hair was looking up at my window. I checked my watch. It was nearly two hours since I'd called Ma, yet here was Sylvia and Ma. Sylvia lived an hour south of East Boston, and Ma lived in Malden, which was north of here. To drive up from Newport to Malden, then drive here meant that Sylvia must have already been well on her way to Ma when we were on the phone.

I stopped at the doorway of the bedroom. "Ma and Sylvia are here, Albert. Do whatever you can to make yourself presentable. I don't think it'll take much, even in your pathetic condition.''

He threw me a weak grin. ''Hey, I get to spend a few hours with my three favorite women. What more can I guy ask for?''

I laughed and headed for the door to let in his two other favorite women.

AFTER SPENDING TWO WEEKS almost exclusively with Reg, I saw him off at the airport. Ma got over seeing Albert's missing finger pretty quickly. I don't know what he said to her in the guestroom when she showed up, but she came out and began bustling around, making hot tea and chicken soup, which is supposed to cure everything, but I doubt it will grow a new finger for him. Anyway, I did see a tear in Ma's eye as she stirred the soup, but she said it was from being near a hot stove.

Sylvia spent a lot of time nursing Albert back to health. In fact, she stayed the night and drove him back to her house in Newport the next day. I kept in daily contact with the couple after that.

Rosa came back from Rome and Albert picked her up at the airport. She was shocked by his appearance and the missing finger, but was glad he was alive.

On the next Sunday dinner, Albert and Sylvia announced plans to remarry, which was met with much enthusiasm by Ma and me. Everyone else fell into line, once Ma gave the approval, of course.

On November seventh, we had a big blowout for Ma's seventieth birthday at her house. Lee was there, as were Joey and Raina, who had begun dating once I introduced them to each other. The attraction was mutual. So much for Joey's other girlfriend.

Sylvia had taken Ma out for lunch and shopping for the day, and before she returned home, the rest of us had decorated the place with crepe paper and balloons. At the sound of the key in the door, we jumped out with "Happy Birthday!" and Ma gave a delayed reaction to me, which told me she'd been expecting it. But she looked pleased anyway, and blew out the candles on her birthday cake with what appeared to be a set of lungs that would make a twenty-year-old green with envy. My birthday gift to her was a set of walkie-talkies. When she opened the gift, she flashed me a wicked smile and said, "Angela Agnes, you shouldn't have. But I'm glad you did."

I knew she'd be making me some stuffed artichokes soon.

Elizabeth Gunn
FIVE CARD STUD

A JAKE HINES MYSTERY

It's a frigid winter in
Minnesota, but detective
Jake Hines has bigger
problems than keeping
warm. The body of a
man, nearly naked and
frozen solid, is discovered
on a highway overpass.

As Hines probes the last days of the victim's life, a
grim picture of betrayal, greed and fear emerges. But
for Jake, solving a murder is a lot like playing cards—
figure out who's bluffing and who's got the perfect
hand, especially when one of the players is a killer.

"This series gets better and better. Gunn keeps her
readers absorbed in the exciting case throughout..."
—*Booklist*

Available July 2001 at your favorite retail outlet.

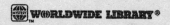

WORLDWIDE LIBRARY®

WEG389

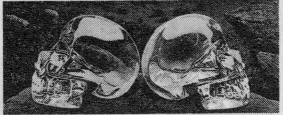